A REVIVED
MODERN
CLASSIC

THREE SHORT NOVELS

KAY BOYLE

THREE SHORT NOVELS

The Crazy Hunter
The Bridegroom's Body
Decision

Introduction by Doris Grumbach

A NEW DIRECTIONS BOOK

To James Stern, no matter how many oceans or hedgerows stand between

This collection first published by Beacon Press in 1958; reissued by Penguin
Books in 1982; reissued as New Directions Paperbook 703 in 1991 as part of
the Revived Modern Classics series.
Manufactured in the United States of America
New Directions Books are printed on acid-free paper.
Published simultaneously in Canada by Penguin Books Canada, Limited

"The Crazy Hunter" and "The Bridegroom's Body" were previously published in a collection called *The Crazy Hunter* by Harcourt, Brace and Company. "Decision" was first published in the *Saturday Evening Post* under the
title "Passport to Doom."

Library of Congress Cataloging-in-Publication Data

Boyle, Kay, 1902–
    [Novels. Selections]
    Three short novels / Kay Boyle ; introduction by Doris Grumbach.
        p.   cm.—(New Directions paperback ; 703) (A Revived modern
    classic)
    "This collection first published by Beacon Press in 1958"—T.p.
    verso.
    Contents: The crazy hunter—The bridegroom's body—Decision.
    ISBN 0-8112-1149-5
    I. Title.   II. Series.
PS3503.09357A6   1991
813'.52—dc20   90–47955
                                                                CIP

New Directions Books are published for James Laughlin
by New Directions Publishing Corporation,
80 Eighth Avenue, New York 10011

cop. 1

CONTENTS

INTRODUCTION

I AM very fond of the first two stories in this collection, "The Crazy Hunter" and "The Bridegroom's Body," and an interested, enthusiastic re-reader of "Decision." If I were to say, as others have, that the first two, representative of Kay Boyle's early work, are "personal" fiction, full of anguish and deeply felt but buried emotion of disconnected and isolated people's lives and loves, and that the last story "Decision" (called, foolishly, by an editor when it first appeared in *The Saturday Evening Post*, "A Passport to Doom") belongs to her later work characterized by strongly held political convictions, I would be making a common distinction about her subject matter, but ignoring as some critics have, the intensity that all three stories—as well as the two kinds of subject matter—share.

For Kay Boyle is a writer who expends the same force of pure feeling whether she is writing about an imprisoned young anti-Fascist (Manuel in "Decision") or the curious and unexpected outpourings of love of one woman for another in "The Bridegroom's Body." Her poetry, novels, and short stories share a style informed by the passion of her utterances, whether for a murdered swan or (as in *Underground Woman*) her opposition to the Vietnam War.

The first two short novels in the collection you have in hand, belong to an early period in Boyle's life and writing, when she was drawing closely upon her own life for her subject matter. In 1936 she and her second husband, Laurence Vail, went to Devon, England, to spend a year. They returned to France in the next year, to a chalet in the French Alps. Here it was, in the next few years, that she wrote her "English" fiction, sometimes in a mode that will remind readers of D. H. Lawrence or more vaguely of Thomas Hardy, but always with that stylistic logo—sophisticated, evocative, elaborate prose—which marks the work as uniquely Boyle's. The wind- and rain-wracked landscape, reminiscent of nineteenth-century English fiction, is there, but the tense, turbulent patterns of human relationships are hers alone.

I have said "patterns of relationships." But Boyle is not content to use these social patterns merely to hold together the persons in the stories. She approaches the hostile, forbidding natural world in the same way, using it for emphasis and symbol (the gelded, trapped, blind horse for Candy Lombe, the triangle of swans for Lord and Lady Glourie and Miss Cafferty). Patterns in the world of nature are propelled by a seemingly mindless and instinctive disorder. They underline the fierce needs, the loneliness and barely controlled passions that tie human beings together, tear them apart and, at crucial moments in the tale, effect some often unexpected resolution. Nowhere is this more apparent than in Miss Cafferty's outbreak in "The Bridegroom's Body." We have been led to suspect she has a sexual alliance with the farmer on the property, or that she has led Lord Glourie on, as they say, but never do we expect the revelation to Lady Glourie of her admiration and love:

> Let me say it! . . . Night after night I've walked the country alone instead of walking it with you, talking out loud to you night and day, asking you to give me everything I haven't . . . asking you to give a little bit of it to take away with me when I have to leave you . . .

and on and on, a passionate outbreak of hopeless longing, adoration, and, a need that is not for men or sex (as we had come to believe) but for womanly "peace and strength" in a savage male world.

The differences in subject matter between the first two short novels and "Decision" are resolved by the recognition that they share, as Margaret Atwood has said "a central preoccupation: the workings of power." It is so. Caught in a web of power from which they lack the strength to escape, characters gather, at last, a show of defiance. Power belongs to the rich, to men, in the upper class they inhabit. Power is at work in the unbalanced war between the sexes and, in "Decision," in the oppression of a fascistic regime against courageous fighters for human freedom. Albert Camus believed that the only weapons men and women had against evil and injustice were individual resistance and rebellion. This is Kay Boyle's view as well: the wonderful last sight we are permitted of drunken Candy in the almost maddened horse's stall, holding off the powers of deceit and threatened death; and Manuel Jeronimo, given the choice of escape or defiance, making his fatal decision. ("If you're a man, you get up on a stage and bellow your heart out, you don't skulk in the wings," says Manuel's friend of him.) It does not matter whether the arena is personal or political resistance to injustice: in the fiction, and in the active public life of Kay Boyle, the gallant human spirit prevails.

* * *

While Boyle says today, and I believe her, that she does not have favorites among her stories and novels, she has in the past been an astute critic of her own work. In 1939 she wrote to her sister Joan, two weeks after she had finished writing "The Crazy Hunter": "I think my 'Crazy Hunter' . . . is the best thing I've ever done, and I do hope you like it." Twenty years later she wrote to a friend, it "remains one of my best, I think." Her acquaintance, Katherine Anne Porter, concurred. My paperback edition of *Three Short Novels*, issued by Beacon Press in 1958, is held together by a yellow strip that reads: "'The Crazy Hunter' is the story closest to perfection that I have ever read," and is signed by Porter.

As far as I can determine, Boyle has not expressed an opinion of "The Bridegroom's Body," except to note that it had been "rejected by every magazine at the time I wrote it." But one critic, Richard C. Carpenter, admired the story as much as I do, seeing its theme as "the perennial human need for love," and noting that, in both this story and in "The Crazy Hunter," the seamlessness of the narrative is accomplished by "a precise tension," a stylistic accomplishment in most of the fifty or more stories she has written in her long lifetime.

Of "Decision" Boyle wrote to her agent: "It will sell no where, but it is one of the most interesting things I have ever written . . . in a class with *Monday Night* and "The Crazy Hunter." She was satisfied with this story because for some time she had been publishing what she regarded as commercial stories to make a living and feared she could no longer write "in a matured, disciplined way."

It is fine when things come full circle: the novel, *Monday Night*, that Boyle mentions in the same breath with "The Crazy Hunter," is my personal favorite among her full-length novels and was originally published by New Directions in 1938. (It is still available in a reprint from Paul P. Appel.) Another New Directions author, Dylan Thomas, wrote to tell her he had reviewed it: "A very grand book indeed." I hope that those fortunate enough to come upon these three short fictions, perhaps for the first time, in this "Revived Modern Classic" reissue will read that early novel and the others still in print. Boyle wears very well indeed.

Sargentville, Maine, June 1990   Doris Grumbach

THE CRAZY HUNTER

Chapter One

THE WOMAN and the girl began undressing in the bushes near the water, modestly taking their garments off at a little distance from each other and with their backs turned so as not to surprise each other's abashed flesh. The sun came thin but warm through the just opening buds and the tight flickering leaves of the branches, dappling the two lowered faces and the bared arms and legs with shadow. The girl had ripped her jersey over her head and flung it aside and kicked her sandals off; the tweed skirt lay discarded behind her on the earth beneath the burgeoning spring-like twigs. When she had pulled the tight blue woolen swimming suit up over her belly and breasts, she straightened up and came out onto the bank, buttoning one strap over the shoulder still, and stood there looking: the white naked legs drawn close together, slender and the flesh delicate as southern dogwood flowers, the head held straight upon the round slender neck, the temples hollow and bare with the black hair drawn back above the ears and falling almost to the shoulders. The hair and the skin's untroubled purity, and the wide, up-tilted, the seemingly drugged or glazed transparent eyes gave her a look un-English as the Orient. And now the woman in her bathing-dress came stooping out, picking her own clothes up carefully and folding them over and laying them in order on the meadow grass above the wall of sedges that grew from the running water.

"Fold your things up, Nan," the woman said. "Pick your clothes up and put them somewhere all together so you'll know where they are when you get out," saying it not so much from will or habit as from the need to stop quickly this or any gap of silence between them. The arms, like the body in the black skirted bathing-dress, were full, powder-white, unblemished: these (with the forebone long and prominent in them, despite their unstained beauty, and the flesh gone slack), and the thickening, sloping shoulders and the neck's yoke signs of the consummation between flesh and time. From now on was the decline, the deterioration towards age, to come. Only the hands, reaching for the plaid blouse to smooth it out and fold it, and the face and the narrow feet in the black tennis shoes, were part still of a thinner, shyer woman's corporeity: perhaps one who had never entered into marriage willingly or given birth but who remained still tentative, still virgin, still unformed. "Nan, pick up your clothes before you go in," she said, the slow, still-innocent eyes searching the ground itself for flaw, saying it hopelessly into youth's deafness and imperviousness.

But the cold was on the girl's feet already, the water rising slowly on the pure legs as she slid down the bank's edge to the stream: the blurred face lowered, part in ecstasy, part fear, to watch the thin silver line of cold pass the ankles and mount the flesh to the knees and pass them, rising, until it had clasped her waist, her breasts, her throat, and for an instant twisted her shocked face in consternation. Then her arms began moving and she was swimming against the pouring current, the teeth shaking in her head with cold. So the last time I did this I was fifteen, two years

4

back, she began thinking quickly against the rushing slabs of water. I hadn't been away yet and I wasn't afraid. I didn't know what it was yet. Now I can feel everything stopping, the heart, the blood, the muscles hardening as if I were working my way through ice and becoming ice and the land and sky congealing tight around me. But the mother standing on her big bare legs on the grass saw the sun falling on the soft short hair that mounted black against the current, and the girl's slim arms falling and rising, the shoulders and the bent arms as they fell chalk-white in motion through the dark water, thrusting it down behind her with small quick strokes like someone quickly mounting a steep ladder or jerking up a greased pole at a country fair.

"How is it, Nan?" she called out. "Cold?" And now her own body slumped over and broke through the sedge and the reed-sweet into the stream's fast deep bed. For a moment she swam strongly, without gasping and her chin high, and then she turned lazily onto her back and rode there, the blue rubber cap edging the longish, pale face, the big arms thrashing backwards. "Warm," she called peacefully across the water's rapid murmuring. "Just the first plunge that takes your breath off. . . ."

The way home takes it from you and doesn't return it, the girl was saying, because every year of youth is still there in the furniture and the rugs and the marks on the glass. There is a school of children everywhere with me here, all of them that one child I was once running along the house's east ivy-covered wall and down through the stables and pastures; home putting short skirts on me and picture-books on the shelves in my room. The child who

5

scratched that drawing with a nursery pin on the inside of the banisters above the sixth bar on the first flight is still your bone, your skin, your muscle of the eye, your nail and tooth, the same physically projected child that dies now in the water's ice. She let the current turn and draw her down-stream towards the blue rubber cap, past the water-beaded floating head with its face turned upward in repose to the sun's light hanging palely on the meadows and trees.

"I'm not so good as I used to be," Nan said. "I'm going to get out, mother. I've forgotten how to swim in cold water after swimming over there."

"Climbing mountains ought to give you wind enough," the woman said, floating quietly with the stream. She lay vast, wide, bloated-seeming, her arms and legs dangling swollen under water.

"Sometimes when you learn one thing you forget another," Nan said, her teeth knocking in her mouth again. She reached up for the willow's roots and pulled herself, straining, out of the water. "I spoke German until I learned French, and in Italy I forgot everything I knew in French." On her hands and knees she sought under the bushes for the towel, tossed the tweed skirt and the jersey aside on the fresh, glinting earth, saying: "One year I know algebra and another year geometry. I never know them both the same winter." In a moment she turned on her knees and came back to the bank and sat there hunched in the towel, shaking, her toe-nails showing bluish at the edge. "Or when I get halfway good in charcoal drawing I forget how to work with oils, and the year I took architectural design I couldn't do life-class afterwards." She started drying her hair at the back with her hand inside the towel, shaking the soft dark locks loose. "And it's the same thing if I admire things," she said, stopping to pick a blade of pressed grass from her knee inside the towel's shade. "When I was so keen on the Renaissance I couldn't—"

"You're tucked up, that's what it is," said the woman smartly from the water, churning backwards with her arms. "You're still growing, you know, and you've been wearing yourself out with all this studying. Yesterday I saw one thing," she said, drifting wide and peaceful. "You haven't forgot how to ride a horse."

Nor have I forgotten to breathe or speak my native tongue, only how to walk into the house and through its rooms as if I belonged there any longer, or swim in water that knew me young, or sit under this tree that knew my legs climbing up it once, or how to look at her and talk to her because she is still talking Then and I am ahead in what there will be for me or in Now. I am home now, this is home, and there is no place for me because every place is taken by that child who will not die.

"I don't think I'm still growing," she said. "Anyway, my feet aren't growing. I've worn the same size shoes for two years now. I got my navy suède brogues to wear on my fifteenth birthday to go to Pellton to Mary's lunch party, and I can still wear them without them hurting."

"Look at your riding-breeches!" said the mother, floating near the sedges. "You've shot up four inches at least since September. That's why I don't want to get you a top-price twill. You'll be out of it in six months. It isn't worth it."

"Yes," she said, "yes," almost in pain, and then as if that was the end of it she sat without speaking, rubbing

7

the damp hair off her neck with her hand inside the towel. Mother, I know my bones, I live in this flesh, I know I have stopped growing. Look at me, I am another woman sitting up here on the grass, only not established, not recognized yet, but I am a woman sitting here watching you refuse the stream its current by your will. Just let me say this and say without looking at you that I've been three days, no, three nights and two days back and I can't stay. It's June, but it's just spring here because things are late this year. That's why the water is cold and the buds hardly open and the sedges the way rushes are in May usually, everything a month or more than that behind the season. But in other countries, in southern countries, things would be different now: the roses out strong and hot and sweet in the gardens, and the students, poets, painters coming back to their rooms along the river not looking like other people, their eyes different, and their voices not like other people's, and their shoes older, and their heads bare the way mine was bare all winter through the galleries and in the art museums and even in the churches, for even in Italy they don't seem to care if you put a handkerchief over your hair in respect any more. You walk in at noon out of the hot streets and the sun and your blood is consecrated, it becomes cool and pious with the devout pace of your feet across the stones, and you kneel down under the rising pillars in the granite dark, believing, believing. It is not religion, or Catholicism, or the belief of the Church of England, but it is your spirit on its knees at last just learning the words for its articulation. Students, she did not say aloud but sat silent rubbing her cold breasts dry beneath the towel, their faces looking different from other

8

faces because they are still on the adventure, looking for a thing nobody here wants or has heard of wanting: knowledge or the way to knowledge or else simply the way, because of what families or convention want, of keeping curious and keeping free. All last winter I wore my clothes the way they did, as if I were a student instead of just making the pretense at it, and walked like that, and now she watched her mother emerge from the water, draw herself out by the feminine thinnish hand which seized the ` damp rope of the tree's uncovered root. The stuff of the wet bathing-skirt shaped the firm muscles in the thighs that gripped toward land, and in some hopeless and unreclaimed contrition, the girl stretched her own bare arm out from the towel and saw the goose-flesh powdering her skin whitely to the wrist as her arm stiffened to aid the other woman up the bank. When their fingers met and clasped, the girl's face flashed suddenly up, fervent, humble, eager, but now the mother burst out laughing, slipping and scrambling there on her broad knees in the mud; either knowing what was to come or else not knowing quite and fearful of what the words might be, she pulled herself finally up laughing onto the grass and ripped the blue rubber casing from her head and shook out her short graying curled hair and glanced quickly across the sky.

"Well, the sun's thinning out all right, Nan. Your hand's as cold as charity," she said, the voice light, inconsequential, speaking merely for the sake of sound. "You're foolish not to have taken your suit right off as soon as you were out. It chills you sitting in it like that." She was moving off, rump-high, groping on wet hands and knees to the pile of folded clothing. "Come along. We'll get our things on and run up to the paddocks," she said.

It was she who led the way along the foot-worn, cattle- and man-marked path that ran between the wild hedge and the rushes in the water, and the daughter followed, listening to the talk which led up to money now and stopped short there. The price of the seventh brood-mare, and the stud fees; on went the mother's voice ahead, talking of buying wider pasture while the big arm and the bathing-bag swung at the foxtails as she passed. Nan came over the pressed grass of the walk behind her, her feet in sandals, the vague, dream-drugged, rapt eyes watching the weeds and the branches move in the sun while the water slid off through the fields and the woman's voice went on before her:

"There's no worse business than this kind of thing we have to do, growing horses on the same ground year after year. I keep racking my brains for some way out of it and how to get hold of another set of paddocks to make use of alternate years like a rich man's stud where money is no object. There's the saying that a sheep's foot is golden and that's what has saved the ground from going horse-proud." The voice went quickly, ceaselessly on, faintly contentious, acrimonious, in the drifting light of afternoon. The back of her neck stood broad and thickening beneath her sailor hat and the cropped hairs lay, wet from swim-ming, flat against the dust-white skin. "Putting cattle on and off the paddocks, in and out while the stud is going on, it's a heartbreaking business. Salting the rough grasses so the cattle will eat them off or mowing the grasses off and getting the sheep in, there's no end to it." She hit out at the foxtails with her bag. "I know what I want," she said savagely, coming closer to the bitter statement of it. "If I had enough money for it. Grassland kept in good heart by resting, d' y' see, Nan? Acres of fresh rested cock's foot and rye grass and fiorin. Ah, I can see it all right in my mind's eye, but what can I do about it? Anyone knowing anything about horses would see it like this, but the one man who has anything to do with it goes using the money up in other ways—"

This was not the beginning of it or anywhere near the beginning: it was merely the high-spot of the story restated so that she could begin to tell it all over again. It had started in those letters written to the young ladies' boarding school in Florence, crossed land and water to another country and begun abruptly in the big wide Italian room with the girls' three beds in it: "Nan, I had put money aside towards buying new pasture and what did your father do but up and buy this stag-faced gelding without any rhyme or reason for doing it, except he'd had too much to drink."

He hasn't any preferences or any real will of his own, it went on in the letters or else in the voice carrying it along the cattle and dairy path ahead. He does it out of, what's the word I want, Nan, I don't mean out of spite but something almost like it only queerer, because I'm the one who has the money, born with it, kept it, doubled it after your grandfather died, and your father has to show he's somebody with something, even if it's only the say-so. He wants to prove to me and everybody else what a man he is by going out and buying an animal I haven't had a finger or an eye on, and drawing the check out to fool them into thinking any of it's his, doing it after a few drinks to show them what it's like, a man's signature and a man's bank account. And he knows I'll stand by him; it's what he trades on, that I won't let him down. Seven, eight years back he spent that fortune on cattle when he knew, sober anyway he knew, that polled cattle were the only kind we could use with horses on the farm. He had the breed names in his notebook when he went off to the fair: Galloways, Red Polls or Aberdeen Angus I'd put down for him, thinking to give him the satisfaction of the responsibility. But after whatever he had at the Ship he must have said to himself, I'll show her. If she's British and the money's hers, I'm Canadian and I'll have the choice and the say. I cried a week over it after but that didn't do any good, and the cattle once re-sold fetched half the price of what he'd paid at the public sales, and I had to swallow that too. And next was the unproved sire he brought home instead of a high-class stallion, without running out its pedigree even. Try always if you can to nick with the *sire's* dam's blood and leave the *sire's* sire's blood as your outcross whenever it's possible to do it, I'd told him since the beginning. I'd written it down for him, but nothing scientific ever mattered to him. If he likes the look of a thing, or if he's had enough of someone knowing better than he does, or after a drink or two, he'll have his head for once whatever the price, so home he comes with this horse and there we were with it, a practical dead-loss on our hands. But even with it down in print before him you can't teach a Canadian anything about a horse's predominate blood. Ah, it's been a heart-breaking business with your father, Nan; if he kept his hands on paints or chess sets it would be one thing, but after he's started drinking at the sales and has the bee in his bonnet that he knows, it would break your heart wide open. But I've never put my foot down about the joint account and that's what I should have done from the beginning. I've always let him go on drawing on the money for the sake of his manliness, or like giving him the tail-end of a career or an occupation because he never had one of his own. And why do I keep on doing it like a fool?—only because he comes back crying over what he's done once he's seen the folly of it, crying and sorry and swearing never to do it again and ready to die for it and willing to pay back every penny out of tobacco money, and swearing to paint a picture worth more than everything he's lost. . . .

"He's only spent the money wrong like that about twice, mother," the girl said. Hatless, stockingless, she walked behind, the dream-rapt eyes watching the weeds and branches stir and quiver in the sun.

"Three times!" the woman ahead cried out. "There were the horned cattle and the worthless sire, and now this time it's this crazy hunter! He brings in this stag-faced hack at the price you'd lay out for a thoroughbred beast, and never thinking after what he'd had to drink, of having him up to pass the vet. Jolly as can be he comes in without a certificate either way, and the man who'd sold it to him out of the country so it happened. And why did your father do it? Just to show me he can get the money out of my hands when he wants! We're stocking a stud-farm, I told him, not a riding-school. But the money was already gone and the price of new paddocks shot again—"

"Was it much? Could it have been as much as that?" the girl said, the black hair back from the hollow temples, the eyes wild-violet soft and tender, the bare blue-veined feet in the sandals wandering dreamily, soundlessly on by the stream.

"Ah, no, not so much as the price of new land, no," said the mother, striking at the tall fox-grasses with her bag. "Nothing like what has been paid for horses, nothing compared to what Sir Mallaby Deeley paid for 'Solario,' for instance," she said with bitter irony. "Never forty-odd thousand pounds, of course, but still for me it was something. It was enough to put off looking at land or even thinking of new paddocks for another year or more until something has had the time to collect and stop the hole up—"

The girl started talking quietly behind her.

"Candy says he bought Brigand for me," she was saying. "He says he wants me to have Brigand to ride and do with as I please. I told Candy I didn't want to hunt any more and he said I could have him anyway for mine—if I wanted him—I mean, if I stay—"

"He's leggy," the mother said quickly, almost quick enough to stop the sound of the last words short before she would have to hear them said, and she went on talking loud and fast. "There's bad blood in him somewhere, sire or dam; he's queer. Your father picked him for his shoulders, but anyone who knows will tell you that's a luxury item. A bad horse can trick a novice time and again with pretty shoulders."

Home three days, the mother began thinking now a little wildly, and already that face as if they'd put her in prison for life, and already the words beginning to be dropped and the hints. She went along the stream's side, irritated now, hitting impatiently at the heads of the weeds, think-

ing of the girl following a little way behind her and thinking It's her good-looks that have done it. None of us
thought she'd turn out like that, and now summer's good
enough to be wasted at home but later she'll have to be
off where the remarks men on the street or men she's met
pass about her will be nourishment enough. Ah, I know
very well what it is you want, she thought slyly, and at
the same time with an impatient recognition of the slyness,
and I'm your mother and I'll keep you from it as long as
I can. It's all very fine for you but it isn't fine enough,
Nan; you're seventeen, you can very well wait till you're
twenty to know what you want and to hear the things
they'll always have to say about your face and figure.

"Your father—" she began, but suddenly, as if wakened
from the walking dream and crying out in sleep, the girl
called:

"Mother, look at that bird up there!"

Once they had been walking along here to the paddocks,
perhaps two years back it was, anyway before the board-
ing-school in Florence, and it was something else that
stopped them short like this on the path, and the mother
now, as then, turned with her bathing-bag in her hand and
the identical sailor hat (which perhaps was not the same
one from summer to summer but which might have been)
shaded her face from what was not sun or even light so
much as merely the absence of rain. I can't look, if I can't
look down there again I can't. I can't bear looking at it,
I can't look again, said Nan's voice over the two years of
almost having forgotten what its shape was and how it
lay against the bottom in the mud.

"What are you talking about, Nan?" said the mother

15

with no alteration in the tone or face, neither more impatient or less, saying it now exactly as she had said it then.

"Mother, look, there's a bird caught up there in the trees," the girl said, thinking: Two years ago the thing was lying in the water and I couldn't look down at it again. I stood staring at her face until she finally turned her face down to see, the hat brim lowering so that I couldn't see her eyes any more, only the nostrils whitening along the edges and her mouth opening as if to make a sound but not making it, and then she threw her bag down on the path. We'll have to get him out quick, she said. Nan, I'll go down and get him and if you can get hold of his arms from the bank while I push him from below we ought to make it. He's got his cap on still, the mother said. Mother, I can't, I can't do anything, said Nan's voice, dying. I can't. I'm too afraid.

So slowly, the act witnessed only by herself because the girl crouched on the path had covered her face with her hands, the mother turned the body over in the water, kneeling in her clothes in the stream while the water ran cold across her doubled-up legs and to her hips. It's Sykes, she said without looking up. What I thought. It's Sykes. He's dead. And slowly, breathing hard with the effort, she got him out over the rushes and up the bank alone, thought Nan, while I sat here shaking and crying and trying not to see. But still I saw, because I remember seeing his head fall backwards on his neck and hit the grass and concrete by the paddock's post and his adam's apple jerk up higher in his throat and stop there and not come down again the way a living man's would. I remember her saying He must have drowned last Saturday night (and this was Monday afternoon), dead drunk, perhaps drinking with your father. She stood up and stood looking down at him, and then she leaned over and pulled the beak of the black-and-white checkered cap he was wearing down across his face. He wasn't a good groom anyway, the mother said wiping her hands in her handkerchief. I've been thinking for two days he'd gone off dishonestly but this was honest enough, the old souse, she said.

Holding her bathing-bag now and looking off in the direction of the trees clumped at a little distance in the meadow, she said:

"Where? A bird caught? I can't see it, Nan. Where?" Because she must turn around to look for it, her back was put now to where the paddocks lay beyond the stream's next bend, masked by the drooping willows, and this was more than she had the patience left for, for she'd already got the smell of horses down the wind. "Where in the world can you possibly see a bird caught?" she said almost in irritation.

"There," the girl said, and the lifted hand was narrow and angular as a boy's hand set strangely at the white arm's extremity. "It's holding onto something in the tree there, or else it's caught by something," she said, the hand lifted, pointing, square at the fingertips and the resolute square nails cut short on a doer's not a dreamer's hand.

The trees they looked at were various and of variable green, standing high and lovely now against the misting heavens, their pale and dark, strong and fanciful greens shaking and beckoning in a breeze that did not touch the woman's or the girl's lifted face. Now that the mother saw the bird hanging too, they set off through the field, walk-

17

ing side by side through the half-grown unbroken weeds
the short way there was to go. Ahead stood the trees: it
might have been that a fistful of seed, no two alike, had
been flung down, years back, upon that place—oak, ash,
beech, juniper, elder and their underbrush—and this almost
circular island of uneven, incongruous mast and foliage had
sprung up there in the open sea of grass. The mother and
the girl did not speak as they walked but watched those
forward branches of the oak where the bird hung, rising
and falling.

"There's a sling on his neck," said the woman, standing
under him now and letting the bag drop behind her into
the grass.

"They've tried to hang him!" the girl cried out in anger.
"Boys, of course! They've strung him up there simply for
the fun of it!"

"Rubbish," said the woman. They stood with their heads
thrown back, the mother taller, stronger, their faces lifted
to the flapping captive bird. "He's got his head tangled in
it somehow. He's a thrush—a silly, thieving thrush, out after
something for his nest and this is the trouble he's got himself into."

As they stood under him watching, he fluttered wildly
upward and lit in panic on the branch above. There he
paused, his beak gaping weakly, his eye, bright, wounded,
desperate, on them. Below him the string that held him
tethered loop down, swinging loose as a hammock on the
delicate air.

"So now I suppose you see what you've got yourself
into?" the woman called up to him from the ground.
"Now you see what it means to go snooping and nosing

around instead of staying in the woods where you belong!"
The bird sat high above them, unmoving on the branch,
his beak as if pried open, his motionless body throbbing
under the leaves like a feathered, stricken heart. "I've a
good mind to leave you right where you are like that,"
she said, and she added: "He's too high to reach from here."

"I can climb to him," the girl said. "I can easily get up
to him."

She leaned and undid her sandals, and then the boy
hands reached up and closed on the oak's lowest bough
and her feet swung off the ground. The bare feet ran
quickly up the trunk's hide and she stood upright in the
first fork with one arm around the tree's girth. Seeing her
there, taller and closer in menace, the bird fell threshing
again from the branch and hung, the eye on her small,
bright, alert, jerking at the string's extremity. It will be
like having a moth fly in the room at night, the girl said
climbing higher; I'll feel the flesh moving up my back and
swear not to shudder and all the time I'll be crawling cold
with terror. When I get my hands around him to lift him
down, I'll have to keep my eyes shut, and even then I
won't be able to bear the feel of his feathers beating and
fluttering on my skin.

"Move out along the branch towards him from where
you are," the mother called up. Her face was lifted and
the sailor-hat brim hung limp across her brow and ears.

"Yes," said the girl, not moving. "That's what I'm going
to do."

Or the feel of his feet, I won't be able to stand it.
They'll be cold, naked, unbearable, like a sick thing's or a
dying baby's fingers. If I touch him I'll have to choke him

in terror, I'll have to break his legs in two, I'll have to do it. She crouched waiting at the tree's second fork before beginning the journey out, her fingers and bare feet holding to the tree's heavy hide. And now, ahead, she could see how the string lay coiled around the branch and the fiber of it, like good fishing-line. Exactly like fishing-gut, she thought, her eyes shifting quickly, steadily from the bird's hanging body beating among the leaves to the way out along the slowly yielding curve of the wood.

"A yard more and you've got him," said the mother, carefully, step by step, keeping pace with her on the ground below; and now the branch sagged gently with the girl's weight, dipped whispering and creaking lower while the mother said cautiously: "Go a little further and then I can reach up and get him."

"But don't pull him!" the girl said. Pausing there, crouched animal-like, wide-eyed on the branch, she saw suddenly what it was. "It is fishing-line!" she said. "Look! He's swallowed the worm and hook, that's what he's done—"

She began unwinding the broken gut string from the bough, squatting on her bare legs and feet and reaching out, and now the terrible, wild, tugging life freed of the branch pulled on the string her hands held, tore through the leaves in frantic terror like a fish leaping underwater with the hook caught in him. In a minute he'll rip his tongue out and I'll go crazy, she thought, feeding the line down to her mother, and below her the woman lifted her arms high and raised her empty hands.

"Can you get him? Have you got him?" the girl said, and she closed her eyes so as to see it no longer and crouched blind, dazed in the tree with the nightmare of frail desperate life tearing, beak, claw, and wing, at the string's vein through her fingers.

"Yes, let the string go," said the mother's hushed voice. "Let it go. I have him," and the movement ceased suddenly, halted with an abruptness closer to extinction than release as the woman took him in her lifted hands.

The girl swung herself from the second branch down to the first, and hung from the first for a moment before dropping to the ground. The woman held him fast, the beak wide open in her fingers while with the right hand she manipulated the hook forked deep within his throat. The breath came audibly through her nostrils as she worked and her face hung over him, and it was at the face the girl looked, not at the bird, as she stood beside her. She looked at the long pale cheek and the lips set and she said, Mother, not speaking aloud, you can touch these things, you can touch death and wipe it off in your handkerchief afterwards and touch pain without shrinking from it but you cannot take me in your arms any more and when I am with you I am afraid. Mother, she said in silence not looking at the bird, come out of your stone flesh and touch me too and see how tall I am, my eye almost up to your eye, and how big my feet and hands are, like a woman's. But the cheek did not alter and did not color, and the girl made herself look down now at the bird. For a while there was no sign of blood, only the stretched gagging throat and tongue, and then suddenly it came, fine as thread and dark across the seemingly unliving substance of the beak and across the cushion of the woman's finger prying it wide.

"There," she said, and she flung the freed hook and the length of the fishing-line from her and lifted the bird closer in her fist to see deeper into the hopelessly defended and betrayed secrets of its throat and sight. And now, eye to eye with her, he closed his beak violently on her finger, the flat tiny poll bristling with outrage, the beak striking and closing and striking again out of the small held feathered body in a paroxysm of hate.

"Now what will he do? Will he be able to eat?" the girl asked in a whisper, watching, and while she said it the woman opened the hand that held him and he struggled queerly forward, his feathers damp from the pressure of the palm and fingers and their human moisture and the thread of black blood streaking across his bill and breast. He did not fly at once: first he soiled the woman's hand and then he wheeled falteringly off under the trees.

"He can't fly straight yet," the mother said, and she stooped and wiped her hand off on the grasses. "Perhaps hanging all night there—"

And now as if the exact hour to speak had struck, as if it were this surprised and perhaps unpermanent moment of tenderness or frailty or default they had been waiting for, the girl put her hand up to the dark hair above her brow, shielding her eyes a little from the absolute committance of sight and began saying:

"Mother, I want to know now, I want to know it so much now so I'll be certain . . . I've been trying to say it to you since I've been back . . . I want to know if you and Candy will let me . . . I want to know it so I can plan about it and talk and write letters . . . I mean, if you will let me go again in September . . . it's June now, I mean in about three months could I . . . I mean, to study somewhere, of course, not just to have a good time but to really learn . . ."

The mother had turned away and stooped, and with her head down picked up the bathing-bag where she had dropped it in the grass.

"Where? Where do you want to go?" she said, her hands dragging the bag's strings tighter, the face turned off under the old hat's brim and the dry lips trembling a little, not speaking loud.

"I thought perhaps back to Florence only not . . . I mean, I don't want to go to Miss Easter's again . . . I thought . . . You see, I want to paint. I thought live with a family in Paris or Florence or somewhere like that and go to classes . . . I thought . . . I mean . . ." She stopped saying it when the mother turned, her chin lifted.

"Nan, don't talk drivel," she said. "Think what you're saying. A girl of your age turned loose in a city. You'd soon enough see the folly of it—"

She was facing the stream again, the path, the willows concealing at the water's bend what lay so richly, ripely, fragrantly beyond. She had begun to move towards it, her back to the girl, the bag swinging, escaping towards the wind's smell, the myriad sound and stamp, the eager substance and heart of horses in their paddocks. Behind her the girl stood waiting, trembling, silent a moment before she too began walking.

"Not loose," she said after her. "Mother, not loose," but the tears rising in her throat stopped the sound of it with pain.

Chapter Two

AFTER she had opened the stable door and let the sun run in she stood watching him an instant: his head was high but quiet, his ears alive, his mahogany flank gleamed richly in the light from the part-opened door. Out of the shallow dimness of the boxes she could hear the groom's voice, continuous in the soothing swageing words of horse-talk as she crossed the floor, hearing it steady as water murmuring while she crossed the separately rounded and hoof-scarred timbers to where the hunter stood beyond his gate. His loins and quarters shone bright and firm and he stood on all four feet, without a hoof cocked, even though at ease. "You Brigand, you troublemaker," she said half-aloud and he turned his head on his shoulder to watch her come inside and close the latch behind her, and then he shifted to one side. At his head she raised her bare arm and laid her hand, gloved to the wrist, beneath his mane.

Now the delusion of darkness was clearing, ebbing fast, as her eyes altered, towards light: she could see the knots in the boards of the stall and the mare's head and neck beyond and her full ripe dappled shoulder over the partitions that stood between, and the strings of white hair, like a witch's, hanging on the brood-mare's neck. "I like this horse, Apby," the girl said, with her hand laid under the hunter's mane. She stood looking beyond into the clearing obscurity at the mare's head and the unseen crouching groom, saying it to his goodafternoon and the voice's low ceaseless cajoling. The windows were open the stable's length and the air was clean with avenues of myriad sparkling light running with sun to the forage of oaten straw and striking there and igniting it like flame. "Apby, I like him. I like the way he went yesterday. He's a good horse," she said. She was wearing breeches, old ones, too tight and darned across the knees, and a sport shirt undone at the neck. The gloves with the buttons missing and the brown leather wearing through white at the fingers' ends were turned inside out at her bare wrists and flapped back loose across her hands.

"Yes, Miss," said the groom, not lifting his voice to say it but letting the sound go murmuring on. "Bees swarming all the morning kept them nervy. They was all over the windows and wood." So hush now, so be still now, it went on gently, gently to the brood-mare as he squatted beside her using the paring-knife on her unshod foot. "Out yonder the wall was black with them, thick," he said in the same low, tempered, wooing tone. "They didn't like them, did you, lady? Oh, not at all, they didn't like them. I got them away with sulphur, burning it here and there in dishes outside and in."

"Apby, what do you think of him as a horse?" the girl said. "What do you think of this animal? He's turned out to be mine." She stood looking into the horse's dark clear eye with the lash, thick, black, fernlike, brushing on the lid, and the blood turned warm, the marrow melted softly in her from the power of the delicate, quick body breathing near. "What do you think of this upstart, this Brigand with his bony face?" she said. The smell of his coat was sweet and the neck's arch sprang firm and meaty underneath her hand.

"I will say he's got a good rein," the groom's voice began saying warily from the brood-mare's side. "He's got quite a bit in front of him, and that gives a horse an air. But I wouldn't—"

"He's got a foolish head, my fine horse has," said the girl with love, and she pulled the near ear gently down and drew the pointed fur tip of it across her face. And now, as if just recognizing the words the groom's voice had shaped or just receiving now their sense on some vague undulation of retarded hearing, she stopped short and stared across the stalls' partitions at the mare's head and shoulder and the unseen groom. "But you wouldn't what?" she said. "You wouldn't what?"

"It might be that I would never have thought of picking him out for a buy," the groom's voice went on. "But if he's stag-faced, as Mrs. Lombe has it, it don't hurt him none for riding. No one's going to ask nothing else of him, the way I understand it." He did not look up, the head, the soiled brown cap lowered over the bent foot as he worked at the mare's side, the same gentle assuaging murmur of contemporation crooning: "If he runs to hollowness towards the nose, there's no foal going to bear it on. Whatever his faults are or his points either, it stops with him there and no harm come to, at least the way I look at it."

She stood with her hand stopped under the black hairs of the mane still, her obsessed rapt gaze moving from the ear's soft flick and the passive brow down the nasal bones to the nostril, her own dream-stupored, half-slumbering eye level with the horse's proud soft brilliant eye. So this is how they think of you, my horse, she said in silence to him. She lifted her other hand and touched the wide hard cheek-bone's blade. Not my first horse or my second or even the third, but this time my horse in protest, my hunter in defiance; not with race and nervousness flickering down your crest and loins, but my bony-legged monster to gentle, to murmur alone to in fortification of my father's errors; the substance of identity and revolt and love to hold to, until I can see you like the oriflamme of what is nothing more violent than Candy and me walking down a street arm in arm together in another country, she said, the gloved hand moving on his neck under the mane's coarse glossy hair. With one finger she lifted the velvet of his lip and looked at the upper teeth laid bare in his mouth, breathing the warm hay-sweetened breath while the physical stab of love thrust in her. He drew his head up from her hand, but tractably, the nostril opening dry as silk and rosy and the hairs quivering on his vulnerable unmottled lip.

"Apby, what age would you give him?" she said, watching in grave passionate pride how his teeth met evenly, touching one on the other almost vertically.

"I'd give him off five," the groom said from the other box, and the girl looked up in sudden sharpness and Brigand's ears flicked on his lifted head.

"Off five!" she said. "What rubbish, Apby! Have you taken the trouble to look at him instead of just making up your mind about him without— Look here, his side front teeth are hardly cut. I'd say he's just off three."

"Come first July I'd give him rising six," the groom said, the peaceful, persistently assuaging voice unaltered. "He's cutting his tush and that's what's maybe thrown you off," but when he heard her jerk the bridle down off the peg he stood up in the mare's box. "I'll have him ready for you straight away, Miss, if you're taking him out," he said.

"No, I'll do it," she said shortly. "I don't see how in the world you handle him at all, feeling about him the way you do." Her hand in its glove lifted the hunter's hair and drew the forelock free of the browband onto his face and buckled the cheek-pieces tighter, working in quick stubborn rebuke. "You'd let them tell you anything and believe it, true or not," she said. She did not look for an instant over the box's panel to where the groom stood, the dwarfed arms hanging from the waistcoat's cramp and the blunt soiled fingers turning the paring-knife in harried, slow humility. He saw the sun coming through the open window onto her hair and head as she loosened the throat-lash on the horse's neck: the dark soft longish hair with the strong light on it and the pale face and throat and the mouth's color warm but pallid and he began saying in expiation:

"They're up to all kinds of tricks you'd never suspect if you wasn't onto them. Copers'll file off the seven-year notch and nobody the wiser if they get hold of a buyer what wouldn't know. You got to keep your eyes open, I tell you, you can't trust anybody, you just got to look sharp." He stood watching her from the other box and turning the paring-knife in his fingers, as if just to keep on talking no matter what the words were would be enough to set it right at last. "Bishoping's another coper's trick," he said. "They'll level the teeth off short and gouge the centers out and blacken them with caustic if they think it'll sell a ten-year old for a six," he said, and then he said abruptly and painfully: "I didn't mean no offense about his age, Miss," standing with the brown cloth cap turned back to front and lending him the look now of a tough stunted gladiator halted in the arena, uncharioted, bewildered, and unarmed. When he said this to her over the box's panel, she raised her lids and looked with the heavy, seemingly drugged wide-spaced eyes across the crib-bitten wood at him, the eyes' substance transparent as glass in the sunlight and clear bright icy blue.

"All right," she said, lifting the saddle over the gate. She stooped to girth it, and now the groom returned to his work again and his voice to cajoling, saying to the mare or the girl or to their quiet This is the way I came to say it or how I came to think it or Here's the explanation of it if you want it and this is the truth, s'help me, soothing them, lulling them, rocking them to sleep with the low half-querulous murmur of his self-palliation as he raised the mare's forefoot onto his lowered knee.

Saddled and bridled the horse waited while she unlatched the gate, and then turned in his box to follow her out. He carried his head down and the reins loose on his neck, but the ears were pointing in expectancy, his hoofs thudding loud and full on the timber as he came. His sloping shoulders flowed under the loose burnished skin and on the left side of his neck his mane hung dark and glossy. At the stable door the girl turned and took the double reins and ran them over her arm; when she lifted the door's handle and pushed the half of it out, the daylight fell like a wedge through the stable's dark.

"Apby," she said, looking back, and the groom stood up and answered, "Yes, Miss," touching his cap as he stood helpless, hopeless in the box by the mare. "Brigand's my show now," she said. "I'll be in to do him every morning," and the groom answered bleakly, "Yes, Miss" again, and touched his cap again with his fingers, and then he suddenly began saying: "Sometimes even old hands at the game'll make a slip, like a breeder I knew of once was thrown off by the corner teeth. You'll see them coming through around four years and rising five, nine times out of ten you will, but like this time I was speaking about, there was the exception proving the rule, as they say, and knowing the horse I knew when he was foaled, a bay colt nice as anything you've seen—"

"All right," the girl said from the doorway, the voice cold, implacable still.

"That Brigand there, he has the kind of look like he might break a rule," the groom said, speaking louder as if the mere sound of his impetration must set it right no matter what the words were. "When Mr. Lombe brought him in a month or something back, I said right off to Mrs. Lombe, I said if ever I saw a horse that looked like he'd—"

"All right," she said, stepping clear of the beam. "All right." She watched the horse pick his way over after her and she said: "All right, Apby, I'll see to him myself when I bring him in. Don't wait around for him," and she closed the door.

✦

Candy Lombe had put his dark green felt on looking at himself, the roundish, soft, bright face, the swollen aggrieved eyes, looking straight into the vestibule's long glass and bringing the brim down right; the small hand with

the signet dark red ring drawing tighter the cravat on which
the beagles ran against his throat, the head held back to
get the light while he slipped his fingers along the short
mustaches' bristles on his upper lip and smelled the bay
rum and the shaving-soap that lingered. He had gone off
from the house in the afternoon feeling the curse lying
heavy on him: the bane and the wrong that there was no
shape to his life and none in the past since youth (and
youth shaped by what, after all, but the imminence of
hope), and now youth gone and the curse of nothing else
to come. The forty-three or forty-four years (he couldn't
or didn't want to remember which) must for a long time
now have been these fragments, discarded over some vague
period of space or time: vestiges of a thing as irreplacable
as life that had been given him entire and that he had let
fall, the separate pieces lost in separate countries, before
knowing there was any value to the thing or even that he
carried anything at all.

Ah, trouble, trouble, there are the two different kinds
of it, he thought, going bitterly alone up through the green
June fields; there's the one you give and the other you
take. I gave, I gave freely, he said to the curse, the bane,
the wrong of his life. It is more blessèd to give than to
receive, so I gave. I gave trouble at home until I was twenty
for the ordeal of art alone; not for the fact or the accomplishment of art but the organized slaughter of what the
idle said was not Art, the Glorified, the Exalted; I gave
trouble year after year for the willful murder of what They
(family) recognized as comfort like a mouse its hole by
Me (individual) who must (for what reason time has never
made clear) be saved from mediocrity for the crowning

and the final wide and loud acclaim. I wore a smock and a beret on the streets of Montreal, did Candy Lombe, by God, and what is he now but a squire in his English squire's jacket strolling up the country with a good felt hat on telling himself he'll get a thumb-nail sketch, a bird's eye view instead of a kick in the seat for his forty-odd years of caring, not making the pretense any more of carrying a water-color box or a palette and tubes and boards but out with his golf hose fitting his ankles right and his heart gone rotten in him.

Because nobody ever made me understand that it was up to me and nobody ever helped me with it or told me what to do, said the petulance, the querulousness which even rising anger could not dignify with heat; me, colonial in England, pauper, painter, each imposing their segregation from country, status, convention. Everyone with their hands lifted hard and high against what I have to be: the intruder on somebody else's soil when I should have stayed home and gone on with what my father was (the visionary, the preacher), and the intruder on some woman's money even if I did give her my name in exchange, and the last tentative intrusion made and abandoned on some other kind of man's career. Me, the painter, tradition of Goya, Velasquez, me, charcoal sketching in night-schools, water-painting landscapes up to thirty like a school-boy, hanging up little canvases in fancy rooms with decorated peasant china and hand-embroidered table linen, all for sale, even the pretty pastel-colored canvases, all at a price for the ladies who come in to tea. Me, an artist, never able to memorize right the lines I wasn't intended to speak or recognizing the cues when I heard them, but somehow trying to take part in the performance, making my exits and entrances blushing, stammering, always backwards and on the wrong side of the stage.

The lane he had come into now had wild hedge growing thick on either side of it and ruts cutting deep and dry into its bed. Long pale grasses sprang up in the crescents marked by draught-horses' feet on the center rise of ground between the stone-hard troughs their cart wheels had hollowed. In a while he knew he would come out onto the dairy farm, not suddenly but piece by piece upon it: first the wall with the moss along it beginning to wind in low, unbroken meandering beyond the orchard trunks, the stones washed light as lime but slightly golden, and after the flash of a white cat with a striped auburn tail past the milk-tins tilted up to sweeten in the sun; step by step coming to it, the familiarly rain-drenched or else the shimmering completely silent, rural scene. It might have been something printed on a postcard, or still more a faintly tinted photograph joined by a silk cord with tassels to a wall calendar for the year. C. Lombe, Esq., he said walking measuredly in silence towards it, taking his forty-three or forty-four years of protest against, dreams of, demands for whispered or spoken or cried aloud at night, to this stage laid for still unaccumulated action, to this hushed homely amphitheater where the classic drama of neurosis might play itself out to destruction; Candy Lombe taking the not even colossal failure of these expended years out for a stroll this afternoon as I did yesterday afternoon and as I will take it out into the air tomorrow, exactly as you'd take a horse out, two hours of gentle exercise a day, to tire him for his body's peace and wear him down to time's passivity for his soul's. Lure the days one after another like this, as the years have been inveigled to a lonely spot where their cries cannot be heard and cut their throats for them and fling them, virgin still, upon the manure-heaps, the stable-rakings, the horse offal of this part of England. They can't stink more than stud-farms do of sex and monstrous matings and foalings brutaler than murders.

Through his shoes he could feel the scars the horses' irons had left in the lane-bed's clay, the shape of them set hard into his shoe leather like in his memory: the calkins, the feather-edge, the plain, the Rodway shoe. Nowhere in this countryside could you get away from the mark of horses on the soil, the smell of horses, of horses' droppings, the rose-headed and counter-sunk shoe-nails found on the roads and lanes and scattered through the pastures. Horses pulled carts when I was young, he thought, walking; they were nothing to me, neither to be liked or not. They never entered into life's substance; their place was allotted, not mine. They were not the established order and I the outcast lost to society and human intercourse for want of a proper name. And now, to elude their wild extravagant possession, Candy Lombe instead of signing canvases walks through a county fetid with horse, rank with horse, pockmarked and stampeded by them; here he is, paddocked at middle-age, hobbled without a choice of pasture or forage, buckled and strapped and gelded and going thick in the wind.

"I feel so sorry for Candy, although he looks such a dandy," he began, making it up, half aloud. "His squire's jacket is black and white, and his something something fits him tight—right—I feel so sorry for Candy," he started over again, "although his color's so—though his color's fresh and dandy. His hair and his mustache are neat, but he's sick of the sight of horses' feet. I feel so VERY sorry for him— tum-te-tum, te-tum-te-tum. He used to be young and his paunch was thin, but rigs and fillys have done him in. I feel so sorry for—"

Now the first sight of the dairy began through the apple trees and he stopped making his verses up and watched for the wings and the dreamy faintly blowing back-drop and the familiar properties set to the right and left. There was the stage, the rural lovely scene, and no players on the boards yet, as yet no sign of horse-dirt fouling the pre- pared ground here where the lane widened slowly towards the farm's court and halted. Oh, Candy Lombe, he used to paint, he said to himself, the idle English gentleman wan- dering towards the picturesque little dairy farm on the June afternoon. But all the praise he got was faint. He thought: if I stop saying this I'm lost, if I stop saying Oh, Candy Lombe, he used to think in the days before he took to—if I stop saying it I'll see the curse hanging there before me, weighted and choked with death and incongruous in the sun as a corpse hanging in his old clothes behind the house there by his neck and swinging gently, or a railway tramp lying iron-dead in a freight-car of red apples. Oh, Nancy, Nancy, give me ear, he went on, like whistling in the dark; oh, hasten to your father, dear! Oh, Candy Lombe stepped out from home, he began rapidly again, and then he saw the first movement of life, furtive and quick as something stirring in the twilight of early morning or evening: the white cat flashing past the up-turned milk- tins as it had done yesterday afternoon, only a little earlier, just as he had been a few yards back crossing the orchard grass. Now, it seemed, had the overture to action been executed at last, and immediately the ducks, neat and immaculate as linen, reeled slowly around the corner of the dairy farm-house and started for the water-trough.

After a time, still standing there in his gray knickerbockers and his trimly gartered wool hose and watching the ducks beguile themselves gravely across the water's surface, their bills dipping and fumbling below the brink, he began to hear the sound of the horse's hoofs coming. For a while he did not turn his head to see or even begin conjecturing, but stood with his hands in his jacket pockets, the narrow, cleanly manicured thumbs showing, the hat-brim smartly down, seeming to watch the ducks in the water but perhaps seeing nothing beyond the lost, corrupted vision of his youth or hearing nothing but the sound of its despair. But when the horse had come close behind him and the rider drew rein, he started and turned in guilt, his right arm involuntarily raised partly in some gesture of greeting and partly as if to ward off the violence of actual sight or being seen by whomever had come on him undefended and unaware.

"Hello, Candy," said Nan from the horse's back, and here were their eyes meeting down the slant of the mahogany shoulder, the same marvelously glazed, indolently cast eyes obliquely and rather shyly spanning the distance's acclivity from mount to ground, and their mouths smiling.

"Why, hello there, Nancy," the father said with an American and disproportionate heartiness that only from uneasiness and hesitation sought to cloak, conceal, secrete nothing but the soul's timidity.

"I was looking for you," the girl said. "I rode him up here because I thought you came this way."

"I've got the habit of walking up here in the afternoons," he said in a bright sociable tone, almost but not quite as if seeking to keep from her some reason for his having come. He laid one hand, palm down, on the horse's shoulder and looked up at her from under the smartly dipping fine felt brim. "Gets me away from the stud," he said, his small mouth and his chin beginning to laugh under his mustache. "I think it's more like country up here and not so much like business. Nobody's doing anything, not even the ducks." He was smiling up at her with this little defense, this eager little reserve between them as if she were a lady he had just met at tea. "I can flâner les boulevards, as it were," he said. When he put out his hand to hold the rein while she dismounted, she stopped and said:

"Don't hold him. Please, don't hold him. He won't stir."

"You've only ridden him two days," said Candy, but he stayed his hand uncertainly and watched her slide to the ground.

"He's been very nicely trained, your horse has," she said. "When I mount he stands without moving a muscle while I fix my reins or gloves or belt or fiddle with the stirrups." She brought the reins forward over the horse's head and ran them up her arm. "We did exercises at the trot this afternoon: the figure of eight on one track and hock turns and the turn about. We're getting on very well together." They walked along side by side, past the dairy farmhouse, the girl with the horse coming docilely behind her and the man with his hands in his jacket pockets, side by side out onto the country road. "Only voices worry him a little. He

likes them soft and low, like you do." Their eyes slid sideways again at each other's faces, and the father laughed.
"He shied twice—once at a fence and at a tree back there a
minute before the dairy. I told him I wouldn't have it."

"Now, listen," said Candy. "I don't want him to get you
into trouble." Here it was, the threat, the menace of horses
again, the monstrous promise in their bone and hide of the
mutilation, the even fatal evil they could wreak on peace
sounding alarm from nerve to nerve and marking it in trepi-
dation on his face. "Look here, Nancy, I want you to be
careful with him."

"It's just a game he likes to play," she said. "He pretended
he couldn't get the look of the fence right and so he shied
off at the jump. He must have seen other horses' dem-
onstrations, you know, and thinks it's smart to imitate them
—you know, the way schoolgirls, I mean some do, you
know, the way they imitate or pretend to talk like picture
actresses they've seen—"

"The silly, adolescent creatures," Candy said severely.

"Ah, don't laugh," his daughter said, and the horse came
gently, meekly on behind. "He's looking for a personality,
you know, the way you have to when you're young. You
can't always decide so quickly what you're going to be like.
Sometimes he plays at being willful and he goes on the way
he must have seen race horses do. But it doesn't mean anything, it's really rather silly of him. Coming up the hill he
stopped walking and stared at a clump of buttercups as if
he'd never seen anything like them before, or perhaps as if
he couldn't *really* see them, and then he just walked on and
I couldn't get a word out of him. But he's really, I mean
underneath everything else, he's really awfully afraid of dis-

pleasing. You can see by looking at him he's very vain," she said.

"Oh, can you?" said Candy, looking back under the brim of his hat at the horse coming on behind. "Now, with all due respect, Nancy, where—"

"Ah, don't make fun of him!" she said in sudden pain. "Everyone ridiculing him and jeering at him as if he were the stable freak simply because he isn't to sire or foal or isn't a colt, or isn't to train, or hasn't a single action he's expected to perform! Simply to look the fool and hack around, but I didn't think you'd feel that about him—"

Walking in silence beside her, he put his arm in the black-and-white patterned sleeve through her bare arm's bend and drew her against him until he felt the ribs and the breast under the sport shirt moving against his squire's cloth, walking in step with her and in silence, the sharp small daughterly hip moving against his thickening hip.

"Nancy, I'm sorry. I'm sorry I said that," he said. "I didn't mean it." A freak and a fool and a hack like me, he thought in bitter, retributive guilt. In this way they walked on for a while through the scallops of shade and sun, shade cast by the thickly arching trees and sun shining palely in the open spaces on the ground; each thinking of the horse, not as it came along behind them at the end of its loose rein, but transformed to symbol for the separateness of two interpretations and two isolate despairs. "I was thinking this afternoon," the father said, "about horses. You were brought up on the brutes but I wasn't. I never had a horse anywhere near me, except pulling a milk-wagon or a tramcar, when I was young. Perhaps I keep on thinking about horses without knowing that I think of them like that, the way someone who has all the equipment bought and ready and has promised to go big-game hunting feels when he starts thinking about the game, you know, the elephants and the lions and all that. Of course, I mean somebody who doesn't like big-game hunting or big game or who doesn't even like shooting. I mean, somebody who just simply doesn't like to think about lions and elephants and other big savage animals and who would rather think about something else. Well, there it is," he said, beginning to smile uneasily under his mustache. "So I have to get out of it by being funny about horses. If I wasn't funny about them I'd have to get up and ride one and I never liked getting anywhere near them. I've climbed up on them for almost twenty years, and I respect them, they stand very high in my opinion, and I think they've got all the qualities the horse authorities claim they have. But I just don't like having much to do with them. I like to watch a good point-to-point race or a steeplechase and have some money on it, but I don't like getting into mix-ups with them. Maybe it's because I'm not really interested in showing them, you know, or anybody I'm the master. I don't like to bully anything into obeying me so that's why I don't like to have to go into their stalls or have too much to do with them. I don't mind this chap coming along behind us here because he's not as arrogant as most, but I wouldn't go out of my way—"

"I met a man last winter," the girl said, his arm through hers as she walked, her eyes watching the ground. "He'd been brought up with them, like me." They went on, arm in arm, silent for a little further and the horse came following on his rein. "At Mrs. Paddington's Wednesday teas in Florence, I met him there," she said after a minute. "He was an Irishman—about twenty or something like that. His people kept hunters and his mother had one of the best seats in Ireland, she was one of the grand women to hounds—you know, he didn't say it to brag but like a joke," she said, looking quickly at the side of her father's face. "As a matter of fact, he couldn't stick hunting. It made him sick. And I knew I felt that way too, after he'd said it, only I'd never been able to explain it before. He'd gone off from home after a row, I think, or something, but anyway he couldn't stick the kind of hunting county people he'd been born with. He was writing a book about them. He was one of the first writers I ever met," she said.

Arm in arm, step by step they went on together, and the father's eyes slipping sideways saw the tender flesh of her neck, and the ear's lobe pale as coral, and the vulnerable temple with life beating visibly, exquisitely there. He made his tone carefully, casually bright so as not to scare her words off.

"Sounds like an interesting sort of chap," he said, clearing his throat and watching the ground below.

"Candy," said the girl in a quick, soft, eager voice, but she did not turn her head. "I want to go back in September. I don't mean back to Miss Easter's but back to Paris or somewhere else. I want to do something. I have to do something. I can't stay here. I mean, I want to go on studying painting or art or maybe how to be a sculptor and I thought after a while I might be able to make my living and then I wouldn't have to stay all the year here. It's not," she said, not looking up from the road but watching it go steadily beneath their walking feet, "I mean, it hasn't anything to do with not— with not loving you or not loving anyone, but in cities and in other places, you know, there're people all over the world, I mean like that Irishman, saying different things all the time and here nobody hears them saying them and—"

"Nancy," said the father in a tight, small, but brightly casual voice. "I suppose—that is, if it's true I thought you just might like to say it—I suppose it's possible you liked him rather well?"

"Oh, no," she said quickly. "I didn't mean that. I only saw him two or three times after that. He wasn't staying long in Florence. He was on his way to Spain." Arm in arm they walked, watching the ground move back beneath their feet, the road slipping back and away in the shade and the light and the shade from the trees as they walked small and human-voiced and human-limbed under the high fresh springing boughs. "He was going to get over there and fight against Franco, only he couldn't let the Italians hear him say it. Here you wouldn't know about anybody doing anything like that, would you, Candy? Or if you read it in the paper you'd forget about it because you wouldn't have the sound of the person's voice when they said it or how their face looked."

"No," said Candy, holding her arm tight in his. "No. I know."

"So I thought if I could do something, do some kind of work, I mean first learn to do something, like painting, the way you did," she went on, watching the ground go; and Like me, he thought, learn to sit waiting in a room alone, face a blank canvas and a notebook with a sketch or two sketches in it, the brushes clean, the paints ready, the light right, the easel set, and sit there making no mark, and fearing to make any, and sit fearing thought as impotently as act. Learn to sit still in terror before nothing, learning, the way a convict learns by heart the words of his sentence, the emptiness of one's own indecision and the elusiveness of the idiom, the pronunciation, the sound even of one's own purposeless intention. "So I thought if I could go back over there, I mean to Paris or Rome or somewhere in September," she was saying, and he went on in silence: Learn it without ever crying out in protest or bringing down in vengeance, and slowly, weakly, gradually meander to the first drink of consolation and the second, until Drink itself becomes the thing to wait for in the room's and soul's void, not the visitation youth promised of the pure and perfect substance of Art. "I thought if it could be decided now so that I'd know," she was saying, "then I could stick it out here this summer without—"

The road moved slowly, unevenly off behind them through light and shade, shade and shimmering afternoon light, poured slowly back over rut and scarcely covered stone as they walked with their heads down, the same shapely, well-turned flesh and bone, the same drugged dreamy eyes watching it run slowly, endlessly back beneath their feet.

"Yes, that's the way I must have felt," said the father. "Just about your age—almost thirty years ago, maybe about twenty-seven or -eight years back—"

"I could get a room with a family or something or live in a club," the girl said. "Then you wouldn't worry about that part of what was happening to me. You could come over with me, Candy, and find the right courses for me to take, and meet the teachers and find the place for me to live in." She was talking faster now, her breath coming quick, as if the name of the street, the size of the room, the utensils of the art itself would be designated in a minute if she could catch up with where they were. "Candy, you could even find out for me what it is I ought to do," she said, and her mouth trembled.

"Yes," said her father, holding her bare arm tight in the up-bend of his arm, his fingers lying on her wrist. "You'll have to find somebody very good; you mustn't have somebody vague to teach you the things you'll have to learn. You know, bone's there, structure's there," he said brightly, his fingers modeling at her wrist where the pulse beat light and quick in the veins. "The old skeleton's there under the rest; under all the fanciness and vagueness you've got to find out in the end that he's there and how he goes together and how he moves. That's what I never paid enough attention to, Nancy. Perhaps that's why I never made a go of things." He glanced quickly, uneasily at the side of her face, and then away, thinking Perhaps it's too late already, perhaps there is nothing more to conceal from her by now. Ever since she could think for herself, maybe, she's laid in her bed at night knowing what I am better than I've ever known it, seeing me clearer, thinking about the one water-color hanging up in the top-hall and the one in the guest room behind the door, and knowing exactly without anyone saying it to her. Out loud he said in bold shy uneasiness: "You've got to dig right down into things from the start if you want to get anywhere. I tried out too many things, got interested in one phase of a thing—you know, experimented with one thing after another, and sometimes that leads you nowhere. I might have done a lot of things if I'd got hold of something certain at the outset. I might have done some good paintings—"

"Candy, you are a great painter," the girl said gravely.

"Oh, no," he said, looking down at the road and the little twitching smile beginning on his lips. "Oh, no."

For a time they had forgotten the horse, hearing without knowing they heard the slow light clopping of his hoofs behind them, but now the rein tightened on her arm and she stopped and looked back to where the horse stood halted on the road. His head was raised and turned a little to one side, away, and when she said his name he shook it gently, then savagely, in bewilderment. He stood fixed at his rein's length, like a beast who has come to water and will not cross, the forefeet planted in advance of the full glossy breast, the shocked hoofs gripping forward for balance to the earth. He had not started to retreat yet and did not venture to come on, but stood, his legs thrusting wider and wider apart, the neck curved back burnished, voluptuous as a swan's, and the raised head tossing, gently, gently, as if seeking to cast the mask of unfamiliar and desperate confusion off.

"Brigand," said the girl softly, drawing in the rein. "Brigand, you foolish thing, be quiet now, be still."

She had turned to him and now began walking to him, but once the rein had slackened on his mouth he reeled slowly, sickeningly backwards on his heels, the last link with human ascendancy and human corporality withdrawn, leaving him staggering masterless, lost, riderless in the obscure and incommunicable reaches of his pain.

"Look out for him!" the father suddenly cried out. "Get away from him, Nancy!" She saw him make the jump forward, the color ebbed from his face and mouth, and jerk the rein from her hand, and saw the horse whirl in panic and totter towards the ditch and trees and falter, as if sensing not seeing danger there, and stop quivering on the brink. "Get away from behind him! He may start kicking, Nancy!" Candy called out. "He's had a stroke! Look out for him! He's going to fall!"

"Hush," she said savagely. "Hush, oh, hush," to man and beast and to the terror that palsied their bones. She was at the horse's head again, taking the man's clutched trembling fingers from the leather and drawing the rein's length from his hand. "Hush, now stop, now listen to me," she said, and at the sound of her voice the horse's head veered awkwardly, but meek, despairing, towards her, the ears quivering antennae-vulnerable, the raised face defeated, directionless, blind, mute. "Hush now," she said, "hush now," standing bare-armed, bare-headed between the man's and the horse's terror of each other and the terror of what mystery, violent, powerful, unstayed, had struck like paralysis with a hand numb as stone and might lift again and strike before them. "Hush now," she said, and she brought the horse's head slowly down and, talking, slipped her gloved fingers under the browband and the fore-lock's length of straight black hair. The gloved leather came away wet, darkened as if from the touch of blood, and the girl stood looking at it. "Sweat," she said, half-aloud, staring at her hand. "He hasn't been running and still sweating like that. . . ."

"Nancy," said the father, running his tongue along his lip. "Nancy, for God's sake, let him go."

"He's got himself into a fever, so he has, my lamb, my lamb," she said, holding his soft mouth and his head firm

46

in the reins caught underneath his chin. "He's been worrying and worrying himself about worms or thinking about
his family tree," she said, stroking the bony, prow-like nasal
peak, thinking In a moment Candy may start shouting again
or the thing that has struck once strike harder like a crop
splitting skull and fiber across the frontal bone. "He's been
eating too much, my horse has, and given himself the mad
and sleepy staggers, so he has. He's got himself into a fit
and he'd like a drink of water, that's what he'd like," she
went on saying, thinking I must go on talking so that there's
no time for anything else and no place for any other sound,
I must go on in this voice because this is the voice that says
to him, "So now we'll just go quietly along home because
nothing has happened to my big foolish man, we'll just give
him some salt and a bucket of warm water to soothe him
and we'll rub his belly for him and rub him down with a
straw wisp—"

"Nancy," said the father, saying it quietly now, not in
a voice from which fear had gone but into which more awe
than fear had come. "Look at him closely, Nancy," he said,
half whispering it. He was fumbling in his pocket for something and the girl looked away from him, wondering, and
up at the horse's head again. Holding him under the quivering soft lip, she looked at the bony brow with the moist
forelock on it and the searching, flicking ears; looked at
the hollows, throbbing and pit-like, above the eyes, and lingered on the fixed brown brilliant eyes themselves before
descending the face's sharp decline to the concave nostrils,
dilated, convulsed now with pain. "Look at his eyes,
Nancy," Candy said, having found the matchbox and holding it in his hand, his fingers shaking still as he drew the

frail match-stem along the box's side and cupped the flame against the air's movement underneath the trees. When he lifted his arm the horse gave no sign, but as the match rose higher in her father's hand, the girl began talking again in precaution, murmuring to him in the ceaseless, gentle, assuaging voice that said:

"So his mother must just take him back to his stable and cool him off and put straw under his rug for him and rub him clean and dry and give him . . ."

"Watch him," said Candy softly, and now the match's flame, made puny by the sun's light through the leaves but steadily burning, came level with the horse's eye and halted and he made no sign. "He can't see it," the father said, awe-stricken, scarcely breathing. "He doesn't even know it's there."

Chapter Three

I KNOW we had quite a time of it," the mother was saying, sitting with her knees spread wide so that the rain would dry from her tweed skirt; talking to them while she smoked the cigarette, but half-musingly, only part given to this communication with other beings and part to her own high scrupulous contriving as she looked into the fire on the hearth. "We had one surprise after another from the moment we set foot on shore. In the first place, nobody'd given us any idea we were going to be sewed up in our clothes—"

"Ha, ha," sounded the vet's uneasy laughter, and perhaps because he caught sight of his boots below him on the rug thick with stable and road muck although he had cleaned them off on the mat outside the door, he shifted in cramped, miserable unease on the edge of the ancient shabbily upholstered chair. "Well, I should think that would have been a bit of a shock," he said, and the pale light-lashed eyes sought rather desperately for comfort around the room.

"I must say, I shan't forget it as long as I live," said Mrs. Lombe. She looked up from her contemplation of this other, this unspoken thing, and went on talking lightly of their trip, some or all of which the vet must have heard at other times, in box or paddock, or seated like this in this room. "They packed our feet and legs up in straw the very first thing," she said, "and then this garment arrangement we

49

each of us had to put on was pulled up over the three layers
of wool around our bodies and arms—" She went on making the gestures, the mouth open in speech, the words coming quickly, almost merrily; only when she looked up at her
husband's and her daughter's faces did it whet to irritation
in the strained, impatient eyes. This is the way to meet it,
the limbs at ease in the wool skirt and the casual, ordinary
cigarette and the conversational manner might have been
saying: if you have to face the truth for once in your lives,
accept it like this with the chin up and all flags flying from
the mast; don't sit there making a tragedy of it. But the eyes
ringed deep with a yearning implacable as intolerance knew
and had for a long time bitterly and irritably known the
uselessness of asking this or anything in reason of them.
There they sat on the sofa, a little back, father and daughter facing across the rug's and the table's interval straight at
the fire without seeming to see it or seeming to hear what
was said. "And then they sewed us right up inside of all
this," she went on saying to the vet, the blond raw-skinned
young man who sat with his arms placed on his knees and
his head extended over his big-wristed, uneasily clasped
hands. "Stitched us up for three weeks," she said with a
snort of amusement at their own audacity. "Three weeks of
it! I tell you, it was an experience to have had."

"Good heavens, three weeks!" the vet echoed in a voice
gone high and unbecoming in this attempt at social grace.
He glanced in hope towards Mr. and Miss Lombe to see if
they were joining in at last, but having seen their faces again
he quickly looked away. He drew one hand slowly over the
light stubble on his clefted buckling chin and swallowed,
thinking now as he had been thinking without interruption

that it wasn't to hear stories about where the family had been one spring that he'd come, but to see the hunter and that he'd seen it and he'd told them and the act to be performed was still there undone. But here they sat with the rain falling down outside, talking of Finland or sitting in silence, and coming no nearer to it.

"Of course, we'd taken all sorts of jackets and warm things up there but we were told to leave them where they were. They told us there wasn't any sense in us taking them out of our boxes, but just to leave them there at the hotel the way they were until we got back." She repeated the word "hotel" in sudden derision, jerking her head up from the fire again and giving the lot of them the same queer, anxious, admonishing look. "Hotel, if you please," she said. "It was a lamentable place, as you can imagine, and even for that part of the world it was just about as bad as anything could be. But that's what they called it, for the sake of appearances, I suppose, and that's where we left all our belongings, and I must say I wondered. Mr. Lombe and I had quite a laugh over it," she said and she dropped her cigarette into the fire and struck the ashes from her skirt. "We had no idea if we'd ever see any of our things again, but apparently that was the way it had to be done. Fortunately for us, there were some other English people in the party and they said they'd heard from friends who'd been out to Finland that it was always done like that. And then in the morning there was another shock in store for me," she went on. "They produced the reindeer and I really had no idea, judging from pictures and photographs where one pays more or less attention, you know, I simply hadn't imagined for a moment that a reindeer would be just about the size of a good-sized dane. I'd always thought of them as quite imposing-looking animals, something rather in the cattle line, of course, not so big as a horse," she said, and then she stopped, leaving the word suddenly there, unexpectedly bleak and alone. For an instant she could not look at any one of them but reached out for the poker's handle and took it and thrust it toward the steadily burning wood. Sitting with her knees spread in her skirt and her face turned from them, she struck the log smartly apart and the vet at least saw from his chair the sparks shower across the deep dead ash in the hearth and the chips of charred wood fall forward, smoking, on the stone. Now at the far end of the room the wind and rain drove hard against the windows, and refusing to think That horse, that crazy hunter is standing out there in the stable, stone-blind, incurable, bat-blind, Mrs. Lombe took up from where it had lapsed her own strained, almost merry locution of the other story. "Then they told us, once we'd got over that shock, that we were to lie flat down on the sleds, each one on his own individual sled, you understand, right behind the reindeer's heels." She hung the poker upright in its place again and with the side of one brogue pushed a charred bit of wood back where it belonged. "We each of us had our own separate sleds and reindeers, you see, and when they got us stretched out like that, more like Egyptian mummies than humans by that time as a matter of fact, they started to tuck us in! I kept looking at Mr. Lombe and wondering how he was going to like it!" Having achieved a certain jocularity again, she could look up at the vet and look at Candy Lombe (perhaps at him because in his fear of the heels and hoofs and the power of beasts she had one on him), but not quite yet at the girl's grave, pale, set face. "I told him I'd heard in Russia you landed the other way 'round, that is with your head to the front, guiding the thing with some kind of contraption with your hands, and your face practically under the reindeer's back heels, but that didn't seem to reassure Mr. Lombe, and I must say there were moments when I wondered how it was all going to turn out. As long as we trotted along on the flat it was clear enough sailing, but when we'd start off down those slopes at the pace they kept up, the sleds would begin going faster than the reindeer did, and that had its drawbacks! But the reindeer were beautifully trained and I must say they managed very cleverly. As soon as they felt you outstripping them from behind, they'd jump to one side of the track, skip into the snow at the side to keep you from running right under their heels. It was quite a lark, I thought," she said. "We were four days and nights on the way, sleeping right out in the snow, and we were told that some years at the roundup the wild deer stampeded. They assured us that nobody, that is, no foreigners had ever come to any harm, but the more I thought about it during that drive, the more relieved I was I hadn't taken my daughter with me." And now, having spoken the word daughter, having avowed in some distorted mimicry of declaration I care, I care! she could raise her head and look over the piece of rug and across the gate-legged table on which the Dresden dancers, the woman in a milk-white petticoat, several layers of china thick and edged with lace, on which hung flowered paniers, and the man in blue silk tails danced in formal motionless precision; looked past the vet's clasped raw uneasy hands, his arms and elbows planted on his breeches' knees, his lowered pale-haired head, to where the girl sat in her dark skirt and jersey on the sofa. There the mother's halted look pressed urgently, compellingly, and finally faded to grievousness on her. "She was about fourteen then, and those nights out in the cold, quite an experience for her of course but not quite, you know, just a bit on the rigorous side for a growing and not very robust girl. In fact, I'm not so sure any of the women liked it as much as they said they did. I loved it, but there were two Frenchwomen among us and I'm sure they must have found it very different from what they were accustomed to, their hairdressing shops and café life and everything like that."

The two others, the father and daughter, sat on the sofa motionless still; still sitting a little apart from each other, seeming to hear nothing, see nothing, like people waiting in a hospital's or prison's halls without hope but in numb unrecalcitrant endurance for the verdict to be given. When I got him into the stable last evening, the girl was repeating to herself, saying it slowly and carefully over and over as if this precision had been exacted by a judge and jury or by the gravity of life or death, I thought I must start right off doing everything for him exactly the way it's always been done so he won't think the thing that's happened to him is going to make him any different. I thought, even if he's lost the power so see, and now the word constricted like a knot jerked tighter in her: blind, gone blind, stone-blind. (Stick to the story, please, said the cold hard silent core of listening in rebuke. Tell us what actually took place, don't tell us what you thought.) I got him into his box, she went on looking straight before her across the room, and I began grooming him right away. I didn't want him to suspect yet there was anything the matter, I mean, I thought if I led him home like that, talking to him, and not riding him, he'd see it wasn't the world and the world's paraphernalia that had been wiped out or had been altered even but something as temporary and personal as a toothache that had occurred. (Very well, said the Court, bringing its mallet impatiently down. Get on with it without any dramatization, please.) I started to brush and comb him hard, the girl went on, and then when I saw the brush was annoying him because the prickles were worn down, I asked Apby for another and he handed me a new one over the gate. Apby was standing there watching me all the time I was doing Brigand down, and I did it thoroughly, it took me an hour to do it. There's a sign hanging up in the stable, my mother had it printed and put up there, and it says, "No one can groom a horse without perspiring over it," and by half an hour I was hot and I stopped and took my handkerchief out and wiped my face dry. I knew when you come into the stable in the morning after the grooming's been done you pass your hand through the coat the reverse way to see if it's been properly done, and if you see the gray line there near the hairs' roots you make the groom start his work over again, and I know Brigand was as clean as anything when I was through. After that I thought I'd never let anyone else ever, as long as I was alive and he was alive, I'd never let anyone put a hand on him again. (Please keep to the facts, said the judge or the jury's silence in jobation to her. The Court cannot admit as evidence the passage of thought, however sentimental its trend, through your mind or that of any witness.) So then I told Apby to bring me the warm water, she said, looking straight ahead. I knew I had to sponge Brig-

and's eyes out because if I avoided doing that, that would
be the worst thing. Maybe he'd just been waiting to see if
I would do it and if I would touch his eyes, and so I did it
and while I did it I spoke to him in a natural tone of voice
and I could see the film that was coming over his eyes now,
a sort of milkiness blurring them all over, but I went right
on sponging out his nostrils and then I did his dock and
washed his feet. While I was drying the heel of one forefoot, he reeled a little as if he had lost his balance and he
trod back on me, catching my shoe underneath his hoof. I
didn't make a sound, I swear I didn't, because I thought it
would be the end of him if he thought that having lost the
power to see had done this other thing to him too, I mean,
had crippled and disabled his legs under him or taken his
sense of gravitation from him. I didn't want him to—(Unless
you are willing to testify in the manner which the Court
has specified, said the controlled cold accents of authority,
the evidence you have given will be struck from the records
as irrelevant.) Then I brushed the mane and tail, the girl repeated slowly and carefully, and took the burrs out, separating as nearly as I could each hair in his mane and bid-
ding him keep his head low which he did. After laying the
mane with water, I brushed the tail out lock by lock from
the roots, talking to him about it. I decided to wash his tail
at the seven o'clock grooming in the morning, that is this
morning, and pick his feet out outside the stable in the sun.
But this morning it began raining early, so I did not do this.
Last evening then, about half-past six it was, I put his feed
down myself for him. I gave him three pounds of corn and
a bit over a pound of chop, and because of what had happened to him I gave him a linseed mash. I put his food on

the ground for him, just the way he always had it. Apby
said it would be better maybe to put his rations up in a man-
ger or hayrack where he could find them easier, and he said
he'd bring the portable rack in, but I wouldn't have it. Our
horses have always eaten from the ground the way they
would if they were turned out to grass and I said I was going to feed him from the ground so he'd go on thinking it
couldn't be as bad as he'd thought at first or else everything
wouldn't be going on exactly the same. My father had put
the call in to Pellton for the veterinary-surgeon to come and
I waited in the stable to see if Brigand was going to eat, and
he snuffed around for a bit and after I'd talked to him he
put his head down to where the food was because he knew
it had always been there although now he was blind, do you
understand, he was stone-blind, he couldn't see it— (Very
well, said the unmoved, the untouched silence, that will be
all, Miss Lombe, that will do.) But I have to tell you this!
the girl cried out, and she jumped up quickly from the sofa
with one hand stretched out as if in the act of arresting the
irrevocable closing of a door. Wait! she cried out. Wait!
You have to listen!

"I'm not going to let them destroy him. I'm not going to
let anybody destroy him," she said out loud, and she stood
looking around the room, bewildered now that she was on
her feet and speaking: looking in fumbling surprise at her
mother sitting by the fire with her face raised in offense,
and at the vet jerking on the chair's edge, his head lowered
as he watched the filth caking dry on the carpet under his
shoes. She did not turn to look at Candy sitting behind her
on the sofa now, but only at the forces mustered there
against them, these two other faces and two bodies, and

57

haltingly, separately, at the different pieces of furniture, the logs burning in the fire, the Dresden figures dancing, as if seeing for the first time what they were. "I don't believe it's something incurable," she said, the heavy, subtly glazed eyes moving off from the faces to object after object, and groping, object by object, as if through darkness, back to the faces again. "Nobody can make me believe you can't cure it if you take the care and trouble."

"There's nothing to stop us from having an opinion down from London," the vet began saying without raising his head. He sat there, bowed forward over his soiled pin-striped riding-breeches, with his arms resting on the cloth drawn tight across his legs. While he talked he wove his blunt big fingers in and out, the knuckles rubbing one against the other, and looked down as if in shame at the mud-splattered calves of his tan leather gaiters. "I'd be the first one to say hold off until we get another opinion. I say it's a clear and simple retinitis, come on maybe after influenza although I'd never have judged him convalescent when Mr. Lombe brought him in two months ago. It's the retina worked loose and the sight goes like that, sudden, and if you don't know to the contrary the history of eye-weakness may go right back through his blood. But I say have another opinion in and that would ease it up all 'round for us. Destroying a horse like that isn't anybody's Bank Holiday," he said.

"Ah," said Mrs. Lombe patiently, evenly, "there it is." She did not look at the vet but into the fire's depths for resolution, watching with calm, man-like resignation the uncertainly flickering flame; but still it was to the vet, the only other of sanity's disciples in the room, she spoke. "In-breeding may very well come to be the tragedy of the country before we know it," she said. "Look at our best dogs now, flying off the mouth with hysteeria because of being in-bred generation after generation. They say you're safe if you put a mother to her son or a father to his daughter, but to keep off in-breeding from own brothers and sisters or even first cousins. But where do general rules ever get you? Here's this hunter out there with a history of eye-weakness, a double history if you look at his in-breeding, and nobody," she said but she did not look at her husband, "would have touched him with a yardstick if they'd taken the trouble to run his pedigree out and had him up to pass the vet. I'm not advocating the general importation of foreign dogs or foreign sires, but a great deal of good might be done by bringing in fresh blood pretty freely from the Dominions." Sit down, Nan, you look a fool standing up there, she did not say out loud, but the girl looked in sudden numb bewilderment from side to side a moment and then sat hesitatingly down. At once and for the first time turning and looking at her face, the father reached out and took his daughter's hand. "I think there should decidedly be a feeling of patriotism brought into it," the mother said, and now the sight of them sitting so hand in hand, drawn closer to each other on the sofa but sitting as invulnerable and grave as statues or wax figures roused her to hot, inexplicable fury. She felt the heat flaming in her face and she pushed back in irritation from the fire, thinking that words like patriotism, and thoroughbred, and blood—a horse's good quick blood— should flay them if there were any natural feeling in them. "This country is the home of the thoroughbred, my father used to say," she said, looking towards the vet's stooped horseman's shoulders and his warped strong horseman's legs in the puttees. "You probably know of him by reputation, you may have heard of Major Husen around Chelton," she said, "although he was before your time. I've often wondered if a man not English born and bred can have any gift or sense for horses." She did not look towards her husband but at the vet still who raised his head uncertainly and looked at her and parted his lips and did not speak but swallowed, the skin of his throat permanently and brightly flushed and covered with stubble as white as a sow's. "Major Husen—your grandfather, Nan," she added in stern arrogative rebuke, "he fought year after year against the exporting of our good classic blood, fought it tooth and nail, in season and out, until he was seventy-odd. He'd go up regularly to the sales and try to keep our classic winners on this side of the water by any means he could, and a dozen or more times he did it. On winter nights at home, he spent his time going through the Stud-book until he as good as knew the whole thing by heart. He knew them as well as if they were horses out of his own stables, those leading sires and the sound mares who shouldn't, for the country's sake, be lost to foreign studs." She shifted around completely from the fire, her knees spread still, and looked at them, the father and the daughter, with proud, bold, but hopelessly defeated eyes. "He kept Navan Flyer from going to the Argentine one year, and the next he kept Phronella from being lost to Germany. He wasn't afraid to stand up there and tell them what he thought!" she said, the proudly and pathetically lifted head and the tongue in her mouth scoring them unsparingly for what was weakness and womanliness far worse than sentiment that kept them sit-

ting silent on the sofa, holding hands. "He brought Peace-
maker home himself for his own stud, and the speech he
made at the sales was printed everywhere. 'Tempting offers,
especially from foreigners,'" she quoted him with the exact
testy and gallant flavor of disvaluation for the foreigner's
name, "'must naturally seem difficult to refuse, but thank
God there is one Englishman at least of patriotic sentiment
among you, and thank God one Englishman's determination
is enough to keep a good horse on its native sod!'"

(One summer, maybe it was the time Candy came home
drunk after buying the horned cattle when he was supposed
to have bought the Galloways or the Red Polls, I was upstairs in bed, maybe I was ten or eleven then, and Candy
went out from down below and laid down on the lawn in
the dark. That was the first time I climbed out the window
and crossed the veranda roof and slid down the drainpipe,
and the stars were out but it was dark and I couldn't see
well, but I knew he was lying there near the hedge, perhaps
because other times, earlier, months back or years back, I
knew he'd laid out there even if I'd never seen him; perhaps
in my sleep I'd heard him year after year when he was
drunk open the downstairs door and go out and then remembered afterwards, like in a dream, the times he'd done
it. I had no slippers or anything but my nightgown on and
I kept out of the window's lights lying yellow on the lawn
and ran over the gravel and the grass to where he was
stretched on his back near the hedge, rolling a little from
side to side with his hands over his face and moaning.
Mother was sitting inside the house, I know she was sitting
inside and knitting although I didn't see her, and the wire-
less was playing, and perhaps Candy didn't see me there

but anyway he knew someone was sitting near him on the grass and he began saying in a low crying voice: "I want my wife. I want my real wife. I want my young little wife to come out and take care of me and save me from what I am. I want her now, my poor thin dying little wife, to start walking up the mountains with me the way she did and not be able to get any further and have to sit down and have to lie down on the pine-needles with me. I want her, I want her," the voice maybe she herself had never heard crying and moaning into his hands. "Out there dying young and living in a house with balconies built in the sun for the dying," he said not to me but to anybody who was sitting there on the cold grass in the dark beside him. "They'd built a café-bar across the road where the dying could get to it easy; before you were dead, you could get down the hall and cross over the road if nobody saw you and get up on a stool if you had enough strength left to do it, and get a drink down or a couple of drinks so later that night you wouldn't meet death too sober." He began shaking with crying now, his shoulders and his raised arms and his body shaking, and his face covered over tight with his hands as he rolled around on the grass. "I used to sit waiting for her there," he said in a moment, "watching the bed on the balcony on the other side of the road for her to be lying on it, and watching the café door for her to come in, and watching the snow on the mountains all summer, waiting and watching like a crazy man for her, my poor little girl, my poor dead dying young wife."

This was the story I had never heard before and I sat shaking with cold in my nightdress and listening to it, holding my teeth tight in my mouth and shaking because now

I knew I wasn't anything to him; there'd been this woman once, this girl, this other wife and none of us knew about her, and now he was drunk he was taking the skeleton out of her bed and out of her grave and hanging these rags of memory on her. I wasn't his child any more because I hadn't been hers, I was nobody, sharing nothing with them, I was just anybody sitting there not far off in the dark for him to say it over and over to. When I thought of her, I set my teeth in the side of my hand to stop their shaking, crying half for her and the other half for what I'd once thought I was to him before I knew about her. "What are you crying for?" he said in a minute, and he had taken his hands away from his face now and was looking towards me although he couldn't have seen me in the dark, only the blurred white nightdress and my knees drawn up and my arms held tight around them. "You haven't anything to cry for. You haven't lost anything," he said, and I said, yes, I've lost something, holding my teeth clenched and not making any sound, I lost something I thought I had. He said the story over and over until I could have repeated it without changing a word or written it down exactly in a copy book, even then that first night I heard it knowing how he must have looked coming up the mountain road that August with his sketch box, and how she looked, the thin young woman standing on the balcony of the sanatorium built there for the ill seeing him for the first time and letting a small bright green feather from a boa or a feather-duster blow down because she wanted him to look up and smile. I sat in my nightgown crying, setting my teeth in the side of my hand and crying in the darkness for her beauty and her affliction and her death.

63

Now he lay without moving, saying the rest of it to me, and for a long time I couldn't understand. "I lost her," he said. "You never knew her young and ill. You knew somebody who came a long time after that." There were the five or six years in between after he'd married her and after he'd stopped painting the pictures and instead took her from one high place to another and into sanatoriums and out; until I began seeing she hadn't died, she couldn't have died because they cured her: the money she had, a lot of money from her father who'd bred horses, or else marrying for love, or else giving birth to the child who sat listening in the dark curing her for life so that she could take it up where her father had left off and go on breeding horses on the land. And Candy turned over on his face again and lay with the side of it against the grass. "Once in a while," he went on saying, his speech thick from the drink still, "just once in a while when she wakes up in the morning or sometimes when she's reading alone in a room, there's something left, something about her neck or her wrist or the way her hair grows, but otherwise she might just as well have died. Can you understand what I'm saying?" he said, his voice drifting off to sleep or stupor in the darkness. "Can you understand what I'm trying to say? If she hadn't wanted to come back here and live in this country there might never have been the two of them, I mean the one I knew first and the one you didn't, and the other one sitting inside the house now. Sometimes when I come home and see her, when I've had something to drink or the light's not good I see my dead young wife sitting there in the room and I walk quietly so I won't frighten her off and I put my arms around her before she has time to turn around and start talking to me, and before I have to learn it again," he said, the words coming slowly across the grass as the drunken, the flagging, drugged lament drifted hypnotically now towards sleep. "I've learned it over and over and I don't want to have to learn it any more, that there isn't any youth and age, there's only life and death," he said.)

Now he looked up from the sofa at them, looked brightly and pleasantly at his wife beyond the Dresden figures on the table, and at the vet whose lowered face watched in blank bewitchment the slow foul havoc wreaked on the carpet by his shoes. Candy Lombe might have been just the bright, fresh-skinned and well-dressed little man sitting holding to his daughter's hand still, his nose short, pretty and narrow at the nostrils, the mouth soft under the just beginning to lighten trim mustache: except for the eyes shaped long to the temples and uncannily weighted with the nameless and unarticulated dream.

"Well, now the thing is we must all try to be as reasonable as we can about this," he said, looking brightly, almost socially at his wife. It might be he had met her at tea just that day and was putting his best foot forward. "Naturally little Nancy here wants to have everything possible done before we come to a definite decision about Brigand. I think Penson's suggestion about—"

"But a blind horse, a horse incurably blind," the mother began, but now as if instead of looking across the Dresden china dancers at her Candy had spoken her name, or spoken a particular name which they had used a long time ago and in another country and in its deepest signification, she ceased speaking.

"How would you like it!" the girl suddenly cried out.

"What would you feel like if sometime when you were ill they'd wanted to—" She sat on the sofa, not looking at anyone but savagely down at the dark stuff of her skirt, her face white, her teeth biting the wild shuddering sound of crying in. "What if just because you couldn't see any more, or couldn't eat any more, or—or—if you hadn't the strength any more to swim—or climb a mountain without—without losing your breath and having—having to stop and sit down —what if—"

"Hush, Nancy," said Candy softly. "Hush, Nancy," holding to the stiff relentless hand.

"What if you were ill once and nobody—nobody happened to come along and take care of you," the strained gulping voice went on, "just said 'put a bullet through where the brains are,' how would you like dying, how would anybody like dying when they're young and not ready for it yet! When you were ill and young sometime, maybe you wouldn't have been ready," she said, with the tears beginning to come down her face but still not looking at anyone, "just because older people said you were incurable and it was better to shoot you, you wouldn't have wanted it just because people who didn't care any more said it was the kindest—"

"Hush, Nancy, hush," said Candy, stroking her hand.

The vet stood up now and cleared his throat and took his watch from his waistcoat pocket and looked at its face, then slipped it back again.

"If you decide on wanting me to ring up London," he said, buttoning his jacket over with his big, blunt, fumbling fingers, and Mrs. Lombe said:

66

"You've been extraordinarily patient with us, Mr. Penson. We'll let you know what decision we—" She was standing now, tall and soft, the eyes a little haggard on him. "I don't suppose you'd know what the fee of a London vet might be for running down?" she asked him.

Chapter Four

A T THE end of the week the two things came: the vet
called down from London and from London as
well the letter from the Irishman. After all these
months the letter came saying he was back from Spain, ten
days back with a wound in his arm, and he would like to
see her but he didn't know if the address would do still or
if she had said Nancy Lombe or Nellie that afternoon.
"You said at Mrs. Paddington's in Florence you might be
back this summer, so I'm taking the chance that you'll remember me," he wrote, and Miss N. Lombe across the envelope outside in a shy quick nervous hand. The letter was
folded in her jersey pocket, doubled over and the corners
held tight and sharp in her fingers when they followed the
London vet out and down the drive, the gravel fresh, wet
underfoot where the rain had been that morning, holding
onto it as if the mere fact of its paper inflexibility would
be enough to hold to no matter what was said. The mother
and the London vet walked slightly in advance and Candy
was in the house still, having called through the bathroom
door: "Nancy, your old pater's still at his ablutions," his
voice amplified by the depth of water in the tub and the
echoing tiles sounding wondrously strong and clear. "I'll be
along when I'm done," he said, and the sound of water
gushed into space. He did not say aloud or articulate it
even to his own soft naked body bending into the bath:

68

I will not walk down that road and into the stable and hear it, but will evade it here muffled in shaving lather as fragrant as the springtime. He did not say: I am afraid to go.

The London vet was no longer the country thing but had become a prosperous, aging man like the accepted figure of capitalism in a political cartoon: there were the well-packed jowls and the paunch and the backs of the hairy, dimpled hands. He went at once into the hunter's stall, the breath ticking in congestion through his nose, and there he forced the lids up from the eyes, first one lusterless blank pearl bulging an instant between his thumbs and then the other while the horse's head lifted sightlessly and warily away. The yellow fall of sunny misty heat poured through the box's window onto the vet's graying hair and onto his spectacles' glass while he said, not to the horse's concepts or perceptions but still in his intuitive hearing: "The poor chap will have to be put down." He looked into the hunter's set milky eye and said the local man could do the trick as he himself had not come prepared to do it. And the mother standing on the oaten bedding said they had promised to give the owner time to decide, they had promised to wait a little. "My daughter," she said of the girl standing out of sight behind him and behind the horse holding to the letter in her pocket and hearing the man's breath clogging in his nose, the thing continuing as they had read of it in textbooks: if there was any doubt in the marksman's mind or if it was to be done by a novice, a line should be drawn in chalk on the horse's forehead from the right ear to the center and from the left ear to the center and a crossline drawn down where they conjoined. "I don't see why it has to be done, I don't see why," the girl said, her voice coming suddenly hoarse and tragic and young out of the stable's shadow.

The vet did not quite turn around to see her when he said the place to aim for and hit was the exact intersection of the chalk lines, the unmistakable center of the frontal bone between the eyes. "No," the girl said, this time only half aloud. "No." She thought This is the illusion and the real time is night, and the condition not waking protest because I am lying in bed asleep with this letter held under the pillow in my hand. The vet is not breathing like that through his nose, but it is my own breathing. I am lying in bed asleep and these are the monsters of childhood: the reptile disguised as authority in dark blue wool with dandruff on his shoulders, the shape my mother has taken now the monument erected to all childhood fear. I am saying "no, no, no" in my sleep and they cannot hear me. The smell of hay and horse is memory and the light is cool and blurred like just-remembered light while the tide of breathing rises and ebbs, rises and ebbs with the strange deep machinations of the heart in sleep. If you cannot give sight to a horse, not only to this horse but any horse, to the finest grandest pedigreed champion of them all, you hand it death like a third eye through the forelock, you give it its peep at paradise through one small black-lipped hole. You do this for the horse, not for the owner nor for the world, but for the bony, mysteriously limbed and soft-mouthed beast who is stumbling in silent panic from darkness to darkness. You shatter his brow at one stroke for him the way a strong man's fist shatters the frail panels of a door to let in the light, and the constant dream of nothing in his inconstant world of rippling skin, twitching shoulder, flicking ear splinters like glass splintering loud at night. You are awake, Brigand, toss your mane. The dream of blindness has ceased, darling. You are no longer sightless, you are dead. "No!" she cried out, putting her knuckles to her teeth. "No! They won't do it! I won't let them do it!"

She ran panting, gasping, not crying yet, out the stable door and up the drying, softly steaming gravel to the house. Behind her the talk went on, armed now with a capable relentless pity: get grooms, the local vet, the huntsman to tell her their experiences with horses gone blind or crippled horses, get her a book on it that will give her the proper viewpoint. If it's her horse, then let the matter go a day or two until she's understood the thing in and out: the mercy first and then the necessity of it. Tell her you can't teach a horse to accept blindness because his world is sight, and in a while she'll come around all right, she'll see the humaneness in doing it as soon as it can be done. Ah, that she'll have to do for all our sakes; we're not a hospital here for the maimed and we need the place for the work I'm trying to get on with against odds. Against God, almost, but anyway against man who was still locked behind the bathroom door and whistling.

"Just coming!" he called out when the girl struck the door with her hand. "Just coming, Nancy!"

She leaned in despair on it in the instant before he opened it to her: first hearing the whistling cease, and then the key turn, and then she saw him there, his lips puckered up to begin the tune again but his eyes through the bathroom's haze recoiling from disaster into their own queer dream-drugged blue. His hands were lifted to smooth the bay rum onto his hair, the sleeves of toweling slipping back on his

71

full womanish arms to the dimpled elbows, and she flung
herself wild and crying against him.

"They'll do it if you don't stop them! They're going to
do it if you don't stop them!"

The tears stopped suddenly at the sound of her own voice
saying what was true. But it was only for a little while she
believed strength could be given or taken, given by Candy
or any man, or taken from the Irishman's letter. She began
seeing how it was now as a savage might have seen it and
made a picture of it with berry stains, or some coloring
as primitive, or stitched it toughly in beads or thread on
cloth: the small helpless lone island of the self out of
voice's call or swimmer's reach lying among the scattered
inaccessible islands of those other selves. In the three nights
that came after with the horse still living and the Irishman
written to, she saw that unpeopled landscape and the vast
waters washing forever unspanned between the separate
islands, and she touched the bones in bed with her, the
bones of the shoulder, the arm, the hand, and the thigh's
bones lying tenacious in her flesh, and the skull's inexora-
bility underneath the hair. If there is any strength it is in
these, it is here, not in running fast to Candy for help or in
writing Dear Mr. Sheehan: It was jolly nice to have a
letter from you and I hope you're wound is getting on
well. I'm feeling very bad because the London vet we
called down here says they'll have to destroy my horse. My
father said to suggest for you to come down here one
afternoon and he would be glad to meet you at the station.
I know you said you knew horses, so maybe . . . lying
awake at night in bed and saying over again these words
that had been written down on paper and would be read

on paper, she thought of the horse's unwritten, unrecorded, uncommitted world of sight and hearing, touch and smell, the horse's moving world of myriad credulous sensation, and lying so night after night the line came clearer through sleeplessness and through the room's dark until its clarity became the impulse to get up and walk with bare feet to the open window and repeat it aloud: "The horse is frightened by the bush because the bush unexpectedly turns and waves a branch."

She put her jersey on but she could not find her slippers at once in the darkness so she climbed over the window-ledge without them and crossed the veranda roof and slid down the drainpipe with the cotton nightdress drawn tight between her legs. It was warm, for once here in England Italian-warm, even the grass warm under her feet as she crossed the corner of the lawn. Because of the bite of the gravel she kept to the grass and beds, going quickly towards the stable, and at the drive's curve she left the soft clipped border and ran painfully and rapidly across. No man, no woman, no girl, no Irishman, no doctor, vet, science, no kind of human knowledge can save him or give his sight back to him, she thought shouldering the door aside; he'll stand there shaking with palsy and funk in that state of incurable blindness and incurable terror until they put him down. She walked barefoot across the stable floor to where he was, and opened the door of his stall in the dark and spoke his name to him. "Brigand," she said out loud, and without seeing it she felt the shudder of fear and anguish that washed down him but he did not shift, perhaps not knowing whether to shift to right or left to let her by. There was no light, only the smell of horse and the taste of sweet clean-kept horse in the air, and she heard his stablemate rousing and moving in her stall beyond. So you'll stand there day after night, night after day, not knowing one from the other until your time's up, she said. She could feel him strong as stone but living as she shoved past him in the stall. You'll stand here, what's in you rearing for death and shaking with fright unless you listen to me. She drew his head down in the curve of her arm, firmly, almost without tenderness. Let the bush unexpectedly turn and touch your flank so you'll get the slap of its leaves like that without sight when the bush turns, she tried saying, and then she began it again: Your eyes, my friend, have clotted in your head. However, the road still flows away under the feet, the fence still bucks under you when you gather up your legs to rise, the house still pivots in the garden showing first one angle and then the other to you, the hedges have not ceased to pour by like water, the trees have never stopped waltzing, the clouds careening. It is you, my steed, who must comprehend motion without sight's limitations as long as we have dispensed with sight. Let the bush slap you full in the face and you will acknowledge its presence the same way as you did when you saw it unexpectedly turn and wave a branch.

The first night she took him out onto the drive only, leading him slowly by the head-rope through the dark. There were no stars, no wind, and the evergreens were a little wet still from the day's rain as they passed under, and the leaves of the wayfaring tree and the laurel brushed light and wet across their faces. It was after one o'clock, perhaps just on two but no bells in the village below, as there would have been in Italy, to say it, and the girl walked near him, her shoulder moving against the· hunter's shoulder as they walked. She said Next time I'll wear slippers, damn it, stepping in pain on the gravel, and now with the great unseeing and unseen beast moving diffidently beside her she began the scheming: "She said they'd let me have two weeks. Because of Candy, she gave me the two weeks. I'll listen to Penson explaining it over again, and I'll hear the grooms out, and I'll read the book. But she's given me two weeks to prepare for death. That's always that. In a fortnight anything can happen."

The third night she put the bit between his teeth and the bridle on him, and on the fourth she took him down past the lower edge of the paddocks and along the path by the stream. Here the way was narrow and they went single file, the girl ahead and the horse coming after on his rein, and where the bank lowered she led him towards the water, saying aloud: "If I know this place in the dark without being able to see it any more than you can, you can believe in it too, you can reconstruct the picture out of chaos and memory's ruins," but the horse stood back, the strong, the monstrously night-magnified body halted and the head raised in bewildered innocence. "Come," she said, "come," and now the sudden jerk as she kicked her slippers off did not startle him as it had the night before when they came to grass. "Come, my man, come," she said, and she gathered the reins up beneath the quivering pendent lip. She stooped, holding him still, and in one hand raised a palmful of water to his nostrils and wet his mouth. "Smell it," she said, "smell water," and now the forefoot advanced with her, and now the other, until the stream washed across his hoofs. She paused with him in the running water, feet on the slippery submerged stones, and he stretched his neck out and then brought his head down, as the rein slackened, to the smell and murmur and the touch of water, and she heard him begin to drink. She put her hand under his cheek and felt the windpipe pull and tauten, and felt in his throat the strong passage of the water, irresistibly and powerfully channeled like the passage of electric current through his neck and jaws. In a moment she said "come" to him again, and they crossed through the stream together, the cold washing to their knees, and reached the sedges and waded through them and clambered up to land. "So you see," she said aloud, and she led him on under the beeches to where the trees grew the thickest and took him in through the underbrush, her bare feet shrinking sideways with pain, but still taking him fiercely through it. First the road that first night, she thought, and after that the grass and the water, and now the trees and what's tripping him up underfoot to say Nothing has gone, blind horse, nothing has altered. When they were through it she stopped again at the edge and drew the mayblossom branches down over his face, gently drawing them down and gently letting them brush upward like veils of some inexplicable substitute for sight. That night she took him back by the marsh where by day the yellow iris could be seen growing, and he did not falter but sought his way with her through the invisible fragrant lilies in the dark.

All day he would stand in the loose box with the mare or a filly for company two stalls away, curried and groomed and the place done out from under him, and the cat coming in through the window and rubbing along his leg. By day he was this thing, the prisoner, the condemned man in the death cell on the final stretch of living, not of a species to play cards and smoke the last cigarettes with the guards while he waited, but silently, motionlessly, completely waiting. But at night the stable door moved back and the latch of the stall gate was lifted and he moved out in blindness and wonder with her into the slowly reconstituted, slowly redeemed and infinite world; until the night came when she did not pick up the reins and bring them forward across his head to turn him in the stall and guide him across the stable out into the insect-murmurous dark. It was the sixth or seventh night and once he was bridled she pushed past him and opened the stall gate and standing alone on the stable floor she said, "Come on, handsome," the voice casual enough, but as she waited there in the stable's complete obscurity her heart began to tremble. She held her hands down fast by her sides, her eyes were closed tight as fists in her face, and she stood scarcely daring to hear the confused stamp of the hoofs seeking position as he turned, not hearing actual sound any more but seeming to hear what might come if he fumbled and missed the narrow way out. It might have been hours—it was less than a minute—before he was clear of the stall and his nostrils came seeking the air for her, the hoofs' sound having altered from their stroke on straw-muffled brick to their thud on timber, and then he lipped her shoulder. "It's as black as your hat," she said as she took him across the threshold's beam. "I can't see any more than you can." She was shaking hard, as if in the teeth of cold.

The Irishman wrote back at once, gravely beginning it "Dear Miss Lombe," and she showed the letter to Candy. "He can't come down on account of his arm, on account

77

of the dressings," she said. Candy had been by the morning bus to Pellton and bought two detective stories in paper covers at Woolworth's shop in Fore Street, and he sat on the veranda in the fan-backed Indian armchair reading *Wanton Killing* in mild, soft-shaven, immaculately accoutred peace (because this would kill the hours of the afternoon and a portion of the evening, this story that did not for an instant deal with people but with the familiarly stamped counterfeits of detective, family, doctor, corpse). On the corner of the ping-pong table lay the other, *Murder in Hand*, still clean and marvelously unread (instrument lying in readiness to slug tomorrow afternoon and evening in their turn into timeless insensibility). "He says he'd like to meet you, Candy, but he can't come down," the girl said, "but look, turn the page," and she turned it for him. "Look what he says about horses." The climbing roses, their leaves and new buds even mildewed by the weather, grew meagerly about them, reaching unblooming up the rusted trelliswork. The afternoon was gray and still, a warm, heavy, iron-dull day with the hawthorn and maples on the lawn standing motionless against it. The single bees that sailed loudly to the laboriously-opening black clots of rose were as incongruous as humming birds boring for succulence in granite flowers. Candy put his detective story face down and open on the end of the ping-pong table and looked at the letter he held in his hand.

" 'I've often seen and ridden horses with "wall" eyes, cataracts (very common), horses blind in one eye, and I've known one or two cases where hunters have been totally blinded by accident. They were not destroyed, though, but put onto farm work, where—' " He stopped reading it aloud, thinking If he did come down I'd meet him at the station, either at Monkton Junction or Eastleigh, and if he came by the late train the pub would be open and over a drink we might get somewhere and for that half hour, in the process of getting somewhere, we'd talk like men. Just for that half hour before we got back here to the house we would be two men talking together, until he saw me for what I am, the one flaw, the single mistake, mistaken as the futile, idle, the evasive must be mistaken in a décor of rearing, stamping, accoupling activity; and as the penniless out of their place and in disguise once unmasked are the mistaken. If he comes down, for a little while my clothes (so much like other men's) will see me through and my receptive manner, for the first half hour over the first drink they'll do; and then he'll see the murder book and the shiftless hours in which no one comes to me, no subordinate or equal, for authority or permission, and at last he'll see the empty glass under the chair.

"Go on," the girl said. "Read the rest of it," and Candy, thinking of murder book and empty glass as weapon and insignia, went on reading aloud:

" 'They were not destroyed, though, but put onto farm work, where they did very well. I don't know anything about retinitis.' " The mother came out through the dining-room door onto the veranda's stone, the basket with the trowel and fork in it on her forearm, and her old gardening gloves pulled on her hands. She paused as if the roses and not the words had stopped her, and touched the blighted leaves with the gardening scissors' beak. " 'I imagine it's not a very common affliction,' " Candy's voice went on. " 'All I know is that the retina's that part at the back of the eye which aches when we come suddenly from darkness into light.' "

"Who's this?" said the mother in a light, inconsequential tone. She stood like a stranger near them under the stricken rose vines, her eyes the perceptive, conjecturing eyes of the human meeting, or only seeking vainly to meet, the cold, unearthly vision of their wide, glazed eyes. The father looked up and cleared his throat and smiled with a sudden little show of daring under his small neat mustache.

"Oh, that's Mr. Sheehan," he said brightly. "Mr. Sheehan calling all stations."

"Who's Mr. Sheehan?" the mother said and she smiled rather bitterly at the dark riddled leaves.

"He's Irish," said Candy, turning the page of the letter as if the actual stamp of his nationality might be set there for the eye to see. "A broth of a boy—"

"I met him in Florence," the girl said. She stood quite still by the ping-pong table, her eyes stopped motionless, her lips ceased moving, her hands and the bare white slender forearms hanging absolutely quiet from the gray jersey's elbow sleeves. I know nothing about her now, nothing, the mother thought bitterly. She looked across, seeking to find and focus the gaze of her daughter's eyes, thinking Ah, yes, here I am as you see me, the old woman who can't think back that far any more, the commander of the ship that would have floundered if I hadn't stepped into the male boots and buckled on the male regalia, an old woman going to fat now in the permanently borrowed paraphernalia that a man, not a woman, should wear.

"That's quite interesting, but you don't have to be sulky about it," she said aloud.

"I'm not sulky," the girl said, and in spite of herself she began to tremble, not only the bones and the flesh but the very marrow shaking and crumbling in her. There was no gooseflesh on her bare hanging arms, but she felt her heart, her substance quaking in her and her teeth chattering in her head. "He knows a lot about horses. He says blind horses don't have to be put down."

"Yes, you are sulking," said the mother, and her hand with the gardening shears in it trembled too. "You've been up to something; now you know you've been up to something you don't want me to know about, Nan."

"He says blind horses can be put onto farm work, so if a blind horse can be put onto work, then I can ride mine, I can teach him," the girl said. She stood looking motionlessly, quietly beyond, beyond her mother and past the lawn, beyond the day even to that irresistible goal perhaps weeks or months ahead, almost visually perceiving the plane of victory on which the horse would pound homeward sightless, outstripping the clear-eyed thoroughbreds, taking the obstacles higher, the ditches wider. "I know I could teach mine," she said, trembling before the still imperfect vision of the truth. "I could take him out a little bit every day, a little bit more all the time—"

The mother reached over and took the Irishman's letter out of Candy's hand and she said:

"I won't have you riding a blind horse and killing yourself and the poor beast. Thank God, there's a more humane way of putting it down—"

"Brigand's a He," said the girl. "He's a man. You might speak of him like that."

"It's a gelding," said the mother. "There's no need to

flatter it with a sex." She turned the three pages of Mr. Sheehan's letter and she said: "He's found time to write you a lot of nonsense, this young gentleman of yours," and in that oddly patient and at the same time oddly grieving voice, her thumb in the split leather, mud-whitened and caked glove holding the sheet, she read the sentences on the last page out. " 'It is easier to change an animal's receptivity of the world abruptly because in his two-dimensional existence everything enters from the outside. For animals a new sun rises every morning and a new morning comes with every dawning day. It is only human reasoning which insists that it is the same sun rising or the same moon waning. That is where Rostand did not understand the psychology of "Chantecler." The cock could not think that he woke up the sun by his crowing. To him the sun does not go to sleep, it goes into the past.' * He is quite an intellectual, your Mr. Sheehan," said the mother, speaking without rancor as if she knew and accepted the end of the story now. " 'So you can quite naturally and I should think with comparative ease give your horse a new world of action by giving him a new discernment for the motions which go on around him. I think this is what you meant, or rather what—' " Suddenly the mother broke off her reading and flicked the letter back to Candy where he sat in the fan-backed chair. "This sort of business isn't going to get us anywhere," she said.

"Come now," said Candy, and he smiled at them both with the same little jerk of summoned courage as before. "From the point of view of that horse costing us anything,

* P. D. Ouspensky, *Tertium Organum*, rev. ed., Knopf, 1922.

if I started in giving up my good tobacco, you know, and my cigars, and stuck to that kind of pipe fodder that makes my head go round, it ought to pay for that chap's food and drink for some months to come." His round neat little chin was lifted clear of his shirt's soft collar and the pale blue knitted tie and his hands held fast to the wicker arms of the chair. "I don't want Nancy to ride him, no, that I don't want," he said. "I don't want to have Nancy stumbling around on a blind horse, but I say let her have him for this summer anyway. She can take him walking up and down the drive if she wants him as badly as all that, Nan. This Irish chap here, this boy Sheehan, he seems to know—"

"Ah, your incurable softness, yours and Nan's incurable false softness," said the mother in a low bitter voice. She looked at his short, helpless hands hanging from the sleeves of the squire's jacket, the nails rounded clean and white on the childlike fingers that held to the chair's arms, and the empty glass put aside carefully beneath the chair. "Keep that animal rotting in blindness out there all the summer? What sort of sentimentality is it? For his health's sake, any horse must have his work-out, but you'd keep him closed out there with a step or two up the drive every day, and you'd break his heart and spirit for him! If you go on, you two," she said, holding onto the anger, "I'll put that crazy horse down myself, with my own hand I'll do it because I'm the only one here who'd have the compassion to do it—"

By the tenth day it was hot, a complete heat had descended on the country and the moon rose clearly at night. At supper Mrs. Lombe said they were leaving the yearlings out all night in the upland pastures, and thinking or dreaming of this the girl awoke as she always awoke now soon after midnight, quickly and without interruption rousing night after summer night as if someone entered the room at the specified hour and touched her arm and said it was time to come. She thought at once of the yearlings out in the grass, and she got up and put on her slippers and her jersey and crossed to the open window on the veranda roof. If they're out he has the right to go up there and graze near them and talk to them across the rails, or even go so far as . . . Or even go loose a while with them, the yet unthought, unspoken thing was shaping; not with the colts, she came near to establishing it as intention as she crossed the grass and the flower-beds to the stable. The colts play as wild as cats together, but the fillies are gentle, she thought, not quite coming to it as she shouldered back the stable door.

They went out the drive, and this time turned up the road towards the stud-farm, the horse waiting while she opened the pale painted gate and then following when she spoke his name. The main buildings stood on the rise ahead, bright white under the moon: the brood-mares' boxes looking south down the pasture-land, the granaries and the men's sleeping quarters to the north, and the stud-groom's cottage nearer, white under its thatch, standing to the right of the road. She thought I used to think jockeys and grooms never married, as if they weren't like men or anyway not whole men, just pieces of men cut down like that to fit a horse, but there's the stud-groom married and sleeping with his wife now behind those windows. I used to think of them all as something less than men because something

more, like immortals, jockeys and grooms and huntsmen
and vets, but whatever they say now I know better. I'm
going to ride my horse, perhaps not tonight or tomorrow
night but in the end I'm going to ride him. They came up
out of the shadow of the firs and beeches, coming out of the
trees' exactly defined darkness and walking into the open
moon-whitened country like walking into the light of day.
The home buildings and the cottage were white as bone, the
fields, the moon-dappled pasture, the blackthorn hedges
wrapped in stillness as they came past them, the girl and
the horse keeping to the grass for quiet and their footfalls
muffled as they passed the closed windows and moved out
again into the open country, the two survivors moving
through a bleached plague-stricken land.

Close to the buildings lay the small enclosures where
the mares were turned out at once after foaling, and near by
them the brood-mares' paddocks, longer, ampler, but like-
wise with the house standing between them and the north.
Stretching farther afield (even in childhood she had felt
in the sweep of the opening land the conditions of youth
and its frenzy) were the yearlings' paddocks, acre on acre
reaching out of sight to the orchards' drop. Far below, unseen, unheard, almost out of the moon's reach, the stream
ran on. The paddocks set close to the home buildings stood
empty under the wide night's light, for the mares and their
foals were closed in until the dew would be off the grass in
the morning: within the walls they were one still, mare
and foal, mare and foal in their boxes, still sharing the same
fodder-fragrant and straw-fragrant air. For a little while
longer foal and dam pressed body to body, moved out in
the early morning limb to limb, the mother sleeping now

with her head lowered and the child with his legs bent under him, folded close, and his nose resting vulnerably on the trampled hay. Weaning time had not come yet and the child still flaunted his willful, wayward lip and eye, his glossy belly propped on stilts, for a little while longer drew milk from her, drank from the same wood bucket, licked the same salt stone. It would come, wax to its peak of sorrow, then wane like the wooing-season: they would be taken from each other, foal from dam, and dam from foal, and for two days they would not eat but run the length of the paddock rails seeking each other and calling out, while the pain numbed slowly and at last died wholly in their flesh. For two more days they would stand with their eyes set on nothing but the memory of each other until the lineaments of that too faded, but when the foal turned down his head to lip the grasses again a part of that fearless, fiery arrogance was gone, already and forever.

The girl and the horse passed by the bright white-painted gates and the posts and rails that marked out the paddocks, following up the road that lay between. And as they walked the colts began coming to the bars and whinnying out to them, first to the sound of footsteps and then to the sight of them passing in the moonlight, and the hunter lifted his head on the rein and turned it towards their high chiming voices. Not here, the girl said and she drew him on; these are the colts and they'd play too hard for you and bruise you, but still the clear foolish voices called out to him to come. It was better than half a mile to the last big paddock where the fillies were turned free on nights like this, and the length of the way the colts ran to the bars and called out after them, running lightly in couples through the moonlit grass. It was only in distances that the moon's power seemed to fail, blotted out in the far maze of firs, myrtles, and the scrub pines grown down the west side against the wind.

At first there were none of the fillies to be seen, lost somewhere in the rich clover down at the meadow's end, or standing asleep in the paddock's eight-acre stretch with their necks curved over one another's. The girl climbed to the top bar of their gate and sat there in the warm, foreign-seeming night, the slippers hanging loose on her bare feet, the short-sleeved jersey undone. "Come," she said, and for an instant he faltered as she drew him forward on the rein, without sight knowing (perhaps because my voice is coming now from above instead of beside him) that the barrier was there. "Come," she said, and now he came carefully forward until the full deep breast came to a pause against the bars. The face hung long and utterly quiet, utterly patient beside her, the long flexible lip seemingly ready to smile if only the gift of humor or whimsy were given, the damp forelock ready to curl in the dew-moist blank soft air. In another while the fillies began coming up the paddock in the moonlight, first one and then another, and now in couples, and now in threes, picking their way like deer with their heads high and their delicate ears tipped forward, until at last the nine of them had come tentatively to the railing, their noses lifted without shyness to lip the smell and substance of horse and human flesh.

None of the men asleep in the home buildings, nor the stud-groom in his cottage heard it, but Apby started suddenly out of sleep remembering the sound of a horse going past on the grass, not running but simply walking quietly by, perhaps in the grass by the roadside. He (who had sought to be a jockey and who had never raced except in country fairs) was dreaming of the colored caps, the striped satin shirts, the narrow pennants flying on the grandstand, and on the fast track of dreams and even through the sound of cheering, he heard the muffled passing of the horse's feet beneath the window. There was no horse in sight by the time he was out of bed and opened the shutters, but still he pulled his trousers on and went down the ladder into the center mixing-room, and unlocked the door and went out onto the road. For a while he stood there waiting to get the sound again, and he heard it, moving farther and farther, fainter and fainter, like two hands clapping slower and farther and fainter, until the sound had ceased completely, and he said There's a horse got loose up by the last paddocks, and he started walking that way.

Chapter Five

B UT AT least he kept the secret, he didn't tell either the other grooms or the masters because by keeping quiet about it the trouble over the hunter's age between him and the girl was finished. She was sitting on the top rail of the gate when he came up the road, and the fillies were galloping wild in the paddock, the group of them wheeling together, first one in the lead and then another; and she started talking to him without turning her head, as if she had expected him to come or just anybody she could say it to to come and stand there below her, a little to one side of her, looking over the top bar at the horses going crazy underneath the moon. She said: "That's my horse in there with them." She had her hands closed into fists and she kept beating her left fist up and down on her knee as she watched them reeling into one corner and out of it and sweeping wildly down the land. "My horse is in there running with them, look, he's with the last three, my blind horse running. . . ."

The fillies came snorting past the rails, their necks and shoulders leaning to the curve, their manes blowing, and galloped down the slope towards where the water passed and out of sight, then up the opposite side of the field they came like the rush of the wind coming, and the hunter with them, the tall, stern, bony body stretching and limbering with them as they swung across the grass. She said: "I

89

took his bridle off and opened the gate for him," her hand clenched tight and beating on her knee as she watched them go. "I gave him a crack and he went straight in to them. I've won," she said, not turning her head to him. "I won against them all, even against you, Apby. I won."

He stood bandy-legged and seemingly dwarfed below her, leaning stubbornly on the painted gate, his arms raised and crossed on the top bar and his chin laid on them, almost classless now as he leaned insolently on the bar below her in this place where, at this hour, they had no right to be.

"No, you didn't win, you didn't win nothing at all," he said, leaning casually and boldly there below her. In a while he might take a cigarette out of his breeches' pocket and strike a match to it and stand there smoking without a saving-your-presence or a grant-your-grace and let it hang dry on his lip while he went on saying in the moonlight: "You didn't win because that's nothing you're giving a horse, that's no life for a grown horse, grazing and romping with yearlings, running like that like maybe a hundred blind horses would run with their kind. That don't get 'im anywheres," he said, and she looked quickly down at him, seeing him like a stranger now that for once the brown-and-white checked soiled cap was absent and the hair showed pressed flat from sleep against the skull; seeing the small elfin-profiled face of the doer for horses, the delicate-boned face of the administrator to their flesh, the inevitable steward to their intimacies. She thought Perhaps no one ever with big bones is good with horses, only these half men, while he said: "What have you won if you haven't found his use for 'im? This kind of thing is all right and all that, but it isn't finding his use for 'im."

"But there's no need to destroy him now," she said. "No one on earth'd put a horse down that can run like that. No one alive—"

"What kind of a deal are you giving him at that?" the groom said, his chin resting on his arms on the bar as he watched the galloping horses take the rise. "You're not offering him much by just turning him out to grass for the time he's got to go. I've known a few horses and I say as he'd rather be dead than in the stable and out year in and year out the way he'd be." The horses came head-on towards the gate, then bent their course and swerved like a flock of birds, and bending still chopped short the corner, and the girl's hair lifted in her neck with the wind of their passing and slowly sank again when they were by. "Grass ain't always the 'appy 'ome of rest," Apby said. "You've got the month of June and that's the best here, and after June the flies start driving the horses off their heads, and when it's late September and on the grass has no more taste than paper."

"Because you want him dead," she said, looking straight ahead down the paddock. "You all want it." And now the groom took his arms from the top bar and fished in his breeches' pocket for the cigarette and brought it out and straightened it in his fingers before he put it in his mouth and struck the match and held it, the fire-bright spark of what might have been life itself cupped in his hand's bones an instant while the lowered head, the tilted mouth leaned to it, and the small jaws sucked quickly at the air. "It's all system with you and all the rest of them," the girl was saying, looking at him now and watching him shake the match's flame out and let it drop into the grass. "So many boxes, so much room, so many hands for the work, so—"

"You get him his own work to do and I'll be the first to groom him," he said, folding his arms on the rail again and the cigarette hanging on his arrogant lip. "Make a horse out of him as long as you can't never now make a sire," he said, the humor turned coarse and free as if it were another groom, not girl and not employer, sitting on the gate above him. "You cut out his work for him and I'd be the first to do for him morning, noon, and night," he said, and the girl said quickly:

"I wouldn't let you touch him."

"Saddle 'im, I'd say, saddle 'im," the groom went on saying. He drew sparingly at the cigarette, letting the ash grow, sparingly letting the smoke rise. "He's queer enough for anything I'd ever seen so he'd likely let you do it. Saddle 'im up and give 'im his paces. Put 'im on a Ward Union double-bridle and just try 'im out."

And now the fillies, as if at a given signal, suddenly broke apart near the fence and quietly scattered; gentle as mares and with the same matured wisdom, they shook their manes on their necks and dropped their heads to graze. Only the throbbing flanks and bellies remained as remnant of their senseless wild abandon, and slowly, step by long-drawn lingering step, they moved off eating at the grass. For a moment the hunter was left there in isolation as they went in their separate, lingering directions, his head raised and searching, perhaps seeking sight now that the comprehensible motion of flight had ceased; and then abruptly he sought it no longer. Whether it was the sound of their still hot unsubsided breathing or the pull of their teeth at the grass that came to his ears now and calmed his heart's equivocal panic, the girl watching him from the top of the gate saw him drop his strong long head and begin to crop the herbage as did the others, and move, as did the others, step after prolonged half-arrested step, grazing at peace in the mysteriously shining night.

Two days after that, when she wrote to Mr. Sheehan again, she wrote:

"At first it didn't go very well because as long as I was on his back my horse got panicky and he wasn't sure about stepping on the road. If I got off and led he went all right, or he'd follow me all right, but when I mounted him again it was the same thing. He'd feel out the ground all the time with his forefoot before he'd go, or he'd stop short, maybe thinking there was a hole he couldn't see in front of him. But I managed to get him around the long way by the stream and into the paddock where there weren't any horses out. It's one of the colts' paddocks and it's more than eight acres square. When he remembered he couldn't see he stopped like a shot and that might be bad if you were going fast but maybe he'll get over that too. I'm trying the half-passage with him because I've seen quite a few horses and I don't see any good in just turning him out to grass," came the predication of youthful authority and youthful plagiarism. "I've noticed that turning them out like that isn't always their happy home of rest. There's only the month of June here and after that the flies begin pestering them, and everybody knows autumn grass tastes like paper to them. But a horse is no good to himself or to anybody if he hasn't got a use or any work to do, and training him to obey can give him a use so even if he's blind he can begin living his life again."

So the battle had another aspect to it now, the ranks were a little altered. On the side of death, the marvelously equipped cohorts of extinction, were the mother, the vets, the stud-groom, precedent; and on the other the Irishman nursing his arm up in London and writing to her, and Apby come to heel. Between the two federations Candy erred as a victim of amnesia might have wandered, the meaning of the issue lost in confusion, the name forgotten, only the sense of urgency, perplexed and sketchily defined but present. He stood at the dining-room window in the evening tapping out the verses with his fingertips on the anciently rain-stained glass: Oh, Nancy, Nancy, your doting parent, is afraid circumstances will warrant. Or If ever you took it into your head, to ride a horse that ought to be— Or If you ever rode that crazy hunter—punter, munter, bunter, runter. His fingertips drummed across the glass with the rhythm of what he was making up, seeking a way, if way there was, to establish a truce between will and will without he himself having to make any declaration or come to any choice. Because there must be an end to it he was almost persuaded now that the alternative lay between two deaths: either the hunter's provoked death or the girl's death if she rode him, and the menace of horse seemed imminent, the threat of equine inhuman power seemed ready to cast the dauntless and the daring down and stamp their life out underfoot. He stood tapping his fingers on the pane and watching the evening coming, the mild June evening in which thundered the defiance of the big-necked, the monstrous-thighed and bony-headed beasts who reeled towards growing timber in their madness (he had read of men willfully killed by horses who took trees as the last resort, low boughs or the trunks

94

themselves, to strike their masters from their backs); he could see the vision of them cracking their legs on fences they'd jumped short and crashing gigantically, massive as floundering whales on the defenseless frail bodies of the mounted young; saw them in steeplechase and point-to-point and hunt, the cripplers, the murderers, striking out left and right and beneath them in their folly, the hard-hoofed, hysterical killers breaking their own backs as they fell, a mass of twisted, writhing tonnage, snapping their own necks as they collapsed across the bars on the still incredulous, still fearless young, the dying monsters killing as they died.

"Tum-te-te-tum, tum-te-te-tum, ta-ta," he hummed aloud now as something like actual physical fear began to shake his soul. He thrummed his fingertips on the window and he thought, The best horse story I ever heard was the one about the cavalry regiment galloping hard, four a-breast, up the village street, young sparks in their uniforms making their mounts take it fast to show the population, in particular the female, how they sat the saddle. Ah, but the street was narrow, lads, and ah, but vanity, that fluctuating current that deflects the blood stream in our hearts, was lashing the horse past all endurance: it seemed the eyes must boil from their heads, and their tongues spume from their jaws, and their lungs burst wide and hang in shreds upon their chests' scaffolding, when what happened but a cob and buggy turned out from a cross street and peacefully came towards them, slowly because it was summer and the driver with his feet propped on the dashboard, half asleep. The horses, remember, left six inches free on either side as they came up

the village street, their necks at the extremity, their legs
stretched reaching for the weapon with which to do the
killing; ah, murderers, lusters, gangsters all, see the horse
coming slowly and flickeringly, like in one of the first moving pictures, his feet seeming to wave from side to side like
slowly waved handkerchiefs as he drew the buggy or else
the buggy pushed him down the street, see the blinders on
the sides of his face, if you can remember that far back, and
the reins hanging slack because the driver had forgotten,
just before meeting death, about the briefness of man's allotted span, and see the last touch, the comic feet propped on
the dashboard. Towards this familiar (if you were alive in
the horse and buggy age) and insignificant (if you did not
admit time's aggregation) and helplessly advancing vehicle
came the cavalry, unarmed except for haste and heat and
savagery, while the buggy's shafts, like spears carried low
and wary by African warriors on the trail, took aim in
measured preparation.

Damn horses, in the name of youth, God damn them,
Candy said, and he turned away from the window to the
sight of his wife through the double-doorway, knitting by
the silent radio. There were six horses less after that de-
bacle, he told himself with pleasure: one man less, the driver
dying with his legs stuck up on the dashboard still like a
dead bird's legs sticking straight up in the air, because he
didn't wake up in time to choose, or if he had chosen what
could he have done with only a couple of yards between
him and the galloping horde? But six horses less, two of
them run through by the buggy's shafts and their hearts
split on the skewers, and four of them with broken shoul-

ders and broken necks trampled to death in headlong panic, six of them less to bolt and rear and stampede, and the officers only badly hurt, only disfigured. She was knitting with pink, and a towel spread over her skirt to keep the delicate wool from soiling, and he thought "badly hurt," how magical, how truly rich and sweet it is, "disfigured" or "badly hurt," the unhoped-for reprieves from death. He sauntered over the worn little islands of the rugs towards his wife, his hands in the pockets of his coat and his neat, well-manicured thumbs out, knitting what? he thought, half-jocularly asking, For God's sake, knitting what? Part of it was humorous and part tender, and part the complete if dimly credited perception that not time itself but the belief that there were lapses in it was the illusion: she might be sitting nearly twenty years back knitting something for Nancy not born yet, the same evening, the same supper, the same twilight outside the windows on which the rain had a long time dried. And at that same time, me beginning what was to be my artistic career, fatherhood the accessory not the keystone to life, envisaging clearly then the now dimmed, wasted features of what was to have been honor and accomplishment year after simultaneous year.

"Nan," he said, coming to the last island on which she sat marooned, "perhaps you ought to be making a confession to me," and he made a gesture with his thumb towards the pale wool and the needles in her hands. She heard the part-jocular, part-tender voice and she looked quickly up at him, at the rather gallant little figure in the squire's coat with the small mouth smiling under the tricky neat mustache, and for once she did not answer as she might have done. Instead she looked down again at her work and for the first time she said to him:

"I would have liked to have had a son."

To be what I'm not and never have been, he thought at once; to do the hard, thrashing, male things I've never done to land or woman or beast; not a son to carry on my blood but hers and Major Husen's, resenting now even her own father's blood in her; the stud, the wooings and the matings, to bear that on, the foalings, the deaths, the cycle turning and returning to the accouplements. He put out his hand and laid it on her shoulder without thinking of the words to use to begin saying it, but simply beginning:

"It's the people we surround ourselves with or get surrounded with, maybe, that seem to make us into something we never would have been. If you'd had a son you wouldn't have had to have been so—so—fearless. That's not quite the word but I mean—"

"I'm not fearless," she said, her head down, her hands working quickly at her knitting.

"Yes, because I'm a coward you had to be fearless," he said. "You found out you had to be fearless a long time ago, too long, and now you don't know how to be afraid any more. But I'm going to be different about things, you've heard me say that before, but this time I'm going to be different. I'm going to try to get into things more, be more active, and make things easier for you. I'd like you to be afraid and come to me afraid, not every day but some days."

"I am afraid," she said, her head down, her eyes on the knitting. For the second that he did not look at her he believed with the same complete perception as before that time did not lapse, in spite of man-conceived divisions

98

neither receded nor advanced, and he heard her voice as his young love's and his young wife's saying:
"I am afraid. I'm afraid for Nan."

✦

The girl worked two hours every night, sometimes longer, with the horse, worked fast with him now that the second week was closing: the half-passage for the first quarter of an hour in the paddock where the cropped grass was resting, and then the turn on the center as the simplest of the three equine turns. "The half-passage," said the textbook she lay reading in the hammock, "consists in making the horse, while keeping his whole body, from nose to croup, parallel with the sides of the enclosure, move sideways, crossing both fore feet and hind feet. The exercise should be performed only when the horse is walking well into his bridle. By asserting a strong pressure of one leg slightly drawn back the horse should move off in the required direction. Both legs on one side should cross the other two (in front, not behind) and he should gain ground all the time. His progression should therefore be at an angle of 45° to the sides of the road or the enclosure."

The second quarter of the hour was the turn on the center, the one turn the horse makes naturally, without instruction: the rider's inner knee the fulcrum, the horse's forehand turning inward, his quarters outward. Not till the last day of the week did she try the circle on two tracks, on the forehand and on the hock, and then "A strong pressure of the inward leg, which should be slightly drawn back, and the hand rein strongly applied," the textbook said. "The

horse should make a complete circle, with his head facing
the center and the hind legs passing along the circumfer-
ence." Or for the hock circle, she read in the warm dim
drowsy afternoon, with the hammock just moving, not
swinging but stirring slightly and nothing more; for this "a
strong pressure of the outward leg, in front of the girth,
and the outward rein, with the hand on the neck pushing
the horse over as it were," and now Candy came across the
lawn, walking quickly, silently on rubber soles, dressed in
white as if just ready for tennis although he had never so
much as thought of tennis in years, but had dressed again,
coolly and freshly, to kill an hour of the afternoon. He sat
down without a sound, without a word, in the canvas chair
by the tin table where the half-empty glass of lemonade was
standing and she looked up from her book at him in the
moment before he spoke and saw the small shocked face
above the polo-shirt's open neck, the color gone from the
mouth even. Although he had been well shaven at lunch,
or must have been, the skin showed ailing as scalp now
through darkish and unexpected bristles.

"Penson," he said, swallowing, and he did not look at her.
His bare elbows were braced on the chair's wooden arms
and his fingers interlocked before him. She put the book
down, closed, and sat up in the hammock, the shape of the
net's sag altering as she moved until it took and held her
buttocks' shape. "Something's happened to Penson," he said,
and his eyes ran from one side to the other, trapped in their
sockets like marbles in a pocket. "A horse almost did him
in last night. I met his wife in Pellton, ran into her on the
street coming from the hospital." His eyes were running
fast from the vision of it, and the girl sat before him in the

scarcely moving hammock, her bare legs hanging slender
and white-skinned out of her skirt and her bare feet, blue-
veined and narrow in the unfastened sandals, swinging
slightly just above the circle of earth worn under the hammock and the trees where feet had always swung. "Around
Buxton, I think she said. He was called in to look at a
horse," he went on saying, his eyes running fast, "and the
damned farmers didn't hold the animal properly. It was a
big draught-horse, heavily shod, and, by God, he got poor
Penson square in the face. One point of the heel right in the
eye, she said, and the other point hooked the roof of his
mouth, and as soon as the brute had him down she says the
farm hands ran a mile. They left Penson lying there in the
stall calling for help until one or two of them collected
their wits and came back and got him out—"

"Bright lads," said the girl, swinging.

"But by that time the horse had trampled his right arm
half off, and she says it was Penson who told them what to
do. 'Get me to the nearest doctor so he can stop the bleed-
ing,' he told them," and Candy's eyes fled wildly from the
sight of it, "but the doctor they got him to took one look
and said he wouldn't touch that skull with a yardstick for
fear of doing Penson in. 'All right,' said Penson, 'then get
me to Pellton Royal Hospital quick as you can,' and she
says the doctor drove him the twenty miles in half an hour."
Candy's breath was shaking in his mouth but he went on
saying: "Penson told the surgeon to give him a local anaes-
thetic but not to put him out completely because it was an
operation he'd always wanted to see done. Trepanning I
think they call it, only this time she said the difference was
they didn't have to saw out a part of the skull because it had

been kicked out already, so all the surgeon had to do was pick out the pieces from the front, and Penson had them put a mirror up where he could see, and there was Penson, Penson, by God, making suggestions!" His tongue came out to run along his lip but it brought no moisture with it, and looking at him from the hammock she thought It's not for Penson he's in a funk like this but for something that might happen to somebody else, perhaps to me or perhaps to himself, something more personal than just fear of theoretic violence but because it's a sample given, not only an instance of what happened to somebody else but of what might happen to him or me sometime, or perhaps just to me. "Three hours on the table," Candy said, "and Penson told the surgeon or the surgeon told Penson, I don't remember which way it was, that the complication could be meningitis. He told him that last night and at four o'clock this morning they recognized the symptoms. He's in for it now," Candy said, the eyes still running from it. "Mrs. Penson says they don't give her any hope. If he comes through, that'll be one more miracle like him having the courage to lie conscious on the operating table telling the surgeon what to do."

"What about the horse?" the girl said. She reached out for the glass of unfinished lemonade and took a swallow of it, but because it was too warm and sour now, she made a face after the first taste, and put it down.

"The horse?" said Candy, for the first time the eyes fixed steadily on her.

"What was wrong with the horse?" she said. "What was Penson called in to look at him for?" She sat swinging slightly in the hammock, the loose, hanging sandals just brushing above the circle worn bare in the grass. "I suppose because of all that stupidity the horse'll go on getting worse, because they'll be afraid to have another vet in to look at him. It wasn't the horse's fault. He was badly managed."

So now the thing is, Candy did not say, his fingers locked together desperately, the thing is we are afraid for you, your mother and I are afraid, we were afraid for you before and now we know exactly: you mustn't go into that blind horse's box any more and groom and feed him. He did not speak but he sat white and shocked before her, his eyes trapped in his face. You'll get Apby or someone else to do it for you, but you can't go in there, you mustn't do it, I forbid you to do it any more. You can't go in there three times a day like that and do all the things you've been doing for him. It's got to stop. Let a man be killed, let a vet die of brain fever, let the entire race of horses stamp out the race of men; but you, my delicate-wristed, my rapt-eyed daughter, you shall stay clear of death by murder, by calculating evil violence, by willful and ruthless vice; you shall remain unstained as the lilies remain pure growing by the water, fragrant as fruit-blossoms, unbruised, unplucked, unsullied. He did not speak but sat before her in his open poloshirt and his white duck tennis trousers, looking out of his blanched face at her and listening to her.

"She said I could have a fortnight to think it over and now I've thought it over," she was saying, swinging just slightly in the hammock. "Today makes the two weeks and I haven't changed my mind about it, I mean I feel exactly the way I did and I won't let them put Brigand down. I mean, it's not just being stubborn about a thing, but the thing itself isn't the same any more, do you see what I'm trying to say Candy? In a little while I'll be able to show you, but now it's too soon. I have to have more time before I can show you. That's what I want to talk to you about. I want you to tell mother I've got to have more time before I can prove it to her, maybe another fortnight would do. You're on my side, Candy, and you've got to tell mother to give me a little more time."

"More time for what?" he said, the eyes coming helplessly to a halt on her face.

"So I can prove they don't have to destroy him," she said. The hammock swung slightly, rhythmically, imperceptibly as breathing. "If I have more time I can show them what's happened and then they'll see there's no need to destroy him. I can't show you now, I want it to be perfect before I show you." The hammock moved her gently towards him and as gently drew her away. "I'm not glad Penson got hurt," she said, the strange, dream-stupored eyes profoundly and motionlessly drifting. "I'm not glad he got hurt, but if he's in hospital then he couldn't put Brigand down. So I want you to ask her to give me more time, just to allow me ten days longer, just enough—"

"He's got an assistant, Penson," Candy said. "He'll have someone replacing him. You needn't count on that," but he knew exactly what he would do: after a while he would get up from the canvas chair and cross the lawn and begin saying it to his wife, standing beside her wherever she was, his hands in his pockets, offering her half in apology and half in challenge the smile that placated nothing. Whether or not the very words in which he would petition the horse's reprieve were asking as well for an extension of the risks of human death, still he would go to where she fought the recalcitrant roses or whatever other insurgent manifestations of life were being chastised by her hand, and he would ask it, smiling, but still in shame and servility of her. "But, look here, Nancy," he said, staving it off a little longer. "What if you go off again in September? What about that blind horse? What would be the point in keeping him hanging on like that if you weren't here?"

"He'll have his own use by that time, he'll have his own life then," she said, swinging. "You'll see."

He thought suddenly I need a drink, that's what I need, a drink, and he stood up and looked at the watch on his warm arm. Bound to her, he thought, by that, "You're on my side," bound and committed to her, to lie for her, plead, connive. He stood looking down at her bare legs and her bare ankles and the sandals open on the blue-veined insteps' bone, and he thought, What if he kicks you to death out there in the box, what if he does, and he said out loud:

"But I want one thing, Nancy," looking rather wistfully and shyly at her as if on the point of asking some favor for himself instead of merely seeking to spare her from death. "I want you to say you won't go out and groom and feed that horse, Nancy. If I ask your mother to allow him to stay on there another fortnight, you can stay away from his heels, Nancy. You can get Apby to do him down and exercise him up the driveway." He stood in uncertainty and almost in humility before her, wanting the drink and at the same time wanting her obedience to be quickly and submissively given. Just not to be the one to wound her, to thwart her, not ever to evoke the balefulness and the defiance (that's for you, Nan, all for you, he thought of his wife; you can have every drop of her resistance, I don't want any of it for me), not now or ever to see the wide floating eyes focus in exprobration on him. "I'm just saying, Nancy, that I don't want to see your face changed, I don't want you dying in a hospital," he said. "I want you to keep on being and looking the way you are. That Irishman," he said, and he accomplished the little smile, "he mightn't like you either any other way."

She sat below him swinging in the hammock for a while, the face meditative, the foot hanging, and then she said, pronouncing the words slowly so there would be no mistake:

"All right, Candy. That's fair enough. I won't groom Brigand and I won't feed him. From now on I'll let Apby do it. I'll let Apby do him down and feed him and walk him up the drive every day. When I go way my horse'll have to get used to someone else, so he might as well start getting used to it now. I'll let Apby groom him and feed him because you ask me to," she said.

Chapter Six

FIRST Mr. Sheehan wrote about his sister marrying and then his aunt wrote: the Hon. Lady Mary Disalt wrote asking if Nancy Lombe would come up to London as house-guest.

"There you are," said Candy. He looked brightly and saucily over the breakfast table. "They want a double wedding."

"Don't put ideas into her head," said the mother. The tone was light enough but she looked up at the girl with a measuring, a quietly conjecturing eye. "What in the world will you wear? What have you got?" she said to the sport-shirt and the fraying jersey and the too-tight riding breeches. "We'll have to go over to Pellton and get you something decent."

"Why doesn't she wear her spotted leopard with the cream lace insert?" said Candy, and the girl began laughing. She lifted her cup of tea to her mouth as if to hide its wide foolish laughing, but once on her tongue the tea spurted in explosions across the dishes. "Try on her old-gold sheath gown with the dimity bodice," Candy said, and the tea splattered onto the marmalade and the silver cover of the warming dish. "Or her emerald-green smock edged with yellow tulle," he went on saying, and the girl cried out:

"Oh, stop, Candy, stop it! You're so silly!"

"Or her pistache velvet with the raccoon slip?" he said.

107

"As we used to say at school, 'was it Daniel Boone or the raccoon that gave the knave the name of Boone.' "

"Possum," the girl cried out, her face bright red with laughing. "I'm sure his hat was possum!"

The mother sat reading the Hon. Lady Mary's letter again, breakfast not done yet, and she did not speak, sitting now in that far and elegantly appointed study in which the words had been penned, perhaps on a russet leather-clasped blotting pad and certainly on Chippendale, with the murmur of London penetrating the bottle-bottomed studded panes and the partially drawn velvet hangings, reading: "So we should like to have her come up on Friday night, the seventh of July. Naturally, she will be met at Waterloo and chaperoned to the house." So that gives us ten days, the mother thought, but not the time for anything to be made; and the time is short like that for the very good reason that this highfaluting Mr. James Sheehan couldn't make up his mind until the last moment, not knowing whether he wanted Nancy Lombe to come or whether he didn't until probably yesterday morning. A wedding as presentable as this one is planned and the house party arranged for and invited six weeks ahead, at least six weeks, but it's plain as day that his royal highness decided just in the nick that Nancy was good enough, that Nancy Lombe, the little girl he'd met in Florence at Mrs. Patterson's one afternoon last winter, would make the grade, and would dear Aunt Mary Disalt write to those squirey people down Pellton-way who had this pretty daughter, and it took a bit of persuading because the guest list had been drawn up months ago, but in the end she did. And at least she had the grace to add: "Please excuse the unavoidable tardiness of this, but my nephew's delayed return from the continent made any planning with him virtually impossible."

"They've given us such short notice, the proper thing would be to turn them down," the mother said, and she put the point of toast crowned richly with Danish butter and bramble-jam into her mouth; but they all knew that the girl was to go. The mother knew it best perhaps, because knowing that friends, just other people found and called by that miraculously transforming name, were enough to change a girl's heart and alter her life for her; knowing this change might be the overture to final propitiation, the way to muffle at last the sound of horse's hoofs, not any horse's or all horses' hoofs, but the hoofs of the crazy hunter on his fruitless hunt galloping unflaggingly towards death through their speech and their silence and their struck bargain's commutation. She began talking of the clothes, shop-bought they'd have to be, and the sound of the galloping horse went on, and the mother thought, In London she'll meet people and she'll see things in their true proportions, but she'll have to have a suit to travel in, and at least two dresses, she's outgrown everything, and the horse's hoofs went galloping endlessly and hopelessly towards the unseen goal. Without pronouncing the name to herself even, the mother decided, It has to be done one day and it can be done without a scene, tears, arguments, if she's out of the house, and then when she comes home she'll have the fact to face, the absolutely done and finished thing. "Three dresses, you'll have to have three," she said to her daughter's bright red convulsed face. Candy was swaying in the arms of the dance, his checked coat humped up across his neck and shoulders as he waltzed between the breakfast table and the sideboard, his eyes half-closed, his head back, singing:

" 'Don't tell my mother I breakfast on gin, Don't let the old folks know. Don't tell my father I'm living in sin, He'd never survive the blo-ow-ow-ow!' "

"For heaven's sake, stop singing that vile song before the servants hear you," the mother said, conjecturing the dresses, three complete outfits it would have to be, a new suit for traveling and two dresses to wear in the city. Candy started jigging, his hands on his hips, across the varnished dining-room floor.

" 'I'm one of the ruins Cromwell knocked abaht a bit,' " he sang. " 'Just *one* of the ruins Cromwell knocked abaht a bit,' " his feet nimbly, quickly, pattering time. " 'Blimey, there reely isn't a doubt of it, All the 'istory books they shout of it—' "

"Is it you who's going up to London to the house party or is it Nancy?" the mother said, and looking at him she began to laugh. But the girl had ceased laughing now. She held her hands down in her lap, watching languidly, drowsily something outside the window perhaps, or perhaps only hearing the same quick, clapping passage of the hunter's feet on road or cobbles or muffled and throbbing across turf. She said:

"I'll go up for the day only. I'll go just for the wedding. I won't stay three days away."

So the argument that never found conclusion began groping anew past the minutiae of this issue as past the others and beyond it to the declaration of probity itself: the mother's voice strained thin with bitterness and hopelessness and, at last, with fury, across the breakfast table and later across the lunch table, before it turned back from the stubborn, outlandish but insoluble pledge the girl had made to some equivocal young honor, to some unperjured but infuriating loyalty. So there it was left, none of the spirit solved nor the will yet broken to will, but in abeyance: the girl would go up on the Friday afternoon and spend the night there, only one night away, and be down on the afternoon train that brought her in just before tea time Saturday. After the first moment of wondering, she knew there was nothing to fear; and now that the mother's voice returned to hopelessness, planning the suit and the one dress instead of the two, the girl lying in the hammock counted the granted days that had not yet elapsed, thinking I can go because I have until Monday and because Apby can feed and water him and perhaps exercise him, perhaps even that. She would go too because of this: because she could see Mr. Sheehan clearly only in profile, sitting beside her on the sofa at Mrs. Patterson's in Florence and leaning forward to lift up the plate of sandwiches and pass it, but the rest of his face had perished; the remembered hairless young hand out of the brown tweed jacket's sleeve, the locks of crinkly, rather difficult hair worn too long for convention, and the lobeless, narrow ear with the hair waving thick above it, light brown, or perhaps only touched with light in places, or perhaps burned light by the Italian sun, had not expired but she could not meet his eyes. Below the concave temple's level were the deep tiny lines (just under the eyebrow's dark delicate extremity), worn there by too much dry chortling at wit (his own or anybody else's) or else from squinting hard against the weather, radiating finely from the eye's tip. But whenever he turned in memory to pass the plate of sandwiches, the vision failed: the mouth, the nose, the eyes went out and only the brow remained with the long wrinkles across it like the marks of tide left on a beach, and the widow's peak giving a heart's shape to the face. Now that he had written her, and the aunt had written, he did not cease leaning in profile, only in profile, over the textbook's page, the hairless, youthful hand following the line as she read it:

"The 'approach' is the three strides the horse makes immediately before taking off. The problem is to get the horse to jump off his hocks, at a suitable distance away from the fence, and to jump completely under the rider's control. The rider must decide in good time upon the last three strides, counting 'one-two-three-up,' and regulate his horse's pace accordingly." She who had ridden and jumped since before she was five now making a study of it and reading: "Keep the horse at a controlled canter up to thirty feet from the fence. The length of a stride in a controlled canter is about six feet. At thirty feet from the fence increase this stride to seven feet, then to eight, and finally to nine. At this point you are six feet from the jump and should then give the horse the office for the leap—" and Mr. Sheehan leaned across the page in profile, the side of his mouth laughing, his eye squeezed up with laughing and the thick dark lashes thrusting forward, and the girl stretched in the librating, the almost imperceptibly moving hammock thought, I don't know whether I like him or not, I don't know if I really like him.

And now the rains returned again, starting in one afternoon as she lay reading the book and swinging slightly, the bare sandaled foot hanging near the ground. First the clouds

gathered up behind the house and then the sun went, half
the visible world lying in yellow murk for a space and half
in blue rich foreboding, and then the first single shafts of
rain came down, slanting long and silvery past the foliage,
falling at intervals beyond her haven like deliberately lanced
spears. Then came the true hard rain, driving down the
lawn all afternoon and streaming along the window panes at
supper; after the first quick stabs of lightning and the thunder had passed, the rain continued swiftly and relentlessly
falling across the country, setting its quiet, dreary pace in
the evening and then buckling down to it for the night.
When the girl awoke at one in the morning, it was still
raining quietly outside. She had brought her mackintosh up
in the evening from below and laid it over the chair with
her riding breeches, and now she put it on and tied the rubber handkerchief over her hair before going out the window. She thought I might have remembered my Welling-
tons, sliding in her breeches and plaid wool bedroom slippers down the spouting drainpipe, but she had forgotten
them the night before and forgot them now by the time she
reached the stable. She was thinking, I just want him to be
there, waiting inside, that's all I ask. I don't care if I'm
soaked to the skin if he'll just understand and be there. And
once inside the stable she saw him leaning beyond the
shaded lantern he had set by the stall: Apby with his own
black mackintosh shining with rain as he saddled the hunter.

"So you did come!" she said, and he looked up and
touched his cap's beak, saying: "You said to be here, Miss,"
and leaned to the girth-straps again.

"I thought maybe when you saw it was raining," she said,
and as she pushed in sideways past the horse's tail and croup

and past the leaning groom, the blind horse turned his head on his shoulder towards the sound of her voice and her approach. She stood by his head, running her wet hand under his forelock, and she said: "I'm going up to London tomorrow. That's why I wanted to see you tonight. I wanted to ask you to carry on without me for the night and day I'm up in the city. I mean, I want you to put Brigand through his work-out the way I've been doing. One to half-past two, say, tomorrow night, and then when I come back I'm going to show them."

"Yes, Miss," said the groom, still leaning, not lifting his head.

"You can keep him on the figure eight with change and the half-passage at the canter," she said. She drew her hand down the short rough hair on the nasal bone. "You can try him out tonight with me on the half-passage and change, and if you can keep him going while I'm away, that'll be saving—" She thought of saying "my life" and then, because this brought it so near to "his life," she suddenly crossed her fingers against bad luck and stopped speaking. As Apby straightened up her eyes slid towards him a little cautiously, in slow, tentative induction. "Look," she said. "Another reason I wanted to see you tonight. I want to make him jump." She watched the groom sideways down the stall, her hand moving under the horse's forelock. "I want to take him over a fence tonight," she said.

The groom stood in his brightly gleaming coat, part in the lantern's light and part in the stable's dark, his cap on and its shadow cast grotesquely to the ceiling's beams, his hands on his hips, his dwarfed legs bowed, facsimile in miniature of tough and indomitable and muscular man.

"You can't do it, Miss," he said. "You can't make a blind horse jump. You can't do more than what nature allows for. You're just fixing him for a broken shoulder or broken neck—"

"I set up a knife-rest in the paddock three nights ago," she said, not paying any heed but standing there half-smiling, bringing her hand slowly down the pan of the hunter's cheek. "He took it. He took it back and forth a dozen times. When I come back I'll stretch him out on broader jumps."

"You can't do it," said Apby. He stood there on the straw bedding, his hands knuckled on his hips and the light shining through the arch and bow of his legs in their leather gaiters. He had shoved the beak of his cloth cap up and now it stood erect from the lining's edge above his creased short brow. "You've done up to now with a crock as what I've never heard of no one else doing, but you nor nobody can't give him the sight the time he needs it quick like that for gauging width and height. You can't do it," he said, and he said it again as he extinguished the lantern and then followed her and the horse out over the beam and into the steadily raining night. "You can't do it," he said, closing the stable door and buttoning his mackintosh's collar up to his chin while she mounted quickly from the ground. "You can't say to any horse, living or dead, this is so high this time and the next time it's so high so get ready for it, not unless he's got the power to see. Not unless you had just one jump fixed for him, say knee-high, and took him over it twenty times running, and even then. Even then," he said, "you couldn't do it."

"What I said to you first about why I wanted you to come out here tonight," she said, turning back to him on the saddle, "that wasn't the whole thing. I could have said that to you tomorrow morning or yesterday afternoon just as well. What I really wanted was for you to be here for the jump. I want you to stand at the thirty-foot mark in the paddock and call out one, two, three at the moment I cross it so I'll know how far it is to the fence."

"You can't do it," Apby said, following the horse's footfalls in the rain, not going up the stud-farm road tonight but the long way around by the running water to the paddocks. "You can't have a horse's eyes go and not pay for it, some way you got to pay for it. There wouldn't be no justice anywheres if a blind horse could do it as good as a horse without a flaw or a failing. You can't do what's impossible, because if you could there wouldn't be no end—" and not hearing the uneasy and exasperated words but only the sound of his complaint, the girl turned in the saddle and went on talking over her shoulder to him in the steadily falling rain.

"That'll tell me and tell him, that'll tell us both when we've got to the approach," she said, "and then I'll know when to give him the rise and take him over. You'll stand at the thirty-foot mark where I laid it out this morning, no, yesterday morning by this time, and you'll call out one, two, three. . . ."

"And to think," the groom's voice went on as he came booted and clopping behind, "it was me that begun this, started you off that night in the paddocks when you had him out with me— If I was to do the right thing by everybody, you and the horse included, what I'd do now is tell Mrs. Lombe what's going on, get 'er up out-a-wer bed no matter if it's middle of the night or tomorrow morning, and

she'd put 'er foot down and seen it was put a stop to. If I
was to do what I ought to be doing now instead of—" He
took one hand out of his mackintosh pocket and wiped the
rain down his cheeks the way a comedian pretends to wipe
the smile from his face, and then he started running clum-
sily forward through the mud and rain, stumbling ahead
until he got to the horse's evenly and rhythmically riding
croup and passed it, and then kept abreast the stirrup with
the girl's plaid wool bedroom slipper thrust soaking in it
while he said: "If I was to go to the house now and tell Mrs.
Lombe, she wouldn't stand for it. She'd put a stop to it all
right before anything worse came to happen, jumping on a
stone-blind horse the way you say on a night that even
frogs would stay home in. If I was to go back to the house
now and get—" .

"Only you wouldn't," the girl said, riding straight ahead.
"You wouldn't do it because I need you to stand at the
thirty-foot mark. If you didn't stand there, then something
might happen because I couldn't judge close enough when
to give him the rise. I worked it out from the book that
maybe he'll jump this way if he won't jump any other. I
wouldn't ask it for any other horse but just give him his
rein and let him take off when he liked, maybe not elegant,
according to the book, but that's the way I've always done
it. The book says—"

"Oh, the book!" said Apby. Either she halted the horse or
he halted of himself, but her voice and his movement ceased
at the same instant and the groom looked up and, under-
standing what it was now, went ahead to open the paddock
gate. She heard the hinges cry out and, waiting, heard Apby

beginning the same arguments over in the same vexed, grieved tone.

"You can't do it no more than anybody could do it, a trainer couldn't do it and no book can tell you how to take a blind, dumb, unwitting, unwilling beast—" and she leaned forward and patted the horse's shoulder on which the rain poured like sweat.

"So you wouldn't let me down," she said as she rode in past Apby. "You'll stand at the thirty-foot mark where I made it this morning. I'll show it to you."

"Anyways," Apby said, letting the gate swing back, "if he breaks his back at it that'll be all right. They'll have to put him down tomorrow then, Mr. Penson or no Mr. Penson."

"Stand here, Apby," she said, bringing the horse to a halt in the grass. "Stand here. You can feel the bricks making a cross. That's it."

"You can't do it," Apby said again, and out of the little distance she had ridden away already, she said:

"I have done it. I did it alone with him over the knife-rest when there was moonlight, ten, fifteen times back and forth. The only difference is neither of us can see tonight. You stay where you are." The rain came quickly, quietly down, not in voluble articulation as on a house's roof or windows, but striking the face, the naked hands in silence, dropping steadily, as if forever, on the head and shoulders, the bent legs, beating softly as a moth's wings in the trees, until it was rain no longer after a while but the accumulated presence of water, more salient than the dark's or any human presence, like the presence of a vast and swiftly flowing, unseen river passing within arm's reach through the night. Apby stood with water trickling from his cap's stuff down across his face, water dripping unceasingly from the now lowered beak, one drop following another in rivulation to the corners of his mouth, into his ears until, like a bather, he put his forefingers into the ears' orifices and wrung them. "Damn the rain," was the last thing he heard her say before he heard the horse coming, and then a little later, either in imagination or in reality, saw coming towards him the dim cantering shape.

"She might have picked any other night to do it," he said half aloud, as if speaking to someone standing there with him for comfort's sake or else to split the blame with. He ran the back of his hand along his upper lip, under his water-beaded nose, and shook the drops off, and now the splatter of the horse's feet, the wind and thrash of his coming was almost ready to pass. He felt the movement of the air, the breath, the throb, heard even the saddle's creaking leather and the tossed bit's jangle, as if someone had opened a window or pushed open a door near him to let in these sounds he had not heard before in a vast darkened and silenced hall; and as the thing rushed past he leapt back and called the words out. "One, two, three!" he called out like a man crying desperately out from shore into the hopeless dark and wind to the floundered and drowning lost in a storm-pounded sea.

Mr. Sheehan, she thought for an instant, said that time in Florence that nobody should start riding too young, children being either too bold or too timid or both at the same time, and then the bold ones crack up going fast and they've no nerve left to go on the rest of their lives with, and the timid ones go on being shy with horses, or danger, or other people, or with themselves; their spirits, not their bodies, crippled. Mr. Sheehan said, England, the horse-growing country and the country as well of all the misfits, the hugger-muggers, the reticent, the mum, the evaders, because why, because what? because what except stuck up on a horse's back since generations and licked from the get-away, the lip set, both upper and lower, the eyes taught not to quail, and the heart broken in two by funk or daring at the age of five or younger. Take away the horses and you would have a fine upstanding race of men, the Britons, said Mr. Sheehan, the side of his face in profile squinted up either against laughing or against the drifting Irish weather, and for an instant she remembered the first time being thrown: the hack had cantered her up the lane to the top of the hill and there he had reared for no reason except "frightened by the bush because the bush unexpectedly turned and waved a branch," without warning dropping her the long way down. I remember being sick, terrifically sick, she thought, perhaps passing Apby at the thitry-foot mark now, and mother made me mount quickly again as soon as I was finished being sick. "If you don't mount right away," mother said, "you'll start crying and then you won't want to get up on a horse again," and now Apby's voice called out, "One, two, three," and she put her teeth together and thought in sudden wild jubilation, Tomorrow I'll be able to tell Mr. Sheehan that at thirty feet from the fence I increased the stride to seven feet, then to eight, and finally to nine, at this point being, as near as I could judge in the dark, six feet from the jump and I gave my horse the office for the leap.

"Bat," she said quickly. "I can't see any more than you

can but we're going to take it." She let the head free then
and the loins free, and her weight moved swiftly into the
knees as they clasped the saddle-flaps. The balls of the feet
were riding lightly in the stirrup irons now and she held
him firmly to the fence with her legs. At once she felt him
rising strongly but sweetly under her, the mouth limber,
the neck pliant even though stretched to go, no sense of
heat or excitement confusing him but the blood as temperate as if he still cantered easily across the paddock. Just
as they cleared what, from conjecture, must have been the
rail though lost and undelineated in the night's and the falling water's obscurity, she thought of the other side and the
wet grass where he might bog or slip at the landing, and
she said again: "Damn it, oh, damn the rain."

She leaned with him, the body that had followed through
the rise and the soaring now bending with him through the
descent, and as his forefeet struck the ground her knees and
ankles caught the shock and broke it but her hands did not
move on the reins. She let him stride on for twenty yards
or more before she pulled him up and turned him on his
hocks, and halted there in the rain and darkness and listening to the coming and going of his breath, she called out to
the groom:

"Apby, I say, Apby, come and open the gate for us," her
own voice sounding ringing and clear. "Apby!" she called,
like someone tipsy with triumph, drunk and reeling with it.
"Apby, hurry up! I want to take him over again."

Chapter Seven

ON FRIDAY afternoon, just after lunch time, the girl went up to London in her new suit, carrying her little overnight bag in her hand, and nothing happened in the country until the Saturday morning. It was then, standing by the sitting-room window and looking into the flowered and damp emptiness of still another day, that Candy saw them emerge from somewhere, perhaps from the main road outside where a two-seated car might now be standing halted close to the bank: the back of a man he had not seen before in khaki riding-breeches and a sport-shirt, and his wife in dark blue spotted all over its broad skirt and blouse with white, and her summer hat on, the sailor hat which came out of some undivulged hiding place each end of May or in the early days of June, depending on the weather. He watched them descend the drive, making the gestures of talk, and pass the rock garden where the purple foxgloves stood nobly if a little shabbily flowering in the moist sunlight, and pass the wayfaring-tree at the curve and go from sight. For a moment, standing at the window, he wondered and then without any feeling of surprise, he knew. He knew it exactly, as if the words had been said to him and knew now, moreover, that it was for this the quiet and lull of the day before and the night had been preparing. Through some irremediable error the sun had come out that morning, but otherwise the unmistakable stage was set.

When they had gone from sight he walked into the dining room and although it was only just gone ten he took the decanter of whiskey out. The ordinary glasses were kept in the pantry, and sadly, quietly he thought, I cannot go out and get one any more than I can go out there and go into the stable and stop them doing it. He opened the sideboard door, stooping to it, and selected one of the small embossed porter glasses and set it on the table, and then he filled it three-quarters full with whiskey and set the decanter down, fitting the glass stopper to it, and he drank the whiskey off at once. He thought, They'll do it humanely, they're bound to do it humanely, and he looked almost peacefully at the bottom of the empty glass. If I had any arguments or any reasons to give them I could go out there, or if I could walk into the stable like a man with a wallet fat in his pocket and slap the sides of it and say, This happens to be, just happens to be my horse, not yours, my lady. He was bought by me, paid for by me, purchased under the rules of warranty (only I never got the certificate because I had two drinks instead), as sound in wind and eyes, quiet to ride, has been hunted and capable of being hunted, so pack up your chalk and your pistol and your vet, whoever he is, in your old kit bag and go back to gardening. They'll do it humanely, he thought, and the feeling of peace spread marvelously through him, something better than mere respite or truce but the final, absolute conciliation through performed and indisputable act. The responsibility is being taken off my shoulders, he thought gently, forbearingly, the issue is being removed from my hands. I have no authority, no jurisdiction, even if I moved now towards the door and out it I could not save that horse, and the sense of actionless, speechless bliss rose richly in him; I am powerless, helpless because they know their business and I have none yet, I never found it; my wife will see that the target is properly indicated and the man in breeches will make use of the humane killer to the conclusion of this drama, this minor but grotesquely aggrandized tragedy which will fade slowly but unerringly into the past. It is not disaster but the one logical solution, he thought, and the voice drifted from some far dim plane of memory to hearing now, repeating as it had years back repeated all day at fifteen-minute intervals across the air, "The King's life is drawing peacefully to a close."

After the second porter-glassful was drunk, Candy put his hand to his back pocket and took his silver and leather hip-flask out. He unscrewed the cap and drew the cork out with his teeth, tipping his head on the side to do it, and then he filled it up from the decanter. He did not spill any, but because a little spread wet at the top, he ran his tongue around the screw-cap's thread, then corked the flask and twisted the top back on and slipped it under his jacket again. Or stamp down there, he thought, and take no nonsense from them, the artist out of pocket, out of luck, but painting alone, accomplishing alone experiments in style, subject, and treatment, working alone and making a name that people listen for in city exhibitions and museums, look for in catalogues and magazines, so that even a wife or even a vet's assistant would listen. He looked at the decanter in dispassionate meditation a moment and then he filled the porter glass again. Penson drawing his last breaths, it may be, while I stand here drinking, kicked towards kingdom come and landing on the threshold, and yet I'd face my

Maker saying they haven't a damned bit of evidence against
that blind staggerer out there in the stable, not a shred of
anything except that he can't see the day ahead to face the
firing squad. You've got to die, he said suddenly, putting
the glass down. Horse, it's your turn to die. This time it's
not Penson or me but you, horse not man, you blank-eyed
espial spying upon the secrets of eternity, you milky-eyed
deserter. You're no good to anyone, he said, but he was
looking at his own face in the sideboard mirror. Because this
was the affair culminated at last between himself and the
very fiber and substance of his going on, he did not begin
thinking of Nancy until after the fifth glass of whiskey;
and when he thought of her he put the glass stopper for
the last time into the decanter and went at once, walking
carefully but without any semblance of drunkenness, upstairs to his own bedroom and pulled open the bottom
drawer of the dresser. From under the neatly folded cardi-
gans, he took out the revolver and made sure that it was
loaded, and then he put it into his jacket pocket. There
were two more glasses of liquid left in the decanter and he
drank them fast.

"That makes everything neat and tidy," he said, but when
he stooped to retrieve the glass stopper which had dropped
to the ground, his head spun slowly, so he helped himself
erect again by holding to the table with one hand. Then
he started walking, careful and trim in his squire's jacket,
his silk kerchief folded on his neck, down the faintly steaming drive.

The sliding door was standing open beyond the wayfaring-
tree and Mrs. Lombe and the young man in breeches were in
the stable. They were not in the hunter's stall but talking to-

gether as they stood on the timber floor, and beyond the box's gate the hunter's quarters shone in the light. At the first sound of Candy's step on the wood, his wife turned her head with her sailor hat on it and said:

"This is Mr. Lombe, Mr. Harrison. I've had Mr. Harrison over this morning while Nan's up in London to do what has to be done."

Candy stood against the daylight in the door, a rather jaunty figure with his hands in his jacket pockets, the back of the wrist and the left thumb showing, but this time the right thumb was out of sight. He nodded his head either in greeting or dismissal and teetered upwards, his legs planted wide apart, on his clean crepe soles.

"Where's Apby?" he said. "Does Apby know what's going on?"

"I sent him off early." She smiled a quick, tolerant, although impatient-seeming smile. "He's having the day off in Pellton. I told him I'd see the hunter got his midday meal. I haven't said anything to anybody. I just want to get it done as quickly and quietly as possible. It's not a pleasant job of work for anyone concerned. I had Richards take the mare to the village to have her shod."

"So there wouldn't be any witnesses, not so much as a mare looking on, what?" said Candy, and now her eye on him altered as she began to suspect it. "Where do you intend to do it?" Candy said. Since that first step over the threshold he had not moved and his eyes had not shifted from her face, so if he had been asked then he could not have said whether the man called Harrison was short or tall, or what the color of his hair or what his age was, only that he remembered the khaki breeches and the gaiters walking down the drive. "Where is justice to be meted out?" he said loudly, sardonically.

"Mr. Harrison is the huntsman from the local hunt," Mrs. Lombe said, saying the words pleasantly and exactly to him, as if it were a child's small, stubborn figure, not a man's and not her husband's, who stood teetering against the light. "He's been kind enough to offer to do it for us. He's an expert at it. I've arranged for the haulers to come at eleven and take the body away."

"Which body?" said Candy, and now as good as if his breath had been wafted to her over the smell of clean horse and fresh bedding and clean mixture in the stable, she knew the bitter and unacceptable truth: that he was drunk, drunk at ten in the morning, that it was not curiosity that held him standing there haranguing but drunken opposition; not only drunk but drunk before lunch for a change and drunk before a stranger.

"Don't be an idiot, Candy," she said, laughing quickly, nervously, and glancing at Mr. Harrison in invitation to him to do the only possible thing and laugh. "You'd better go back to the house so Mr. Harrison can get on with it."

But Candy began crossing the stable now, walking blank-eyed, blank-faced, deliberately toward them, not swaying or deviating from the invisible line his intention had drawn, but walking carefully and deliberately at them as if they were no longer there now that he had started walking directly to where he wanted to go. They did not obstruct his way, but as he came they drew apart, each of them drawing to one side as a crowd might have drawn apart to allow the passage of a vehicle that ran on tracks and could not alter its course, and Candy passed between the two people who stared, the man in curiosity and the woman in wonder at him, and walked to the stall where the horse stood, its head hanging peacefully now across the gate. Candy took his left hand from his pocket and put it on the latch, and the horse threw his head up and Candy hesitated an instant, and then turned his head too and looked back at the two people standing, in their turn outlined and faceless, against the sunlight in the open stable-door.

"I just wanted to know," he said, almost imperceptibly swaying. "I just wanted to ask you before I go in there how Mr. Penson is, Mr. Har— I'd like to know."

The young man took a step or two towards him—young, thought Candy, seeing him for the first time now as he stood in relief against the yellowish brightness of the day outside, young only because the legs tapered in the breeches and the shoulders were broad and unsloping, for he could not see the features of the face or the color of the hair.

"I was just telling Mrs. Lombe," the man said in a strangely gentle, girl-like voice. "I was just telling her he died. He died last night."

"So an eye for an eye, a horse for a man, that's the way you look at it," said Candy, sardonically, but the whiskey was swinging hard and sickening in his head now and he held to the gate's wood for support. "A life for a life is what you think—" He saw Mrs. Lombe with the old sailor hat on coming towards him and he remembered I mustn't take my right hand out of my pocket until I'm ready. I can get the gate open with my left hand, like this, and now he had come through it and he stood on the oaten straw bedding by the horse now, and the gate was closed between him and his wife and the man she called Mr. Harrison.

"He's so expert," he said, holding to the wood and pressing away from the horse's shoulder in the stall, "that he could probably do it without drawing the chalkline or do it with his eyes closed only he's not going to. The minute he takes out his revolver, I take out mine."

"Candy, come out," said Mrs. Lombe, but the conviction had lapsed from her voice. Candy was standing as far from the horse as he could get, the bordeaux-red silk kerchief around his throat because he hadn't shaved yet, the small of his back against the rough wood of the stall. "Please be reasonable, please come out," she said, but the power had gone from her. She stood with the straw hat pushed up off her forehead, seeking to say it with dignity.

"I'll come out when Nancy gets back," he said. "My little girl will come out here and she'll understand what I'm trying to do. She'll take shifts here with me, all summer if it has to be, hunger-strike, sleep-strike, drink-strike," he said, and at the last words the feeling of tears welled in him; and oh, heavens, heavens, thought the woman standing on the other side of the gate, what have I done that I should have to stand here before a stranger and hear him turning maudlin? What have I done that it should have to happen like this? Oh, spare me, spare me. "And if you try to stop Nancy's marriage it'll be the same thing. I won't have you interfering with her and stopping her whatever she wants to do, lift a finger, go to a dance, have a horse of her own like—" And ah, unjust, unjust, thought the mother bitterly. Who was it picked out the clothes for her to go up to London, who was it had found the school for her in Florence last year? But there had been so many years of it now that it was for nothing else but the stranger's presence that she

cared. "I'll wait here for my little girl," Candy went on saying in the same low-pitched and vagrant and scarcely defiant voice, "and you can't do anything to me because this
time I've got the upper hand, for once I've got it. You've
got the money but this time I tricked you, I fooled you,
you can't field marshal me out of here, you can't major-
domo me, you can't even bribe me—" Oh, sordid, sordid,
thought the mother in grief as she looked at the small contorted flushed face, ageless and queer as a dwarf's, turning
from one side to the other in fear of death and fear of life
on the other side of the gate. In a moment she looked towards Mr. Harrison and whether the actual word was said
or merely indicated, they both moved in simultaneous dignity and forbearance towards the door, crossing the timber
to the threshold, and there the young man stood differen-
tially to one side to let her pass before him out into the
light. "You can go, but it won't make any difference to
me," Candy called out, but then as the blind horse shifted
a little nervously on the straw, he lowered his voice. "That's
all right," he said, but when he looked at the massive shoulder and the strong hanging head his blood swooned in him.
He stood leaning against the side of the stall, his hands in
his pockets, seeking not to see the great, living, breathing
beast with its eyes clogged blue and milky beneath the
long, luxuriant lash, and then he took his left hand from the
jacket's pocket and felt out the flask, and braced it against
his ribs with his palm, the left hand's fingers fumbling off
the cap. He did not stir his right hand but drew the cork
out with his teeth and drank, and while he drank the horse
brought his lowered head across the straw, the wide, soft
nostrils seeking quiveringly for cognizance until the nose

reached the shoes' tips and lipped across them, the monstrous, vacuous, ingesting suction of a snail mounting the ankles and the trousers to the jacket, and when the man brought his arm carefully down and his hand with the flask in it he dared move no longer but stood flattened against the stall's wood, waiting, the flask extended in his stricken hand. The horse's head lifted slowly, searchingly, the ears back, the hairs in the nostrils trembling in the blasts of breath, and now that the lips came blindly fumbling across his shoulder to his face, the cry of terror ripped from Candy's throat. "For Christ's sake!" he screamed, and the horse flung his head away in fright, swinging in the box until his quarters stood trembling now before the man, the long black tail twitching across his buttocks and the points of his hocks. "I can't, I can't," Candy said under his breath and he began whimpering as he leaned against the boards. "I'm afraid, I have a right to be afraid," he said, but now that the horse had ceased to move he managed to cork the flask, his left hand shaking, and slip it into his back pocket. Then he stood quiet there better than a quarter of an hour, his hands out of sight in his pockets, the dream of dauntlessness and sedulity vaguely augmenting and as vaguely waning, and at the last instant of fading reversing to a stronger, clearer, dizzier amplification. At the end of that little while, Mrs. Lombe and the huntsman came through the door and crossed the stable again.

"Mr. Harrison and I have been talking things over," she began in the measured, pleasant voice that must bring concurrence to logic in its wake. "Mr. Harrirson thinks it might be very dangerous for you to stay in there with that horse. I explained to him the horse was not accustomed to being handled by you and he says that's where the great danger lies. It's strangers that worry them when there's anything wrong." He stood with the small of his back held against the boards, his eyes fixed sightless on the horse's rump and the long black tail that swept at intervals across it, and he did not speak. "If you're making this absurd scene for Nancy's sake," she went on, "I assure you she'd rather come home to find her ailing horse dead than to find her father in hospital—"

"Mr. Lombe," said the huntsman in his girl-like wounded voice, "it's scarcely taking the long view of things to—"

It was not Candy's passive opposition now that stopped them both, but without any warning he began to sing, lifting his head so that the back of it rested against the stall's boards, and his throat came free of the silk kerchief as he sang loudlessly, tunelessly what words he remembered of what remnants of song he salvaged from the cahotage of terror and drink and despair.

" 'I saw England's king from the top of a bus, He was riding in state so he didn't see us,' " he sang, bawling it out, and the horse flicked his ears. " 'And though—oh, tra, tra, tra, te-de-dum—oh, by the Saxons we once were oppressed, I cheered, God forgive me, oh, God, oh, God, forgive me, I cheered with the rest, I—' "

Mrs. Lombe stepped a little nearer and spoke his name, and he glanced quickly at her and began at once:

" 'I'm one of the ruins Cromwell knocked abaht a bit, I'm *one* of the ruins Cromwell knocked abaht a bit, oh, tra, la, la, la! Outside the Cromwell Arms last Saturday night I was one of the—' "

When the haulers came a little after eleven, Mrs. Lombe

went to the door with dignity and sent them off, offering
to pay them extra if they would be kind enough to come
back in the afternoon. Candy had been singing: " 'You remember young Peter O'Loughlin, of course? Well, here he
is now at the head of the force! I met him one day while
crossing the Strand—oh, God, oh, God bless him, he held
up the street with one wave of his hand,' " but when he
heard the men speaking outside and saw her go, proudly
and discreetly as a lady might, to give them their directions, he turned his head towards the open door and
shouted: " 'Don't tell my mother I'm living in sin, Don't
let the old folks—' " and they closed the door and left him
to it. All through lunch time he stood motionless in the
stall with the small of his back against the boards, and at
two he had finished the whiskey. The horse had dropped
his head and began eating his bedding for they had not
watered or fed him since the morning meal. It was almost
three o'clock when the haulers came back: he heard their
horses and their voices outside in the sunlight, and then Mr.
Harrison opened the stable door and he and Mrs. Lombe
crossed the timber briskly together. At a little distance from
the box they came to a stop.

"You must be very hungry," she said, standing there
slightly in advance of the huntsman. "I had them put out
some roastbeef sandwiches and beer on the veranda for you,
so if you'll just come along—"

"No," said Candy, looking at the horse. "No, it's all right.
You can't trick me." He was talking thick now, leaning
against the side of the stall. "I'm waiting here for my little
girl, I'm waiting, I'm on the side of civilization. This horse,
he isn't a horse any moren any of us are horses, he's the

forces of good against the forces of destruction, he's me, just as much me as artist, foreigner, just as much an outcast, he's freak and he's love, he's got something to do with love as it works out against—against this, this empire building and this susspression of the native, what you said the other night about Gandhi being so ugly himself, thin and his teeth out and his gums like that the way you would talk about a horse, you said he was such a freak you didn't care what his beliefs were and didn't think he could have any looking like—well, this horse is against that sort of thing. He's for love. All right," he said, "now we've got it straight. This horse, he's all wrong and wherebyfore he's against everything that is your right and the world's right and Mr. Har— He's me by this time, and he's Nancy I think, or he's me and Nancy getting off to another country where everybody who speaks English is a foreigner, not only me. He's my horse, if he's a horse any more, and I bought him with your money, yes, all right, all rr-r-r-right, your money, but I bought something else at the same time, making the same purchase, my dear, something you haven't seen yet but it's there keeping me in the stable and in the stall until you get out of it and there doesn't have to be any explanation for him," mumbling it, half-crying it as he stood with his hands in his pockets staring at the horse's rump.

Mrs. Lombe made the imperceptible sign to the huntsman or spoke the unheard word, and immediately he stepped forward.

"Mr. Lombe," he said in his winning, girl-like voice, "won't you come out with us now and let events take their course?"

Candy turned his head and looked at them, perhaps assuring himself that he had heard it right, and then he began to laugh. With the small of his back pressed in against the stall's boards he began shaking with silent grotesque laughter.

"Let events *what?*" he wheezed through his laughing. "Let them do what?" He leaned his shoulders back now, his mouth half open, growing sick with laughter. "Let events—"

Mrs. Lombe again made the immediately understood sign to the young man, and again he began speaking.

"Mr. Lombe," he said, "we don't want to do it at all but if you don't come out we shall have to ask the hauler's men outside to help us. This horse has been condemned by two leading veterinary-surgeons, one of them dead now, killed in the act of discharging his duty—". and Candy's fit of strangling laughter cut off the sound of the huntsman's voice and the color came up his girlish throat and spread across his jaws. "Killed," he went on after a moment, with his eyes dropped now, "because he stood behind a horse the way you're standing now, Mr. Lombe, in the stall of an ailing, unpredictable animal," and Candy lay weak with laughing against the boards. "I said he was killed in the discharge of his duty," said the huntsman, his high voice trembling as he raised it to be heard. "While you, Mr. Lombe, are obstructing mine and wasting my Saturday for me—" and Candy's hilarious gasps rose now to cries of laughter and then stopped short in incredulous amazement.

"*Your* Satur— Mr. Har—? Your—?" he began, and the laughter convulsed him again. "Oh, please, pull-ease, stop being funny! Oh, pll-ease, pll-ease, Mr. Har—" He threw back his smooth neat little head again and the laughter squeezed out of his eyes and out of the strange contortion of his mouth. "For Christ's sake, pll-ease!" he said, and Mrs. Lombe turned and walked to the stable door and opened it. When she came back the hauler's men were with her, three good, stout countrymen who came through the door after her and stood waiting, ill-at-ease, beside her.

"Will you be so kind," she said quietly to them, but her spirit was bowed in grief and humility in her: so it has come to this, it has come to this. "Will you be good enough to assist the gentleman outside so that he will be out of danger," she said.

The three men stood awkwardly there a moment, their arms bare in their short-sleeved collarless shirts, their shoes good and almost stylish-looking as the shoes of Devonshire workmen are likely to be. They looked uncertainly at one another, and at Mrs. Lombe in her sailor hat, awkwardly seeking, and in too much of a dilemma to feign any other emotion, the unmistakable side of respectability. And then the huntsman made the gesture before them: standing with his face and his right arm averted from Candy's sight in case Candy had turned his head to see, he lifted his hand as if it held a glass in it, raised it to drink, once, twice, and then a third time. His mouth shaped the one word but he did not say it to them: drunk. Here was the shared joke now, the inaudibly communicated truth, and once in on it with the gentry the three hauler's men smiled, neither broadly nor sheepishly but simply in recognition, and after looking once more at one another for confirmation, they took the thing on. First Mrs. Lombe stepped forward, the huntsman walking to one side of her and a little back, perhaps out of native and habitual precaution, and close behind them followed the hauler's men. For an instant Candy did not see them as the march across the boards began but stood leaning back against the wood, his eyes fixed on the horse's motionless rump as if subduing and mastering it by sight alone. He leaned against the stall's side, his hands clenched in his pockets, having entered now another and more violent plane of fear. If I take my eyes off these quarters, this catapult of death, I'm done for, he thought, I'm finished, I'll die with the sight of Penson lying with his skull oozing its sense and memory out on horse's bedding. The dream-stupored and desperate eyes saw on the hunter's cool burnished croup the mark, raw as if only just branded on the flesh, of the horse's iron, the identical stamp they had found on Penson's face, with the hook of one heel jerked through the eyeball and the other heel caught in the palate's vertebrates. But when he felt their purpose advancing on him, he took his right hand out of his pocket for the first time and they saw the pistol in it.

"Don't touch the gate," he said, watching the horse's croup. "Don't touch it."

He did not shoot until Mrs. Lombe put her hand out to the latch, seeing or perhaps only divining the raising of her hand towards the box's gate, and then, without taking his eyes off the horse, he shot wildly out across them, the detonation splitting loud through the stable. The hauler's men and the huntsman ducked, but Mrs. Lombe did not stir but watched with clear stark eyes the blind horse as he whirled in his stall, spinning with forefeet slightly lifted, the tail arched and thrashing in panic across Candy's face and passing, and then the strong brutal head swinging across Candy's skull in its demented quest for sight.

"Come out, Candy," she whispered, but no one heard her. The hauler's men were out the door already and the huntsman was smoothing back his hair. "Come out, Candy," she said. "Come out."

He stood braced against the stall's side, the smoking pistol hanging in his fallen hand, his head pressed back against the board, the face small and fresh-looking, the eyes closed in an attitude of resigned and terrible waiting. He felt himself so, his body like something growing now to the wood and waiting, not for release any more in the gate's opening or Nancy's coming from the rapidly gyrating and seemingly illuminated wheels of fear, but release, as he swooned and drowned in terror, in the actual splinter of the complete and unalterably ordained end. But when he heard the huntsman's voice speaking again beyond the tide in which his body sank and perished, saying, "Let me by, Mrs. Lombe, let me by. This has got to be dealt with. This can't go on. Let me by"—he lifted the revolver again and again, but this time with his eyes closed fast against the vision of his own violent death, he fired out across the stable. And this time the horse shot upward, upright on its hocks, swung madly over him, and, whirling, smashed its heels savagely against the wooden gate. Mrs. Lombe's hand fell suddenly on Mr. Harrison's arm and her fingers clutched in anguish on his flesh, and they stood watching the horse spin, watched it fling itself from side to side in wild despair, while the little man lay pressed against the stall's side, his hands down, his head lifted, so far untouched and perhaps immuned by this passive, abeyant, this almost ludicrous posture of martyrdom.

They stood a while watching Candy pressed back against

the planks, his eyes closed, his right hand hanging with the pistol in it, and watched the horse quieting again and beginning to pace restlessly back and forth, its head swinging, pacing quickly, nervously back and forth across the straw with its head lifted and swinging and its nostrils quivering as they lipped the air for warning. Then Mrs. Lombe and the huntsman, as if the inaudible word had again been said, took up their positions at the open stable door. They did not speak much, only now and again a word about the weather, and at twenty past four Mrs. Lombe said in a low voice:

"There's Nancy. There's my daughter coming," and she went forward to meet her, neither the thoughts or the words ready yet, nor the emotion nameable that shook her heart.

Checkout Receipt

Friends of the Library Book Sale
Sept. 10th: 10AM-8PM
Sept. 11th 10AM-5:30PM
Sept. 12th 12PM-5PM
W. Clarke Swanson Branch
omahalibraryfriends@gmail.com

Main Library
09/11/10 05:10PM

PATRON: 179373

Three short novels [of Ka
33149001254503 Due: 10/02/10

TOTAL: 1

Return Items to Any
Omaha Public Library
For 24 Hour Automated
Renewal Call 444-4100

THE BRIDEGROOM'S BODY

Chapter One

THE SWANNERY had been established there, just on the edge of Lord Glourie's grounds, because it was here the swans had come of themselves since years, since centuries maybe, to feed on the weeds and to lead their own strong violent life in the lagoon. It lay a little piece beyond the swanherd's cottage, a narrow strip of brackish water running for a mile between the bank of shingles and the green swampy soil of England. In late April or early May, depending on how the year was, the swans began working and weaving anew, the old cobs staking their old claims out on the land and the water, and the newly mated birds, a little uncertain still, casting about for virgin ground in the rotting swamp of the lagoon.

On the tenth of May this year the swanherd, who had been up since light, was standing in his rubber boots in the water when Lady Glourie came along the path that ran high and dry through the towers of the swans' nests. He was a slight little man with a lock of graying hair thrusting from under the beak of his cloth cap, and his eyes light blue looking up at her coming, uneasy and faded like a beggar's or a drunkard's eyes to what was authority or charity or law.

"There's a bit of a hack-up going on," he said, and Lady Glourie said, "Ho, ho."

She was a woman of thirty-five or six with a big pair

of shoulders strong as a wood yoke set across her freckled neck. She slapped the breast pocket of her green suède jacket and took the package of Gold Flakes out.

"Young brat fighting for the same bit of ground as old Hitches," said the swanherd. With the back of his miniature hand he set the hanging shreds of his mustaches off his mouth. "One or other of the cobs puts so much as a foot in the lake and they're off. Been up after them twice this morning till now." He stood small as a child below her, looking up to her in weakness and for hope from under his twin shaggy brows. "Got a blow from Hitches this morning trying to get between them near took me off my feet," he said. "Bang down come Hitches with one wing thought a hammer'd struck me proper. Iron couldn't have done it better."

"I'll have a talk with them," said Lady Glourie, snapping her lighter open. The swanherd stood below her, in the water still, watching her underlip pushed up against the white paper of the cigarette, and the little flame of the lighter perishing in the rain. All about them over the trees and the sea and the pasture-land the rain was falling, endlessly falling. As if the island had not had enough of it all winter, the rain was going to keep on falling right through the spring.

With the cigarette fast on her unpainted lip, Lady Glourie started back up the path again, and the swanherd lifted his feet from the muck lying deep on the roots of the zosteria weeds, drew them slowly from the separately heard kiss of the water and swamp and followed her quickly towards the rhododendron trees. Just beyond the forest of leathery leaves on which the rain stood and the wire-run down which Lord Glourie and the others drove the wild ducks in season, the swanherd called to her and pointed out across the full water of the little artificial lake.

"There beyond's old Hitches," he said. Lady Glourie halted and looked, her head lifted, her eyes narrowed, the rain loading the dark green rim of her felt hat until it drooped in scallops around her short-nosed, long-lipped face.

"I'll just give him a piece of my mind," she said. She stood squinting against the cigarette smoke and the rain and the distance there still was between her and the white floating bird. He was close to the other shore, gyrating slowly on the surface of the lake, the imperious head lifted, quick as the finger of a compass to sight or sound. "You there," Lady Glourie called out to the big bird across the water. She took the cigarette out of her mouth and held it down, shielded in her broad white ungloved hand. Behind the swan, sitting on the high throne of the nest, sat the bold-eyed pen, no longer young, who year after year had been his mate, his love, his freshly seduced bride. "You there," Lady Glourie called out again. "You, Hitches," and the swan's body curved the water as he turned, his bright menacing eye fixed on her like a jewel, the supple neck arched, the webbed feet fanning just below the surface as he came. "If that's your end, then you can leave this end to the young ones, can't you?" Lady Glourie cried, and the woman sitting on the nest behind him looked in venom across the water at Lady Glourie and the swanherd, then stretched her powerful throat forth and spoke her husband's name.

On the other side of the little neck of water where the

lake narrowed quickly into the stream, Lady Glourie saw the young couple now, pure white among the rushes, slender as young girls and working eagerly, hesitantly together, building their first nest higher, higher out of the fringe of ruppia grasses.

"What harm are they doing you?" Lady Glourie called out to the old ones far at the other end. "What harm on earth?" The cigarette dropped from her hand and she looked quickly down at it and, thinking of this other thing, she ground its fire out.

All the way back along the path towards the swanherd's cottage these monuments to love the swans had built stood near them, some on the right hand and some to the left, and some unfinished yet and others with the serene white birds already enthroned on them. The path wound through the labyrinth of the swannery land, and there, close enough to be touched with the hand, rode the fiery-eyed young cobs on the swamp's water guarding their brides and their territory from the approach of man or one another. Here in this passionately mated life where bird cleaved violently to bird, the beetling old navigators followed the narrow veins of water through the reeds, slowly and arrogantly tracing the limits of their own domains in inexplicably savage perpetuation of the past. Here it was shared, as nothing else is, by the young and old alike, and for an instant Lady Glourie felt it moving, like a hand, across her heart.

Then the roof of the swanherd's cottage showed suddenly through the trees and Lady Glourie's face changed.

"I say, how's Mrs. Lucky today?" she said to the swanherd and they stopped just before the cottage.

"I can't say as there's been much of a change," he said.

His faded uncertain eyes went from her face to the mucked toes of his rubber-boots and took on the resolution of his grief. "She can't do much about getting onto her feet at all."

"I'll just pop in and have a look then," said Lady Glourie. She stood with her hands in her pockets, looking at the rain. "I've been thinking we'll have to write up to London for a woman-sort-of-thing to come down and help, give a hand for a fortnight . . . probably more trouble than they're worth. . . ."

On the morning of the eleventh of May she wrote to London for a trained nurse to come down, writing to Mrs. Wolf-Laxtern at the nursing home for someone who would not mind the country life so far from every kind of thing for a time.

"They'res no cinema with in five miles," she wrote, scratching the words in a bold strong man-like hand across the paper. She could never remember the spelling of things or when the end of a sentence seemed likely to come along. If anything looked too wrong to the eye, she struck it out and began it again on the same line, farther on. "I wouldn't be bother with women down here atall if it wasn't for this that my swanherd got married last summer and his wife is not so young and not well atall and is expecting to be confined in a few weeks time any time atall really."

Chapter Two

EVEN in May the fires must still be lit, and Lady Glourie wearing her tweed skirt and her cardigan and the heavy brogues a man might have worn stood eating her morning egg with one foot on the iron head of the firedog, watching the flame on the wood and spooning the yellow quickly out of the shell held in her hand.

"Says rain again, what?" she said, standing eating. She knew it was Glourie who came in through the double-doors at the other end although she did not turn her head to see.

"Let it," said Glourie as he came across the room. "Let it, says I." He gave a little moan of weariness as he came up behind her and she felt his forehead rest for an instant, hard as stone, against her shoulder. "I've got a head like nobody ever had," he said, and Lady Glourie dropped the empty eggshell into the fire and wiped her fingers in her handkerchief. "A head, a head," he said, but even so there was the smell of the damp outdoors already on him. He came around before the fire, rubbing his lean, red-knuckled hands together, the cheekbones high and raw in his face and the darkish mustache clipped neatly the length of the naked-looking upper lip. It will be a good day on the river, he was saying to himself. The clouds will be low all day. It will be lively on the river. Every morning he would be out before breakfast on the drive to see which way the wind was moving and stand there on the gravel with the wet heavy air clinging to his face and his hair, smiling with pleasure, smiling into the mist and not seeking to peer through it. "I'll take the car and run up to Coppington-Fenwick," he said, scarcely seeing his wife before him for his own escape in the day. "Just pick up my rods and coat and a snack for lunch."

Lady Glourie stood with one foot on the firedog still, watching the flame along the log and thinking of the salmon, and Glourie said again: "I've got a head. There's nothing else to do with it. If I keep it out in the air all day, it'll clear of itself."

"And then you'll start in again tonight," said Lady Glourie. For a minute she thought of pulling her rubber-boots on and going out with him without another word into the late wet morning's dark.

"No," said Glourie, rubbing his hands over. "Not tonight. There'll be no one coming in. I'll take one before dinner and that will be the end of it."

The sound of men, all day, all year without a break, the sound of men: a man serving at the table, a man in the kitchen, as if it were not only the wild cold countryside that drew men to it but as if all life itself and right to life were man's. At night, there it was: the sound of men talking and drinking in the downstairs halls, as if the house like the country around were too much the coarse hardy master ever to turn wooer and urge any but men to share the granite indifference to ease that struck to the marrow like the cold. Even in May the cold was there, like in September, but in the autumn it was the wild ducks instead of the salmon the men hungered for. At the stream-end of the swans' lake had been fixed a corridor of poultry-wire, open wide at the mouth so that the ducks who came down, drawn by the decoys, could be startled into it off the spread of quiet water. Concealed by the rhododendron trees, the hunters waited with the canvas bag held open at the one small outlet at the extremity of what seemed escape. There Glourie and his guests, down for the week-end, would wait for the wild ducks, fifty or more at a time, to drive into the wide deceptive mouth and down the tunnel of wire to the death that waited at the other end. Even from the house could be heard the tremendous wild beating of the trapped ducks' wings, and the panic and compulsion of their advance. The men's voices could be heard shouting up from the lagoon, and the firing of their guns through the orchard and the pasture to the house. All day, month after month, the sound of living men, and at night when the men's voices were too loud, Lady Glourie got up from her bed and walked down the paved hallway to the brink of the uncarpeted stone stairs and from there called down to them, standing barefooted in her white nightdress.

"If the lot of you don't stop your row, I'll turn you out of the house," she would call down the stairs to them, and the stone of the stair-pit and the arches sent back her voice with another sound to it, like the voice of a choir-boy singing in church is given a double, purer sound. Or if it were vacation time and the children home, she called down: "Do you want to wake Mary and Ferris with your racket, Glourie? Now, call it a night and come up to bed."

There he stood at the bottom of the stairs, holding his glass in his hand and looking up at his wife in her night-dress with her reddish hair planted handsomely on her brow and cut short as a man's hair on her ears and neck.

"Better come down and we'll get another bottle up," he might say to her. His bright glazed intoxicated eyes would look up at her over the smile in his face as he stood there, a tall angular-boned man in hunting-breeches, his lean shoulders rounded and stooping a little from his riding and his height.

When he had done speaking the men out of sight would burst into laughter, having ceased a moment as if in waiting for his cue. Up the stairs and through the hall would come the sound of their guffawing, and Glourie would turn his head to look back at them, his glass held up in his hand still, and she would see the side of his thin cheek and his mouth beginning to laugh.

"If you open another bottle, I swear I'll come down," Lady Glourie would call out and there would be nothing but laughter to answer, Glourie's guffawing and the guffawing of the other men like sound from the throats of a species that had since generations lost the power of speech and could only lift its voice now in this clamor that expressed neither pleasure nor derision, great howls of what could not be taken for jocosity giving vent to the soul's shyness and embarrassment.

"If the swans had quieted down I would've gone with you," said Lady Glourie with her foot on the firedog. Watching the fire she could see the cold belligerent eye of the great evil swan fixed on her, a bubble of tree sap or gum eyeing her beadlike from the burning wood. "Jo Lucky wants to put a wiring across the pond to keep old Hitches and the young couple apart, but I won't have it," she said. "Dividing the whole place up before we're done. I say let the cobs fight it out if they can't keep peace."

She knew Glourie was moving behind her towards the doors again, setting the newspaper straight on the table, putting his hands in his pockets and taking them out, listening and not listening, thinking, Now I'll get out through the door, the rods, Coppington-Fenwick, the salmon. . . .

"There's Jo Lucky's wife too," she said, watching the licks of fire tremble along the wood. "Might want a woman around. . . ."

"I thought you wrote for someone," said Glourie, clearing his throat at the door.

"I did. Yes. Three or four days back," said Lady Glourie.

"Right-o," said Glourie. "I'll be getting on then."

Chapter Three

WHEN Lady Glourie walked up from the swannery and took the path over the downs she saw how many of the sheep, the great thick-coated ancient ones as well as the young, were limping with foot-plague as they grazed. The pasture-land came to the edge of the cliffs and there halted; the short-cropped pasture grass that turned suddenly to white caustic earth, too friable for stone, dropped precipitously to the sea a quarter of a mile below. Before, behind, and to one side stood the half-circle of the iron sea curving inflated to the skyline. On the one side as she climbed was the green wringing land and on the other the twilight darkness of the water rising unbroken to the twilight darkness of the morning heavens.

Because of the continued weather, foot-rot was spreading faster than ever before among the flocks this spring. The crippled sheep and the lambs even were hobbling everywhere among the new thistles and the clumps of bramble-bush and brier that marked with continents of dwarfed impenetrable jungle the open miles of green close-nibbled pasture-land. Green, green, almost painful to the eye in its greenness was the grass underfoot, and then it stopped quickly, without hesitation at the edge. Far below was the uneven coast line, broken by monstrous boulders that had crashed down in other years, or suddenly flowering with dark emerald islands mounted by oaks and tors in full luxuriant leaf and rocks on which the gulls stood thick.

It might have been a detached universe she saw below, visible as if static under glass. There was the far line of the shingles on which the seemingly motionless surf continuously broke, the white thread-like edge of foam as if painted there by hand; and the single gulls that might set out in flight, so rare, so farly seen that they were birds no longer but chalk-white splinters falling in retarded motion a long time towards the water's bleak gray becalmment. Climbing still, she came past the little semaphore, and she saw that with the spring a wash of new color had begun to rise in the dry sticks of the gorse that stood around it.

She began thinking about the nurse who was coming down from London to tend Mrs. Lucky, thinking quietly and securely of her. There might be times, in the afternoons maybe, when the nurse would have an hour to walk out with her over the country like this; they would be talking and not go as fast as she was going but stop and look down at the gulls, speaking about something else it might be, but looking down at the life and the languorous drifting half-movement of the birds and at the smugglers' black abandoned caves, blank as blind eyes in the cliff's face. Or it might be an older woman sent down to a place like this, too old and too unused for the climb. But even so they could walk along the lagoon together, on the flat, and she could talk about Mary and Ferris to her. I never thought I'd be able to have them off to school like this and live, but then it happens, you can bear anything, anything, and there you are. . . .

Or if the old woman could put one foot before the other without doubling up, she'd get her as far as this. Why, Mrs.

Gilfooley, or Miss Williams it might be, or Mrs. Kennedy, Ferris used to walk as far as this when he was five; I used to come up here with him three times in the week at least ever since he could hold a gun. Or tell her Mary had never liked dolls for a minute, mind you, never once, never at any time. Or else the story of the day Glourie's farmer died of the injuries done him by the ram. It was right here, Miss Smith or Mrs. Penny, that old Mathone was killed by the ram in tupping season. It was one afternoon when the sun was out for a change and old Mathone came up the way we've just been coming, walking with his dog, and the ram was making his choice with his blood on fire when the dog set on him without warning. . . .

Or if the nurse were not young enough for this or to get this far, they'd stay where the ground was flat as your hand and damn the sucking wet. It might be there would be parcels of pain tied up in the old woman's legs from having stood thirty years too long by bedsides, piously running with bottles, pans, pots on rubber-soled shoes down hospital halls. Now, you've seen a lot of life and a lot of different people, and what do you think of Ferris going off to school like that, making up his mind to it overnight? It isn't as if he were like every other boy you meet up with, but with Ferris there's something particular, something especially shy that makes you wonder how he gets on at all with anyone. Yes, yes, I'm sure, said Mrs. Gilfooley's voice to her as she climbed. In the first place, take his underwear now. He has no idea of the weather or whether it's cold in or out and which shirt or jacket. He's been writing home all the winter about a blazer. He wants a school blazer, mind you, and the matron writes me back the blazers are only for the summer term, something thin as cotton, it seems, and left to himself he'd wear the thing all year around. She could hear it, the cluck of the old trained nurse's tongue in her head. I thought he wouldn't be going to school until next year any way, Miss Perry or Mrs. Appleby, so it really took me unawares. But you knew he had to go sometime. All boys go sometime, said the trained nurse with that maturing of kindness that becomes almost a severity. Yes, I knew he had to go sometime, Lady Glourie said.

Why am I thinking like this about you, she suddenly asked the facelessness, the vacancy that was the nurse, the woman old or young or however she was, who might be at this instant packing her bag in London, putting her traveling shoes on, breathing hard in her corsets, middle-aged, as she tiptoed down an absolutely silent nursing-home hall. Why am I saying these things to you, said Lady Glourie shortly, and she fumbled her cigarettes out of her pocket and put one in her mouth. She stopped walking to put the lighter to the end of it and with her eyes half-closed the sense, if not the words, of explanation came abruptly, bitterly into her heart. Miss Smith, Miss Kennedy, Miss Forthright, there is nobody left, no one. I have put flowers in your room seeking to disguise the look of it. If I change the flowers every day and keep on talking to you, perhaps I can keep it from you for a little while that there is nothing left here, that everyone here has died. If I take you out to see the swans and the sheep with foot-rot you may not find out at once that everything has succumbed to the sound of glasses, bottles, guns, to the smell of stone and fish dying with hooks through their gills. I might even do one more thing, she did not say. I might look for the poems I wrote at school and say them to you. Poetry, mind you, poetry. Can you picture me sitting down and writing it, or if you were not too old we might be able to laugh out loud, uproariously, senselessly, stand shouting with laughter at something the way men scream with laughter together.

It was a gray day, the weather soft and drifting and wet, in which only the bright color of green survived. Lady Glourie had set out looking for the farmer and seeing him now kneeling beyond the gorse robbed the unarticulated speech suddenly and completely of its power. He was kneeling down in the wet grass with a lamb caught between his thighs, held fast there by the incapacitation of its spine with its four legs thrust out. He himself was young. He had been only five years with them, having come to them with his wife and child from near Dartmoor to take on the work when Glourie's farmer was killed by the ram. As soon as he saw her coming he lifted his head from what he was doing and spoke.

"There's more'n half of them lame with it," he said at once, and he smeared the salve deep into the heart of the hoof and pressed it down firmly with his thumb. "You can do and do but there had ought to be something made as holds better'n what we know."

"I was looking at some pictures in a magazine last night," Lady Glourie said, smoking her cigarette and watching what he did. "There's a kind of boot thing comes that they're showing up in London. It's a rubber casing, coming in several sizes, and you fit it right on fast over the hoof. I thought of getting some down here to have a try. What do you think? I thought I might get them if I do go up to town next week."

The young man stopped what he was doing and looked up at her, the knife he had been working with hanging loose now in his hand. He had no collar to his shirt and the neck of it was fastened neat and close with a separate collar button of bone and above it his brown strong neck swelled out, darker seeming because of the clean linen below it with the fine black stripe running through the stuff, and the throat a little full in the front with great veins of life lashed to it. His face was lifted, rather pretty and narrow on the strong workman's neck, the chin cleft, the lips parted so that the teeth showed bright white between them, the eyes black, ardent and shining, fixed on her in sheer amazement.

"Look at that!" he said in a low voice of wonder. Two furrows from squinting a long time against rain and the blind misted sun stood just above his nose in that space where a few scattered black hairs almost drew his eyebrows into one. He spoke just above a whisper, as if the breath had left him for the moment in surprise.

"I'll be sure to be going up to see the children," Lady Glourie said. "It wouldn't do any harm to bring some back with me for a try." The farmer freed the lamb he held and they both watched it stumble and fall on its knees and lift itself and go, bleating and seeking to run, towards the sheep nibbling in concert, quietly, steadily, at the grass. The young .man stood up now, sturdy and heavy on his feet, and tall but not as tall as she was. She could see the bits of gray that were coming in the strong thick locks of hair that sprang from his forehead. "Never can tell," she said, taking the packet of Gold Flakes out. "Maybe thingamabobs not worth the paper they're wrapped in. But if I go see the children . . ."

Thinking of the two separate things they went on, hardly knowing that they were going towards the sheep until the farmer suddenly leaned and caught one. With a jerk, like that of a subtle pugilist, he tossed the animal to its back before him and kneeled quickly and grasped it fast between his thighs. Lady Glourie stopped beside him and lit her cigarette, shielding the lighter's flame in her palm, and then she stood quiet, watching the knife's point work deeply into the soft black rot. With one hand the kneeling farmer held steady the yellowish woolen and wooden leg while the knife held in the other hand worked savagely, carefully, deep into the core of pain.

"I had a letter from Master Ferris this morning," Lady Glourie said, and the farmer said, "Yes, my Lady?" with a smile, scraping away at the hoof's rot still. "Pellet-shooting seems to be taking up more time than anything else as far as I can make out," she said, pulling hard at the cigarette. The farmer threw back his head and laughed out loud and the sheep started and writhed with terror between his thighs.

"That's it, that's what I always says!" he said. "Best schools in the country and—ha, ha, ha!" He settled his knife again in his hand and looked up at Lady Glourie, laughing. She knew what it was that Glourie did not like in him: the humility that was not there, the question in him of what was best and what was not nothing short of challenge when flung into a master's teeth. There had once been talk at the beginning when he and his wife and his child had first come; there had been some kind of story about him staying out all night, one story and then another but all of them agreeing that he did not drink and it was not that, but that he stayed out for someone else, one night for one woman and another night for another. Things had blown over and it was over and almost forgotten now, but when she saw these signs of arrogance and beauty in his face she remembered. She stood watching him, smoking, remembering, recognizing the youth and life in his hands and in the swelling of his neck as if the spring had enrichened them again. She stood looking without womanly shyness because without womanly awareness at him as he worked, smoking and far too much the hard-bitten lady to acknowledge or believe in the stubborn power of his flesh, but experiencing the strange deep pang, or echo of it, that his wife must suffer seeing these things awaking in him, beginning again, endlessly re-beginning like the seasons' continual returning.

"How's Mrs. Panrandall?" she asked him in a moment. She watched him press the salve into the hoof, plug the hollow with cotton and lay hold of the foreleg of the sheep he held. At once the youthful, reckless look went out of his face and he said:

"Oh, she's keeping well, thank you, my Lady." His knife worked sharply at the rot, and then he began speaking of his daughter. "Violet's been having worms again," he said. "It's always like that this time o' year."

"There's a trained nurse coming down from London for Jo Lucky's wife," said Lady Glourie. She spoke before she knew the words were coming into her mouth but once she had spoken she felt the relief and the faint sense of excitement a lover feels when he has at last, after a long time of waiting, brought the loved name into a conversation of

other things. Ah, Mrs. Gilfooley, Miss Williams, Mrs. Far-
low, is it possible this is loneliness?

"Yes, I'd heard tell of that," said Panrandall. Lady
Glourie stood holding fast to her cigarette and trying to
say it quietly to him.

"I'm expecting her any day now, and she might as well
have a look at Violet when she comes. She'd know exactly
with her experience in nursing homes and hospitals." The
name "trained nurse" had taken on a subtle meaning now, it
was sweet with mystery, like a name whispered tenderly
across the dark. "It'll seem strange to me having another
woman at the manor, y'know," said Lady Glourie. "Someone who knows about children like that. . . ." She felt the
smile on her own face, stretched foolish as a girl's grin. She
ceased speaking because there seemed nothing more to say.

It was past four o'clock, just before time for tea, when
Lady Glourie, coming up from the swannery, saw the old
one-seated unwieldy car taking the curve of the drive
around the beds. The fishing rods traveled the length of the
near fender, the sensitive tips of them out quivering and
jerking on the air ahead, and the flapping hood of the car
was back like a cloak slipped from the shoulders of the two
people who rode in it. They were seated high and seen so
peculiarly distinctly: the man behind the wheel was Glourie with no hat on and the woman beside him was wearing a
navy coat such as schoolgirls wear and a bright red beret.
Because of the reckless sweep with which Glourie took the
corner, Lady Glourie knew the woman riding beside him
must be young.

Chapter Four

"OF COURSE, there are other swans," Glourie was saying at the table, leaning back in his chair and eyeing the two women as he told them what they ought to know. "There's the Whopper or Hooper, the whistling swan. They come down from the north—Iceland, Scandinavia, Lapland. You can see them here in the autumn some days feeding with the others on their way migrating to Lower Egypt, stopping off here for a snack of zosteria and a bit of pow-wow. . . ."

It had been decided from the first that Miss Cafferty should take her meals with Lord and Lady Glourie at the house. She was to come up at the end of the morning after Mrs. Lucky was made comfortable and clean, eat at table with them, and then go back to the swanherd's cottage in the afternoon. Then she would come up at dinner time again, at half-past six or seven, for Miss Cafferty was not an ordinary girl; it was evident she came of good middle-class family and her father had been a scientist, in Dublin, but still a scientist, or so she said. If Lord and Lady Glourie had not wanted her there, there would have been no need to have her. They could not ask her to cook her own meals in Jo Lucky's cottage, seeing the rather superior girl she was, but they could have put her to eat in the servants' hall, not at table with the servants who all were males, but served before the others ate, and quite apart. However it came to be decided, there she was at the child's place at the table, sitting modestly between the two grown people, the parents, the master and mistress of the house. She wore a green silk dress that buttoned up to her throat, and her arms, bare from the elbow, rested round and white as a child's arm on the cloth. Her head, with the light hair parted in the middle, was turned in respect to Lord Glourie, harking as a child might docilely incline its head and listen to him, her fresh lips curved up a little, her guileless soft eyes resting on his narrow face with a half-mocking, half-prestigious awe. The clear look she turned now and again to Lady Glourie held almost the same measure of respect, the same deferential, slightly amused look for the lady at the head of her own table struggling to slice the joint of cold mutton on the platter.

"You can hear them passing over at night some times," Lord Glourie was saying. "Certain times you can hear them whistling away as they go flying over the house."

"And over England," said Miss Cafferty quietly. "Over England to something else."

"Yes. Yes, of course," said Lord Glourie, taken aback. "Of course, over England."

He looked at Miss Cafferty a little uncertainly but there was no alteration or intent expressed in the sweet, oddly quiet, oddly childlike face which, despite her youth (she must have been twenty-six or twenty-seven at the most), could not logically and yet seemed to have survived even that long without losing any of its first innocent decorum, its first absolutely untouched guiltlessness.

"What would happen, do you suppose," said Miss Cafferty, moving her soft white arms as the serving-man put her plate before her, "if one of the tame swans down on the lagoon decided to pair off with a wild one who was just passing over? How do you think they'd fix it up?" she asked. "Do you think the wild one would give everything up and settle down here or would the poor old tame one have to hump itself and go on with the others?"

"Now, there's a question for you," said Glourie, and he looked towards his wife, laughing. Turning his head, he took the plate from the serving-man's hands and set it down himself before him and quickly stabbed the meat with his fork. "Now, that's something to put to old Lucky, I must say. There may have been something like that come up in his father's time or his grandfather's time and there's maybe some record of it." He talked with the potato and meat in his mouth and his lean jaws grinding. "Now, that's a thing it would take someone like you to come along and put up to us, Miss Cafferty. I must say, it's a thing that would never come into my head if I lived to be a hundred."

"It's the corruption of the city, then, Lord Glourie," said Miss Cafferty gently. She gave a shy soft little laugh and her eyes shone mistily, almost tenderly, from one to the other of them. She glanced for an instant across the cloth for the Worcester sauce and Lord Glourie's hand set it quickly down before her. "Thank you," she said in a low voice and she screwed the little stopper off with her pink-cushioned finger and thumb.

The farm-horse was standing on the other side of the pasture fence as they came down the hill in the rain, a great thick horse with a wide back and shoulders plump as a woman's. His coat was tan and his mane and tail the color of unbleached linen; the same shade of hair but of another texture hung long at his fetlocks. He stood with his neck and head reaching over the top bar of the gate, watching the three people come down the grassy path among the apple trees growing on the hill.

"I managed to avoid him coming up," Miss Cafferty said. "I saw him at the other end of the field and I kept walking as fast as I could and tried to think of something else. I even think I said a prayer, just a little one, one big enough to keep him from turning around and seeing me."

She had stopped still for a moment, looking uneasily towards the fence and the horse on the other side of it at the bottom, and Lord Glourie stopped in front of her, below her on the hillside, and looked up at her face. Her yellow oilskin was buttoned to her neck and a bandanna handkerchief, soaked dark with wet now, was knotted on her hair. Between the smooth skin of her forehead and the red bandanna there was a space, two inches perhaps, of light shining hair divided in the center and smoothed back and Lord Glourie stood below her smiling and watching the falling rain cling in it.

"What do you think he'd do if he did see you?" Lord Glourie asked, and Lady Glourie with her hands in her pockets and a cigarette on her lip said nothing but went on down the hill.

"He might trample me. Isn't that what horses do?" Miss Cafferty said, smiling dreamily at him. Lord Glourie gave a hoot of laughter.

"Trample!" he shouted. "Trample! Oh, that's wonderful! That's too good to be true! Do you really imagine—do you think for a moment—"

"I was quite brave coming up because he was way at the

other end," Miss Cafferty said in her calm young voice. Their eyes came together and suddenly they both laughed. Lord Glourie with his jacket collar turned up to his ears and the brim of his hat pulled down stood grinning and roaring like a fool at her.

"Well, what are you going to do about it now?" he said in a minute. He could not take his eyes off her hair and the cluster of drops, like dew, fallen in it.

"I'll just follow Lady Glourie," Miss Cafferty said with decision. "Look, she's wonderful. She doesn't mind him in the slightest."

"I must say, you're behaving very well," said Lord Glourie. They were coming side by side now down the land. "You're coming through the cattle here without a word—"

"Ah, but it's different when you're here," said Miss Cafferty gently. "It's not the same as walking up alone."

One of the young black bulls, his brow pressed fast to another's was forced backwards across the path before them but Miss Cafferty did not falter.

"Perhaps it was the drink you had before lunch," said Lord Glourie with a grin and Miss Cafferty answered:

"No. I've made up my mind to get used to them of myself now."

In the silence that might have been taken as rebuke to what he had thought and said, they watched the little bull, still battling with his knobby ungrown horns, be forced backwards into an apple tree in blossom on the slope, and there the bigger bull tossed his insolent childish head and veered away. The small one stood swinging the black tassel of his tail, absorbed in looking at the people now. There was a short thick lighter fringe of hair as if cut straight across his forehead and from under it his eyes looked boldly at them.

"He likes you," said Lord Glourie and Miss Cafferty turned in surprise and looked quickly at him. "Does he?" she said, as if truly pleased, astonished. "Does he, do you think?" She held out one hand towards the bull, her fingers rubbing softly together in a wooing gesture to the little animal planted motionless before them in the grass. "Come here, come, my darling, my baby, come," she said softly to him. His fresh naked nose seemed vulnerable as a living heart, arrogantly and timorously exposed before them. "Come, my darling," she murmured.

"I'll have to remember what you had," said Lord Glourie to cover his embarrassment. "A Gin and It, wasn't it? After a Gin and It taken before lunch, you're not afraid of bulls any more and you might even be persuaded to go through a field with a horse standing in it—"

A slight rush of wind struck the branches of the apple tree and a shower of unbroken drops scattered down from the leaves and fell on the young bull's broad obstinate brow. Lady Glourie had reached the gate below and lifted the bars down and out of some emotion speechless as failure she could not look back and recognize Miss Cafferty there coming down the hill, Miss Cafferty instead of all those other women, old or young, with varicose veins or with voices that never faltered, talking about the cases they had had, the Mrs. Michaelmases, the Miss Mitchells, the Mrs. Doghertys who were to come with ears to lend, with Cockney voices ready to confirm, This is the first year that Ferris, this is the first term that Mary hasn't written every week. This is the first time I've ever needed anyone, the first time in my life, Miss Weatherby. . . .

The big horse on the other side was arching now with impatience, shaking his mane eagerly at her and stroking with one forefoot the sodden earth. There he was, as she let the bars down, chafing from one end to the other, waiting to shoulder her aside when the moment came and to canter free up the hill through the young cattle grazing underneath the trees.

"Look here, my lad," said Lady Glourie in a loud bold voice, "the other side of this fence is exactly like the side you're on. . . ."

She stood in the opening where the horse sought to pass and when he seemed ready to rise above her and break across her like a wave, she lifted her hand and slapped his wet naked shoulder a crack with her open palm. They saw him veer on the points of his hoofs, the muscles tighten in the strong ballet-dancer legs, and then he cantered away, snorting, across the flowering mustard-yellow and pansy-faced field.

"Isn't Lady Glourie amazing?" Miss Cafferty said in a low wondering voice. They were almost down the hill now and she stopped to watch the horse spin and go. "Oh, if only I could do things like that. . . ." Even Lord Glourie, or any man, Lady Glourie thought turning to look back at the nurse, must hear the repudiation the silence gave the passionately and deceptively uttered words, but Lord Glourie said: "Yes, she is, isn't she?"; responding not to the silence but to what the nurse had said in the rapt voice of one who has not listened to the sense but only to the voice that spoke them. In a moment he might say: "I'm awfully afraid I didn't hear what you said, Miss Cafferty. I'm afraid I was thinking of something else. . . ." And Miss Cafferty might turn her young, tender, unbaffled eyes to his and answer: "Oh, it wasn't anything of any importance. I was just talking about Lady Glourie. I was just speaking of your wife. That's all."

"Come on," Lady Glourie called out, as if impatient. "Get the bars up again before he takes it into his head again to make a dash—"

"Right-o," Glourie sang out. He came quickly along, up to her now on the other side of the fence, a necklace of raindrops sliding bead by bead along the knife-fine brim of his brown hat. "I'll take care of it," he said, looking back to see if Miss Cafferty was there. But Lady Glourie had lost her patience now.

"Here you are, Miss Cafferty," she said. "Take up the bar once you're over and fetch it up where it belongs."

"Hold on a minute, I've got it," said Glourie, stooping, but Lady Glourie had already put the long weathered pole of the fencing into the little nurse's hand. She saw the sudden fluttered look of deference in Miss Cafferty's eyes, the flickering across her eyes of humility or guilt or fear as she genuflected to take the cross-bar up and lay it in its place. When they were all three on the same side of the fence Lady Glourie took the packet of cigarettes out, put one in her mouth and snapped her lighter open.

"There's just one word I wanted to say to you about Jo Lucky," she said. She started walking down the path through the meadow and they followed obediently, like children, watching her foot-marks falling firm, regular, one by one on the mud and grass before them. "If anything happens to his wife," she was saying, "he'll never go after a new one. It took him forty-five years to make up his mind to it and once it's done he's through forever. He's been off his head for weeks about her now. Out the door he goes to look to the swans and then back to do for her as best he can. He's been doing that all alone, except for when I could get down there to help him."

Glourie gave a laugh and chewed with his lower teeth at his mustache.

"Doctor says something about her staying in bed," he said to Miss Cafferty's back. "Rigamarole about keeping her feet off the ground."

"And another thing," said Lady Glourie so sharply that Miss Cafferty started, "he's got to have a boy, y'see. If it's a girl, then the swannery's through for his family. It has to go on after him to somebody else. Y'see, it goes from father to son, from father to son. It's been four generations Lucky, but he isn't so young now, and he's an old man for his age, and if he hasn't a son this time then it's probably the last time."

Glourie burst into a guffaw behind them and Miss Cafferty half turned to him, as she walked, and smiled.

"Seems to me you're asking an awful lot of Miss Cafferty," Glourie said.

"I'm not asking anything of her she can't do," said Lady Glourie without humor. "I'm telling her how things are here. If he don't have a boy it'll be the finish of him." The path broadened near the cottage and Lady Glourie waited, smoking, until the others caught her up. Then she said: "Those shoes, Miss Cafferty. You'll catch your death in them. You ought to get something better for the country."

"I will, Lady Glourie," said Miss Cafferty humbly.

Chapter Five

MISS CAFFERTY came on a Tuesday and it was a week later in the afternoon when Lady Glourie was standing up by the fire drinking her tea that she believed she saw where the fault lay. Lady Glourie put her cup quickly down for now she saw Miss Cafferty suddenly and piteously clear, touchingly and bitterly in need not only of money but of the other things to which no name came voluntarily: those effects which were a family's and a life's accumulation and which Miss Cafferty had none of. With the taste of jam in her mouth still she put on her jacket and her hat, scarcely waiting in her haste to seek out the packet of cigarettes, and then she set out under the rain for the swanherd's cottage. Whatever might have happened in time here, the thing went on quick, sure and unbewildered now, whatever it might have been it would all have been my fault for I can see this place as nobody else here sees it. She believed she was seeing Miss Cafferty for the first time now, taking her by surprise as if she had never before clapped eye on her, and the sense of recognition grew stronger, louder like a tide rising to its fullest power. It was this, whether truly shaped by thought or unenunciated vehemence, which took her in nervous haste down through the orchard and the pasture-land.

She saw them now as wilderness to which only the vaguest outline of order had been given, this place they gave a name like "home" to and what must seem nothing but dereliction after streets of tidy semi-detached residences in the outskirts of London or of Dublin even; the whole restless malevolent estate abandoned to the willfulness of wind and rain and the sea-birds' scavenging and to the willfulness of purely male desire. She was on the path to the swanherd's cottage, walking fast between the rounded pyramids of nests on which the swans sat lightly, their white bodies softly spread, their heads alert and upright in the rain; and still the process of minute recognition went on, object by object rising on the relentlessly rising tide on which the swans now floated and which swept Miss Cafferty on with this sudden and unforeseen vortex of compassion. Even me, a woman, too hard, too defiant, so that she came into this domain of locked, welded mates an outcast, to be kicked up and down the hill from one wedded couple to another, the Jo Luckys, the Panrandalls, the Glouries, the violently mated swans, and nothing but suspicion offered her. A poor little Irishwoman with nowhere to go but to other people's houses in other people's countries, a living to make with other people's clothes on her back, a green dress somebody had handed down to her and pointed shoes too narrow for her feet with heels too high for the country she was in. Lady Glourie saw her for an instant gentle as a young lamb to be nursed in the heart and she knew the words to say at once to her. The cottage door was standing open and Lady Glourie took her cigarette from her mouth and ground it out under heel on the mossy ground.

"How's Mrs. Lucky doing?" Lady Glourie asked. The swanherd had come out of the cottage-dark to the threshold, wiping the tea from his mustaches.

"There's no change, my Lady," Jo Lucky said, "unless it might be she's stronger some from lying in bed and her mind more at peace like."

"So she likes Miss Cafferty, then, does she?" said Lady Glourie pleasantly and boldly.

"Oh, yes," said Jo Lucky, but saying it so quietly that he might have been saying nothing. Then he looked up and said: "Old Hitches near took the breast offen the young cob this morning. Let it be the pen in the water and Hitches don't stir a feather, but soon as the cob comes down off the nest they're at it."

The young pen had laid her five olive-green eggs and when she left them to feed in the ruppia grasses the cob would mount the nest and take her place, was what Jo Lucky was saying. Nothing had changed, not Mrs. Lucky's health, nor the warring on the lake where a wreath of fallen swan feathers floated on the water's black glass, drifting slowly towards the stream's mouth in the rain.

"I just wanted to speak a word or two with Miss Cafferty," Lady Glourie said and Jo Lucky's face seemed suddenly to stop short, stopped absolutely as if he had drawn a curtain down across it, and he looked away towards the lagoon.

"I reckon she's out," he said. "She said something as she was going out for a bit of air like."

"Which way did she go?" asked Lady Glourie. The swanherd waited a moment, as if making a choice, perhaps between what was true and what he was going to say. Then he said, still looking towards the water:

"Hard to say."

Lady Glourie took the time to light another cigarette be-

fore setting off across the fields, not towards the house or
the lagoon but in the direction of the cliffs, towards the
path to the semaphore where the flocks grazed out and
where the farm stood. For a week I've been thinking of the
things I haven't said to you, Miss Cafferty, the tide ran on.
I'm doing a sweater for Ferris now and I'm awfully clumsy
always around the shoulders. I'm not good at getting the
sleeves in and time and again it's come into my head to ask
you if you've done very much knitting and if you could
help me out. There's nothing at all to rolling up wool if
there's a girl or even a boy in the house, but ask a man to
hold it and where do you get? I thought perhaps in the evening after supper if I brought the wool out, because it's
like talking to the wall to ask Lord Glourie . . . Miss Cafferty, I come to you in apology, I ask you not to do death
to those imaginary figures the name "trained nurse" gave
birth to. . . . I ask you. . . ."

She had climbed faster than she knew and now Panrandall
standing near the semaphore startled her out of it and she
cleared her throat to speak.

"If you hadn't come up," he said, "I'd have been down
this evening." He had lifted his cap from his head and they
stood facing each other. It was a week since she had been
up and now the gorse was beginning to bud brightly and
tenderly about them. The sheep with their heads lowered
to the wet herbage grazed slowly, step by limping step,
away. "It's getting very bad now," he said. His mouth with
the white teeth in it seemed charmed to her as she watched
him speaking, charmed and damned with the great burden,
the terrific gift of beauty he had to give. He hasn't the look
of a man who stays home, there must be something still;

even now there must be something going on. She thought of Mrs. Panrandall and the sister-pang of compassion struck her heart again and she said quickly:

"I know, I know. I'm sure I'll have to be going up to town about it. But just now it's not so easy. The swans are kicking up a row for one thing. And then I don't feel right going till Mrs. Lucky's time is over." (Is this true? Is there a word of the truth in it? Is it only because I'm afraid of leaving Glourie now?) "The nurse has come, y'know, a Miss Cafferty," she said in a natural, pleasant voice, saying the name out frankly. Panrandall lifted his hand and put his hair back from his forehead.

"Yes, my Lady," he said. "I know."

"I'll come up and have a cup of tea with Mrs. Panrandall tomorrow or Thursday," said Lady Glourie. They started down the land together, walking a little apart through the sound of the sheeps' lips tearing strongly at the grasses.

"I'll tell her, Lady Glourie. She'll be ready for you," the farmer said. As they came to the path Lady Glourie's eyes fell suddenly on the footsteps: the perfectly preserved marks of a woman's narrow high-heeled shoe in which a foot had gone leisurely, elegantly down the hill. She halted, staring down at the footmarks in the wet clayey earth, and Panrandall stopped too beside her. There they both stood, not speaking, looking down.

"Now who would that be?" Lady Glourie said in a moment. Both thought and suspicion had gone instantaneously from her head in surprise.

"Well, that's funny," the farmer said in a low voice. They both stood quiet, reading the history of delicately, perfectly made prints. "It wouldn't be your own shoe, my Lady?"

Lady Glourie gave a snort of laughter.

"Take a look at my foot, Panrandall," she said. The farmer looked down at the long broad foot in its brogue that she lifted sideways for him to see and slowly shook his head.

"Perhaps someone from the manor," he said, and with that Lady Glourie knew. Whether from the side of his face or the blood smiting strong in her own heart, she knew. She saw the color rise in his cheek and run dark and sullen underneath his skin.

"Well, that might be, of course," she said. "Yes, I'm quite sure it might."

Ah, yes, she said, ah, yes, and in a moment she went down the hill with her eyes fixed on the traces of it, walking quickly where this other woman had seemed to saunter down under the falling rain. Ah, yes, Miss Cafferty coming up here at night, every night perhaps, walking along slowly with an arm fast around her, this was probably exactly how it was; and here further along near the stile where the steps paused and mingled, the man's with the woman's, here doubtless a mouth had suddenly ceased to speak, perhaps ceased laughing or singing, while a man's mouth that might be anyone's but must be Panrandall's had closed in passion on Miss Cafferty's thirsting mouth.

Chapter Six

WHEN she had hung up her wet jacket and hat in the hall and put house-shoes on she walked into the big room and found them. They were sitting in the inglenook and Glourie must have been reading or reading aloud for the book was open on his knees still. The chimney had been heaped with monstrous slabs of wood flung in a half-a-dozen deep with no thought of economy, whole logs that split with flame and fell disastrously as Lady Glourie crossed the room, like falling trees that tore their roots and hearts out as they crashed.

"We tried to make it warm enough to bring him back to life," Miss Cafferty said as she stood up in the glowing jagged shape of light. Lady Glourie had begun to comb her hair up from her ears, sharply, severely in her fingers, and she stood still this way with her big white hands spread looking at the sea gull Miss Cafferty held. "We found him blown down, wounded, on the shingles," Miss Cafferty said, and Lady Glourie looked, wondering, at the sign of tears left on her face. "It doesn't seem to be his wings," Miss Cafferty went on. She was holding the bird in one bare arm against the green tidy dress that day after day emerged out of some immaculately kept if almost destitute wardrobe, the cool clinging green dress worn regardless or in defiance of the weather. "But still it died," she said.

"As soon as you found it?" Lady Glourie asked without

sentiment, as a doctor or a nurse might have said it. She had gone close enough to see how the feathers had begun to dry in yellowish pointed wisps that hardened upon its breast, and she ran one finger now along its lifeless throat.

"No, it was alive, it was able to flutter off when we found it," said Miss Cafferty. "We were taking a walk along the beach and I saw it a little way ahead. I didn't think it was badly hurt. I thought I could easily save it."

"It died as soon as I gave it the whiskey," said Lord Glourie with a low uneasy laugh. Both women looked at him a moment, at the face strangely contorted, twisted as if in pain, as he sat there laughing.

"Lord Glourie gave it a spoonful of whiskey," said Miss Cafferty. Her face hung over the bird's dead body, the wax-like apples of her cheekbones just visible under her lowered lids. "And then it died at once," she said quietly. Lady Glourie stood like one enchanted, unable to move hand or foot, watching bewildered the tears slip from under Miss Cafferty's lashes and disappear down the pale flesh of her cheeks.

"I've been trying to relieve her mind with some statute, case and customary law," said Lord Glourie, and Lady Glourie sat down on the other side of the inglenook knowing that she herself was not only not required to speak but not even to be present to look on. The pace had already been set from the beginning, like the rush of the favorite from the post who could only be watched romping home without effort and without rival. She sat quiet, watching Miss Cafferty across the firelight while Glourie read on again from where he had left off; watching Miss Cafferty not with envy or even dislike but with hopeless acknowl-

edgement of that line which had from their first meal together been finally, unalterably drawn between spectator
and those who ran. When she had looked a long time at
Miss Cafferty, her eyes, like those of the other woman,
fastened on the body of the dead white gull and remained
there while Glourie's voice went on in what might have
been uncomfortable imitation, half-jocular, half-tragic, of
someone else's nonchalance. ". . . 'item where as well our
said Sovereign Lord the King, as other Lords, Knights,
Esquires, and other noble men of this noble Realm of
England, have been heretofore greatly stored of Marks and
Games of Swans in divers Parts of this Realm, until of
late that divers Keepers of Swans have bought or made
to them Marks and Games in the Fens and Marshes and
other Places and under Colour of the same, and of Sur-
veying and Search for Swans and Cygnets for their Lords
and Masters have stolen Cygnets and put upon them their
own Mark, by which unlawful Means the Substance of
Swans be in the Hands and Possession of Yeomen and Hus-
bandmen and other Persons of little Reputation.' " Lord
Glourie cleared his throat and laughed at this while the
two women on opposite sides of the fire looked unceasingly
at the sea gull with its head fallen to one side on the green
stuff of the nurse's dress. " 'Wherefore it is ordained that
no Person of what Estate, Degree, or Consideration he be
other than the Son of our Sovereign Lord the King from
the feast of St. Michael next coming,' " Lord Glourie read
on, " 'shall have or possess any such Mark of Game except
he have Lands and Tenements of Estate of Freehold to the
yearly Value of Five Marks above all yearly charges.' The
penalty for breaking this law," said Lord Glourie, "was

'forfeiture of the swans, one moiety to the King and the other to any qualified person who made the seizure.'"

"They used to put the marks on the swans' bills," Lady Glourie said in spite of herself, but Miss Cafferty did not lift her head.

" 'It was resolved that all white swans not marked which had gained their natural liberty and were swimming in an open and common river might be seized to the King's use by his prerogative,'" Lord Glourie read out. " 'A man may prescribe to have a game of swans within his manor, as well as a warren or a park, and he who hath such a game of swans may prescribe that his swans may swim within the manor of another and that a swan may be an estray. In such case, the cygnets do belong to both owners in common equally, sic, to the owner of the cock and the owner of the hen and the cygnets shall be divided betwixt them. And the law thereof is founded on a reason of nature, for the cock swan is an emblem and representation of an affectionate and true husband to his wife. . . .'" Lord Glourie's voice muted slowly into silence and his hand turned the page. "This isn't such an interesting part of the treatise," he said, looking on ahead.

"Please," said Miss Cafferty in a scarcely audible voice. "Please read it all, Lord Glourie."

The color rose in Glourie's face but he turned back the page again and again began the mocking loud accompaniment to Miss Cafferty's silent implacable grief. The tears had begun to slip down her cheeks and fell singly and bitterly upon the lifeless bird.

" '. . . for the cock swan holdeth himself to one female only,'" Glourie's voice read out sardonically, " 'and for this cause nature hath conferred on him a gift beyond all others; that is, to die so joyfully that he sings sweetly as he dies. . . .' "

"Of course, swans make mistakes sometimes," said Lady Glourie, speaking rapidly as if to save or hide them all from implication. "We've seen them, Glourie and me here. One autumn a couple of cobs paired off together, went through all the song and dance of meeting each other on the water and dipping their heads under, first one and then the other a dozen times or more the way they do, and then sank under the surface for the pairing. And in the spring, mind you," said Lady Glourie, staring with inexplicable sorrow into the fire, "the two cobs took turns sitting on the empty nest they'd built together."

Lord Glourie closed the book smartly and stood up and stretched before the flames, his legs long, narrow, the knee-caps delicate and prominent as teacups above the leather of his puttees.

"Oh, it isn't only the cobs that make fools of themselves by a long shot!" he said in annoyance. "There were two pens made a sight of themselves one spring, last year I think it was, laying infertile eggs and sitting a month on them trying to hatch them out!"

"Jo Lucky said there was nothing for it but to introduce the two cobs to the pens," said Lady Glourie, and Miss Cafferty looked up for the first time across the fire to her.

"Do you think that would have helped?" she said in a low passionate voice. "Do you think that would have changed anything at all?"

Chapter Seven

LORD GLOURIE had a glass of whiskey and soda in a minute and the ladies each a glass of sherry, and when they looked out of the windows now they saw that the rain had stopped. For the first time in the fortnight the clouds had drawn away and the sky was a faint but marvelous blue beyond the branches, perishable as the tinting of a robin's egg it seemed and with the same fragile quality of an eggshell blown clean of any future purpose in life. Because of the drink, something festive became of the evening at once and they went into supper with the sense of gaiety like a fourth person who had joined them there.

"Now I feel young again, I feel saved from old age," said Miss Cafferty, taking the same place at the table, the child's place between the two people of authority. "One little drink has saved me and the rain has stopped."

"Save me, then," said Lord Glourie, crossing his legs and laughing. "Look at the gray hairs I have. Whiskey and soda doesn't change them."

"Ah, but you don't need to be saved," said Miss Cafferty. "Two people together don't starve, don't drown, don't flounder. It's only alone that one perishes. You're two people always, but I'm one person very quietly but very steadily getting old alone."

"Old!" exclaimed Lord Glourie, savagely uncrossing his legs.

"Last night I went to bed very late," Miss Cafferty said. She sat with her hands clasped on the cloth before her, her clear candid eyes watching Lady Glourie worrying the joint. "I was very dissipated," she said. "I couldn't bear to stay in the house, and black as it was after Lord Glourie walked me home, I went out on my own."

Lord Glourie put his fork down.

"You mean you went out by yourself?" he said.

"Yes," said Miss Cafferty. Her eyes were shining and her chin was lifted in defiance or triumph at him. "You see, when I was a child and after, when I was growing up at home, I used to go off walking like that at night alone. Sometimes I have to do it. I can't help it. Something happens inside me and I have to go." She helped herself from the platter of smoking greens the man held at her elbow. "Something happens and there's no help for it," she said in a cheerful voice. "It's like a bird that suddenly comes alive inside my head and starts beating and beating at the windows. I know what I have to do when it happens. There's no escape for it unless I go out and walk it off. So last night I didn't get to bed till almost dawn. There was nothing else for it. I went out and up along the cliffs, walking and walking like mad, I don't know where, way up past the lighthouse somewhere—"

"You were alone?" repeated Lord Glourie, scarcely aloud. He cleared his throat and he could not take his eyes from her face. "Were you by yourself?" he said.

"Yes, yes, of course. Why not alone?" said Miss Cafferty, smiling at him.

"Look, Glourie, they're passing the greens to you," said

Lady Glourie. But it was as if he no longer cared who saw it nor how perfectly it might be seen.

"You walked up around the farm, I suppose," he said bitterly.

Miss Cafferty shrugged her shoulders and turned her attention to the food on her plate.

"I don't know," she said. "It was so dark I couldn't see anything. I just wanted to get out, don't you see, breathe the air, feel the wind on my face, the rain even, smell the sea. Doesn't it ever happen to you?" she said, and she turned in appeal to Lady Glourie. "Don't you feel that thing, that kind of desperation I mean, that desperation of the heart as well as of the flesh, and you must get out however late it is or whatever the weather's doing?" She looked at both their faces, waiting a minute, and then she said without shame: "I believe sometimes I'm damned, I'm cursed, perhaps by my country or by the blood in my veins, because no one else feels this, no one. I've never met anyone who has this madness. I'm no longer a human when this thing begins. There's no identity left to me, it's swept away on the torrent or by the devastating fire or whatever the thing is. I have to go out and walk all night, no matter if a gale is blowing—"

"Well, the weather's broken now," said Lady Glourie, cutting the slice of mutton on her plate. "If it'd gone on like this the sheep would've been done in and no mistake. Pan-randall was sick at heart this afternoon when I saw him."

Glourie did not speak, did not stir, but sat there leaning back in his chair, his jaw set, his eyes fixed motionless on Miss Cafferty's face.

"Well, if you were up by the semaphore you must have

seen the farm, Miss Cafferty," he said in the same low dry voice, taking it up where he had left off, as if no one had spoken.

"I assure you I saw nothing," said Miss Cafferty. "It was absolutely black. I saw nothing at all."

Lord Glourie waited before he spoke again, his eyes still fixed on her, preparing himself and his voice for what the answer might be. On the other side of the table Lady Glourie stirred as if she must rise from her place and save him from it. Don't speak, don't ask any more, don't try to know, Glourie. She knew the story as well now as if it had been told her over and over again. Glourie, said her agitation across the table, don't ask it, don't say it. But there was no stopping him now, there was no way to halt him.

"Have you met up with the farmer?" he said. He did not smile but his whole being made the effort towards nonchalance, the terrific gesture towards lightness to detach those words from all his voice foreboded. "I suppose you must have run into Panrandall up there?" he said.

Miss Cafferty went on chewing her dinner and then she looked at him with her little up-turned smile.

"Met up with whom?" she said politely.

"With Panrandall." Lord Glourie's hand played with his fork on the cloth. He had not touched the food before him. "With the farmer," he said.

"Oh, the farmer!" said Miss Cafferty. "Perhaps he would be the man who brought the eggs to the cottage one morning?"

"What was he like?" asked Glourie, still making the bitter, the despairing effort towards ease. "What would you say he was like? How would you describe him?"

Miss Cafferty sat quite still, her eyes lowered, the little point of hair growing off golden from her white childish brow.

"I don't know that I could say exactly," she said while the two others watched her. "It's rather difficult to remember."

"Difficult to remember!" Glourie cried out. "How many days ago was it—three? Four?"

"I suppose it was something of that sort," said Miss Cafferty in a slow quiet voice. She looked at Lord Glourie, smiling in soft tantalizing surprise. "I can't say that I took much notice of him, really. I know I went down to the door when I heard someone knocking because Jo Lucky was out with the swans already. It was very early. He was there with a little basket of eggs, the farmer, Panrandall, as you call him. I think I asked him in for a cup of tea—"

"Oh, you did, did you?" exploded Lord Glourie. He shifted in anger in his chair and his thin fox-face pointed wildly and helplessly at her. "So you asked the farmer in for a cup of tea, did you?" he said.

"Yes, I did," said Miss Cafferty in her low musical voice. "And if you mean, Lord Glourie, that it was not the thing for me to do then I feel I cannot agree with you. You see, I believe we have very different feelings about people. I'm sure we don't see things at all in the same way. I haven't the least bit of snobbishness in me, not an atom. I'd just as soon ask a farmer in to tea as the vicar." She looked at Lady Glourie with her softly defiant eye, playing so spiritedly the rôle of the proud Irish rebel at bay in their midst. Her eyes swept the lordly table and she said: "I wonder if it has occurred to you, Lord Glourie, that things are changing everywhere in the world and that you'll probably wake up one morning and find everything quite different. Some day that egg just won't be there for breakfast, and that will only be the beginning. There'll be much worse to follow. Everything is going to be so altered that you may have to learn a new language. The wars they're fighting now aren't just the same old wars, the same old tiresome story. It's that man, the man you think one should not sit down at table with, who's coming to be the most important person in the new arrangement. I can't see any place for your vicars in this new thing the world's coming to."

"Ho, ho," cried Lord Glourie, slapping his leg. "You talk like Dartington Hall, Miss Cafferty, I must say you do!" Suddenly he uncrossed his long legs and leaned forward in the candle-light with his eyes fixed, shining, on her face. "I'll take my oath on it Lady Glourie's sat down to table with more farmers than you ever have!" he said sharply.

"That's very easy," said Miss Cafferty quietly. "I've never sat down with any."

"Oh, you haven't?" said Lord Glourie. He leaned back in his chair again. "Then I take it Panrandall didn't step into the cottage with you after all?" he said.

"No," said Miss Cafferty, looking at him in gentle surprise. "I thought I said that. Mrs. Lucky called me from upstairs and that was the end of it."

"Mrs. Panrandall does our washing for us," said Lady Glourie deliberately. The pudding had been set down before her and she began helping it out in great steaming chunks. "I remember when they first came here to work for us and Panrandall was a stranger in the village. He couldn't go out but all the girls were making eyes at him along the road. Then it came out he was a married man and a father and that put a stop to that."

"There was some to-do about a chamber-maid down at the Clarence," Glourie said, spooning the pudding into his mouth. "I gave him what-for then, I can tell you. I wasn't going to have anything like that going on here on my place, and since then he's kept to the straight and narrow."

Lady Glourie thought for a moment then of speaking to Miss Cafferty about Violet's worms but when she looked at the gentle guileless face she could not bring herself to speak. *She is not a trained nurse, she has nothing to do with nursing; she is a witch, she would only know how to charm them away.* But as if she had read her thoughts, Miss Cafferty began reciting in a clear derisive voice:

> *"When Hebrews lived on lizard pies*
> *And fed their children worms and flies,*
> *Who were God-fearing, kindly, wise?*
> *The Dunns, O'Tools and Flanigans."*

"What's that?" asked Lord Glourie, bewildered. His head was flung up like a horse's, the white eyes cocked, the mouth ready to roar with laughter, no dignity, no annoyance even left, but only the sheer terrible sense of his deliverance because Panrandall had not gone into the cottage, because there was time yet, because Miss Cafferty was there, for the moment there before him, to be seen, to be listened to. . . .

> *"Who cheered up Eve when things were dark,*
> *Drew up the plans for Eden Park,*
> *Helped Noah navigate the ark?*
> *The Dunns, O'Tools and Flanigans."*

"That's a poem about the Irish, is it?" asked Lord Glourie in terrific delight, and Miss Cafferty laughed and nodded her head.

"Yes, it is," she said. "I recited it to the farmer the other day and that's how it came to my mind now. We had a little tiff about the Irish one afternoon but he brought me a bunch of violets to make up for it after."

Lord Glourie put his spoon down slowly and carefully on his plate while Miss Cafferty's voice went on:

> *"Who was it that invented war,*
> *Whose praise is sung in ancient lore,*
> *Who was the world created for?*
> *The Dunns, O'Tools and Flanigans."*

Chapter Eight

AFTER supper was done, Miss Cafferty told them she would go home alone. There was no dissuading her. She had never done it before but now her mind was set on walking down through the orchard and the pasture to the swanherd's cottage quite by herself, and she put her coat on saying it.

"I'm more at home in the country now," she said, "and besides the moon is coming through. It isn't as if it were one of these black stormy nights."

"I think you said at dinner you didn't mind the weather any way, Miss Cafferty," Lord Glourie said, and then he turned his back on them both and walked into the sitting-room and started the radio going. In his face as he went Lady Glourie saw the mark the truth had left, the stony stricken look of impotence and of despair. The thing was finished for him now, finished, finished. Through the thin sucking cheeks and the small flushed grinding jowls she could see it as he passed her: the look of the truth stuck fast in his crop, as bitter and terrible as gall.

"It'd be better if you didn't go alone, Miss Cafferty, Lady Glourie said. "I'm only too willing to go with you if you feel at all nervous in the dark."

She turned the big iron handle of the door, talking quietly to the nurse, and as she pulled the heavy door inwards the cool night air came strong and fresh into the hall, moved pure and clear, almost palpable between them.

"Ah," said Miss Cafferty softly, "there's nothing to fear, really, is there?" She stood small and girl-like on the step, her coat buttoned up, her head uncovered. "You see how it is, Lady Glourie," she said. "I haven't anything of value that might be taken away from me, not a single thing any one might want to take. Even my life isn't of any value, if someone wanted to take that, because of the stupid things I have to do with it."

There was no light outside, only the clear moon-flooded night without the house and the far little finger of the semaphore's ray from the cliff swinging, blue as glass, once, then twice, then three times across the unseen land and sea. Miss Cafferty lifted her face, as tender as a flower's, to look at Lady Glourie and then she stepped at once out into the moon-sculptured darkness, so small, so young, so child-like in the schoolgirl coat that something like misgiving smote Lady Glourie's heart before she closed and locked the manor door.

Lord Glourie sat in the cushioned armchair with his legs in the riding-breeches stretched out before him, deliberately not listening for the door to close and the feet to sound out on the gravel. The fire was dying slowly and Lady Glourie came back into the room and picked up her knitting and sat down in the inglenook by the small perishing flames.

And "This is the National Program," the broadcaster's voice said. "There is one S O S message tonight before the news summary." The casual cultivated voice spoke clearly but discreetly to them over the unseen waves of air, reaching from the long way out of civilization to them across the country's wilderness to this house made of stone massive enough to last forever. "There is a message for Barnes," said the perfectly articulated voice. "B-a-r-n-e-s. Will Alec R. Barnes, last heard of in Manchester three years ago—"

The voice did not falter in the grim stone-ribbed comfortless room but, resonant, impregnable, continued and Glourie got abruptly up from his chair and began walking the floor, pacing from one end to the other of the sitting room with his hands in the pockets of his breeches. He walked up and down in agitation while the voice of the broadcaster asked without pity or appeal that Alec R. Barnes, last heard of in Manchester three years ago, return to his wife Margaret Barnes, lying dangerously ill at the Middlesex Hospital. Lady Glourie's needles worked rapidly through the green wool of the sweater that would be for Ferris and as the fire trembled and gasped in death the joke began to take on its proportions. Wives calling out across the country at night, broadcasting their names and their addresses with their despair. She looked up from her work towards where Glourie walked wildly in his solitude between the two extremities of what confined him.

"Glourie, we might have a game of something. What about a game of 'Sorry' or 'Monopoly'?" she said.

But Glourie burst out:

"I'll have to get rid of that fellow if he's cutting up again!" His apoplectic face whirled towards her. "We've had enough trouble with him. I tell you, I'm fed up. He's got a wife, he's got a child. I swear I don't know what he's after."

"Who?" said Lady Glourie, looking blindly at her work.

So it wasn't finished, so it might be only the beginning. Glourie stepped quickly to the radio and switched it suddenly into silence.

"Panrandall," he said shortly. He stood in the middle of the room doing the buttons of his jacket over his lean belly, and they did not look directly at each other. Between them, like a veil, was the substance of Miss Cafferty descending the hill alone, going without him but still accompanied it might be into the darkness of the trees, descending through the moonlight into what obscurity, into what depths of pollution. "Think I'll step out a minute for a breath of air," he said, and even when he crossed to where she sat and leaned over and put his thin lips against her cheek, they did not look into each other's faces. "I suppose you'll be going up to bed soon," he said, straightening up, and Lady Glourie answered:

"Yes, in a minute or two. I'll leave the front door unlocked."

After he had gone she sat for a while knitting the green wool in and out for Ferris, thinking of the shape of the sweater, up the back of it to where the sleeves would begin and the trouble there would be casting the shoulder on, and then the cold of the room or of her premonition began to gain inch by inch and minute by minute until it had outstripped her endurance and she could not sit quiet any more. She stood up and the chill ran down her spine. She thought of nights when she had gone to the head of the stairs in her nightdress in the winter and stood barefoot on the stone and called down to Glourie, but she had never before felt the cold as she now felt it. Even the words came back to her that she had called; but now their meaning was lost for they were words to be shouted out to and to be heard by men, not to be called in supplication after a woman. Because of the way the absolute male life had altered here she could no longer call his name as another man might call it into the darkness, shouting, "Now, come back, Glourie! Come up to bed before I go out there in the dark and get you!" She stood mutely rolling the length of the knitting up and thrusting the two needles slowly through the yarn, almost without thought or choice discarding the words that could no longer serve and which dropped voluntarily away as withered leaves will—seeking elsewhere, deeper, farther, beyond the forcing sense of cold and latency into what might be capacity not needed before, judgment that had not yet been required to be. For this, as for everything else, there must be some sound that is not complaint to utter. . . .

Lady Glourie had jumped out of bed and pulled her dressing-gown on before the knocking on the door had quite stopped, and now as she went at a run down the sloping orchard the night air felt sudden as winter on her naked legs. She had not taken the time to pull any stockings on, but in the white nightdress and the woolen gown she went running a little ahead of Jo Lucky through the moon-bleached orchard.

"She was feeling queer all evening long," Jo Lucky was saying with his breath coming short. "But I kept thinking Miss Cafferty'd be in and I was afeard to put a foot out of the house and leave her there all to herself." He was coming along, laboring close behind her in his hobnailed boots. "I kept thinking Miss Cafferty'd be coming in—mind now," he said as Lady Glourie slid on her bedroom slippers in the mud.

"I'm all right," she said quickly. "Go on."

"But when it got on to twelve and she wasn't in yet I went out like I was telling you." He stopped talking to draw his breath in deep again and Lady Glourie said:

"Are you sure one of them's dead?" She felt her teeth beginning to chatter as she ran. On either side of the steep-dropping path the small apple trees stood shimmering, their leaves and blossoms done delicately in milky foil and the grass at their feet as white as if frost had fallen on it.

"It must be dead," said Lucky running behind her. "It wouldn't be lying still like that. I kept thinking it wouldn't be a minute before Miss Cafferty'd be in or I'd have been out there when I heard them starting. If it hadn't been for fear of leaving my missis alone there wouldn't of been no holding me. I was caught there between the two things." They had reached the cattle gate at the foot and Jo Lucky, with his wind crying in his throat, took down the top bar of it. "I was helpless as a child—"

"Let it go at that," said Lady Glourie when he laid hold of the second bar. She threw one long bare leg in the night-dress quickly over the poles and swung the other after. Now they were in the pasture-fields and the meadow they waded through was lit by the moon wide and far around them, the grasses starred with dim flower faces stretching away pale and perishable with light. "I'll go straight out to the lake," said Lady Glourie. She walked quickly before him with the tassels of her dressing-gown's cord tapping lightly, rapidly at her knee. "You go in and put Mrs. Lucky's mind at rest and see if Miss Cafferty's there. You'll catch me up by the water."

Just inside the cottage gate their ways diverged and Lady

Glourie took the path along the covered stream towards the lake. Here in the sudden darkness under the rhododendron trees the stream's water rang loud and musical among the stones, and Lady Glourie went quickly and silently over the wet, fresh, buoyant moss. At the end the shrubbery ceased and the oval of still water sprang without warning into being. It lay flat as metal between the black banks of earth, glassily, uncannily becalmed except for those instants when the breeze passed over it and combed the imperceptible current back to its untroubled heart.

At first there was just this to be seen and Lady Glourie paused a while in the gloom the trees cast and peered across the water. And then the shapes of the two swans began to emerge in the milky, deceptive light, the two enthroned birds sitting upright, pure and immobile as if hewn from marble and set at a distance from each other on their nests. The young bride was not far from Lady Glourie, seated white and still against the farther foliage, and the old pen could be seen beyond, across the whole length of the water, and with a flash of impatience Lady Glourie thought Jo Lucky had been mistaken. She followed the gradual curving of the lake, seeking guardedly under the bushes rooted in the sedge, watching steadfastly but almost without credence for what Jo Lucky said was there.

Five minutes must have passed before she heard the ripple of the water breaking, and she lifted her eyes toward it and saw the great unmistakable bird issue from the rivulet at the lake's head and ride slowly and supremely forward, his immaculate breast kissing the surface and pressing the reeds aside as he advanced. He did not ride into the open lake, but once freed of the thickest rushes he veered into the shallows. There he languidly came to anchor, and with the same profound, satiated languor opened first one and then the other of his wings. Lady Glourie stood motionless watching the ceremony of the bath begin.

He was just across the lake with the moon shining fully on him, and presently she began walking panther-swift and soft along the path that led her to where he bent and dipped and shook under the lambent dripping veils of mingled water and light. Her eyes did not leave him; as if it was his own luminosity that drew her like a sleepwalker to him she moved, seemingly stepless, seemingly mindless, towards him. Now that she was near she could see the dark blotches on his pate and throat, staining the incredible purity as blood might have stained it, and she could see the feathers scattered like petals around on the metallic rings his ablutions flung quivering across the lake's perfect sheen. When she was almost behind him on the bank he was still unaware and he rose, treading water, and lifted the full reach of his pinions on high and threshed the beads of wet mightily from them. The great throbbing of his wings beat startlingly upon the silence, and as Lady Glourie watched she perceived someone else standing near, another woman standing among the densely flourishing, leather-leaved trees half-way, it might have been, between her and the bathing swan.

"Look, he's dead, he's dead over there," said the other woman in a whisper. She came towards Lady Glourie, moving silently across the moss until the white oval that was the face was there within hand's reach before her, and still the swan did not perceive them and did not falter in his dance. "Look at him, look," she said in a pained wild whisper, and Lady Glourie said scarcely aloud:

"What are you talking about, Miss Cafferty?"

"Oh, help him, help him," the nurse's voice implored, issuing strangely from that disembodied face which still retained the power of speech. Whatever else had been its corporeal being before was blotted out by the dark coat that buttoned to the chin and left the head detached but still articulate to drift towards Lady Glourie in invocation. "He's lying there, just over there, in the reeds. I saw it happen. I saw the old one get him and take the whole night killing him. I couldn't move. I just had to stand here like this and see it happen." The voice just missed the reach of sound for a moment, gasped and sank like the missing of the distantly heard motor of an aeroplane that is flying high and failing fast and has a long way to fall. Then she said with sudden breath: "I couldn't call anyone, I couldn't go. I just had to stay here, I must have been paralyzed, I had to see it happen." Her hand moved, seemingly without warmth or volition, into Lady Glourie's hand and quickly closed upon the fingers of it. "He's over there," she whispered, choking. "If you go back up the path a little and then down into the water you'll see."

"Stay here while I go and fetch him out," Lady Glourie said. "Perhaps it isn't too late after all."

"Oh, yes, it's too late, it's too late," whispered Miss Cafferty, wildly. "And he didn't sing as he died so that's just another lie they tell you! He died horribly, horribly, screaming with pain and terror—" Lady Glourie felt the whole body shuddering, tremor after tremor shaking the nurse's flesh down to the extremity of her quaking hand.

"I've been praying for you to come, I've been saying your name over and over," she said in anguish. "I've been saying you were to come, that you had to come. . . ."

Lady Glourie slipped her hand out of Miss Cafferty's and turned and went up through the bushes again and the little Irish nurse came running after her as a child might have run. She could hear the sobs gasping and crying in Miss Cafferty's throat.

"Now don't cry," said Lady Glourie sternly and she kicked her bedroom slippers off onto the moss in the moonlight and stepped from the moss into the rushes. Step by step as she went the cold lake water rose from calf to knee from knee to thigh and as she walked her hands twisted the ends of the nightdress and the woolen dressing-gown tighter and higher, higher and higher from the water's touch until they formed a swollen tire-like shape around her buttocks. It was hard, wary going, the slogging advance forward through the mud: first one leg drawn strongly up out of the suck at the roots of the weeds and then the other pulled mightily from the thick shifting leeching cold. She had gone three yards or more before the big swan turned his head and saw her, and his neck arched swiftly in passion. He spun on the water, his wings slightly raised and spread, and rode towards her, hissing his venom from his poised snake-like head.

"Lady Glourie, Lady Glourie!" Miss Cafferty cried out in warning from the bank and Lady Glourie called savagely back:

"Don't worry, I know Hitches!" She strode fiercely on through the shining water, shouting at him: "Damn you, damn you, Hitches, you murderer, you killer!"

She had water to her waist now and she was walking swiftly, the undone twist of her night garments floating drenched behind her, the strong legs pulling their weight of water forward. She lifted each separate step and dragged it powerfully on until she perceived the floating body of the bridegroom. The dead young cob lay between her and Hitches, the neck drifting long and lifeless under water. She put out her hand to him and Hitches rose to his full height before her, the smell of his evil spit on the air, his wings and feathers busking. Just as he lifted his pinion above her arm to smite her, Lady Glourie seized the body of the bridegroom and took it swiftly to her breast.

She turned in the water and faced the land again, and as she went she felt the swan's fury rising like a wind behind her. With the dead swan's body held against her she fled before the passion of the living swan. As she swung to one side the tip of his wing swept from her shoulder down her arm and struck the water like a plank, and not only strength but movement itself seemed to leave her and the figure of herself she saw as if it were another's, a woman knee-deep in slough like a statue capturing the attitude but not the motion of flight. She felt him gathering power again, heard the thunder of his presence behind her as he rose again to strike.

"Lady Glourie, my darling, my darling," Miss Cafferty's voice cried out, and Lady Glourie saw her coming through the water to her. She was still buttoned up in her schoolgirl coat deep in the icy liquid of the lake, reeling and staggering through the muck and the reeds towards her.

"Go back, go back!" shouted Lady Glourie, but Miss Cafferty came on through the water crying:

"If he touches you, I'll kill him. I'll kill him!" She had reached her now and flung herself on her. "Are you hurt, my darling, are you hurt?" she cried.

"Here now, take the bird and go as fast as you can with it," said Lady Glourie quickly. She put the limp feathered bridegroom in Miss Cafferty's arms and turned her back to land, and then she swung on Hitches. He was rising again on his tough legs from the surface of the water, his wings full like a ship's sails with the wind packed hard in them, and as the old bird towered on her Lady Glourie lifted her fist and brought it fiercely upon the side of his white rearing head. He paused a moment and swerved, but not in fear; it might have been stone striking stone for all it mattered to him. But Miss Cafferty had gained the bank again and in the moment the swan faltered, Lady Glourie climbed bare-legged, dripping, out of the reeds and up onto the land.

"He's dead," said Lady Glourie quietly and with the swan the two women moved off towards the trees.

He lay in Miss Cafferty's arms, the long neck hanging a soft white silken rope across the dark sleeve of her coat, the weight of the strong-billed head swinging it like a clock's dying pendulum, gently to and fro.

"I killed him," said Miss Cafferty in a whisper. "I couldn't go and get help. It was my fault. I couldn't move. I just had to stand and watch it happen. I couldn't go for you."

"Don't," said Lady Glourie. "It's no use thinking of all that. It's no good talking like that." She laid her open hand on the dead swan's breast and Miss Cafferty's tears fell on her fingers, warm and quick as blood falling from the heart.

"I couldn't sleep and I came out," Miss Cafferty was saying in a broken voice. "I came out thinking about you.

Let me say it!" she cried in sudden passion. "Let me say it! I came out to think about you here alone where there might be something left of you somebody hadn't touched —some place you were in the daytime—some mark of you on the ground. . . . I couldn't sleep in the room, I couldn't bear closing the door after I'd left you, just one more door closed between what you are and what I am! And then this, this," said the wild whisper, "this, this!" The enormous white bird lay shining against the schoolgirl coat. "There wasn't any need for this, there didn't have to be any death if I'd had the courage to call your name out!" The tears still falling down her face fell hot and violent on Lady Glourie's hand. "Night after night I've walked the country alone instead of walking it with you, talking out loud to you night and day, asking you to give me everything I haven't, peace and strength and that look in your eyes, asking you to give me a little bit of it to take away with me when I have to leave you, asking you for just one drop of it, one hint of what it is you have that I haven't got, that nobody else has, just one weapon to fight the others—"

"Hush, hush," said Lady Glourie, but she could not move away. For now the words seemed no longer Miss Cafferty's, or the voice Miss Cafferty's speaking, but these were things she had heard once or once imagined and had for a long time only dimly remembered, and this declaration was shape given them at last in the moving and terrible statement of memory. "You mustn't speak like this," said Lady Glourie blankly, and her blank eyes looked straight before her, like a statue's. She stood waiting; scarcely breathing, waiting for the words to start again.

"Don't you think I see you as you are?" Miss Cafferty

said passionately. "Don't you think I see you living in this place alone, alone the way you're alone in your bed at night, with butchers, murderers—men stalking every corner of the grounds by day and night? Don't you think I know? Don't you think I fought them all off because of you, because I knew that fighting them was taking your side against them?" There they stood back from the water in the darkness as any two women might stand on a street corner talking or in a still unlighted room and with the same lack of drama in their limbs and posture. The one with her head lowered was the only one who spoke now, speaking in hot broken fury as if directly to the dead swan who lay heavy in her arms. "Every night since I've come here I've walked out in the rain through the fields or up on the cliffs thinking of how I could tell you, or ever make you see your beauty, or how I could ever make you know. . . ." Lady Glourie heard the voice stop again and with it her own hand ceased moving on the dead bird's breast and she stood bleakly waiting. The chill that she had not yet felt on her flesh entered her heart for the instant that the words abandoned this anonymous but exact description of love. "Every night I've asked everything of you," it began again at last, "asking you to escape from this, getting down on my knees to you asking you to lend me what you can spare, what you have left over, like the little piece of courage you lent me for a minute when I went into the water after you—"

They had not seen the yellow funnel of light that had been moving through the silver variegated shadows and the trees, but now it came clearer, closer, and they heard the men's voices speaking. Lord Glourie was walking just behind the swanherd and Jo Lucky was carrying the lighted lantern in one hand.

"Hallo there," Lord Glourie suddenly called. "What's up?"

The voice that answered was Lady Glourie's, but strangely transported, strangely reverberant and high.

"The swans," she called back, "the swans," as if this were explanation. The two women did not move or speak again until the lantern's light fell first between them, like a barrier falling, and then on them, as if someone had switched on the illumination in a room. Lady Glourie looked through the clear honey-yellow flood straight at the other woman's brow, at the lowered quivering lids, at the pale cheeks, and the mouth. There was no record, no sign, no history marked on them.

"You're wet, my God, you're drenched to the skin, the two of you!" said Lord Glourie in annoyance.

Lady Glourie looked down at the nightdress clinging to her own strange flesh and suddenly she began shaking with the cold.

DECISION

This novel was first published by the *Saturday Evening Post* in 1948, under the title *Passport to Doom*.

Chapter One

THE FIRST morning in Madrid I went to Manuel's address off the Calle de Goya, and it was exactly as his sister had told me it would be. The apartment was two flights up, and the staircase was made of stone, but the tall dark stooping boy who opened the door a little warily said that Manuel was not there. I told him I had a letter from Manuel's sister, the one in Paris, and the boy's dark soft eyes watched my lips move, and his regard was filled with eloquence, but he was still not certain. There was a shadow of down along his lip, and the hair hung longish and black behind his ears, and he stood there, his shoulders stooped in the white rayon shirt, his full moist lips half smiling, his eyes watching my face. Behind him, in the hallway of the apartment, hung a tier of shelves crowded with bright miniature tambourines and toy accordions and mandolins, and in a room beyond, a piano was playing ballet music—the same sprightly measure repeated as if it led group after group of dancers in flight across a stage. After an instant, the boy motioned me hesitantly into the hallway where the empty coat rack and the shelves of ornaments were, with the smell of lilacs strong and sweet in the semi-darkness, and he carefully closed the door.

"*Por favor*," he said in a low voice, "wait here."

He turned and walked lightly as a cat toward the sound of the piano playing at the end of the hall, and through the door that framed the brilliant panel of day. When he had stepped into the light, the music ceased as abruptly as if someone had lifted a finger for silence. It may have been that he said, "There is a stranger from Paris here," or, "A woman has come from Manuel's sister in Paris," or it may merely have been because of what was written in his face that the music ceased to play. In a moment, he came down the passage, his head bent, his eyes lowered, and he led me toward the light.

It was a small room into which the sunlight flooded, and it had been cleared nearly bare for dancing, with an upright piano, on which the vase of lilacs stood, pushed across one corner, and a sofa set against the inside wall. Between the two windows that stood open above the hot, silent street hung a long mirror which reflected the figure of the young woman who sat on the sofa, as startling in her nakedness as an artist's model seated upon a model stand. But she was not naked; it was only her arms and throat and breast and legs that were uncovered, the flesh of them white, voluptuous and firm. She wore a pink tulle ballet skirt, and her smooth thighs were crossed beneath the limp, soiled tulle of her dress, and her feet were encased in red toe shoes, with the silk of them split, and the red ribbons binding her ankles were frayed. There was no one seated at the piano but the curtain beside it still stirred a little as if the pianist had, just a moment before, opened the glass partition and gone quickly out that way.

"Will you sit down, please?" said the young woman, and she got to her feet. She had picked up an embroidered scarf from the sofa and drawn it around her shoulders, and her palm was soft and moist as she shook my hand. She stood smiling in uneasy, tentative welcome, committing herself to nothing yet, and there was no access to her face because of the dark glasses which masked the scrutiny and color of her eyes. It was she who had been dancing, and a dew of perspiration stood on her upper lip, and the knot of her soft golden hair had slipped a little sideways on her head. "You will excuse me. I have been practicing," she said.

I said I had a letter for Manuel from his sister; that I had come from the station with it here.

"I had hoped to be able to see Manuel today," I said.

"So you know his sister well?" said the young woman in the ballet dress, and the smile was there in uneasiness on her mouth still as we sat down on the sofa together.

"Yes, very well. I've known her for eight years," I said.

The boy had seated himself on the piano stool, his back turned to the keyboard, and the sunlight poured, shimmering with dust, over his lank, black hair and his yellowish, naked arms as he leaned forward to watch us.

"Then you must know something of his family?" said the young woman, asking that the words of peace and quiet be spoken between us without delay.

"I know about Manuel, and about his cousin Alfonso. I know what they have believed in all these years," I said. "I have a letter from Manuel, and papers to give him—papers he has been waiting a long time for."

The young woman stirred on the sofa, and however her eyes may have altered behind the dark lenses I could not know. But she leaned toward me and laid one soft, damp hand upon my arm, and she spoke in a gentler voice now as if to spare me from pain.

"You are going to be disappointed," she said, speaking

quickly. "You have come so far, and neither of them are here. Alfonso was arrested again, ten days ago. There was a new roundup of people—professors, intellectuals. They simply walked up the stairs and rang the bell and asked for both of them. Alfonso was here and they took him off, but Manuel had not been home since the day before. Perhaps he is still safe somewhere, hiding." She had not taken her soft-tipped fingers from my arm, and with the handkerchief held in her other hand she wiped the drops of perspiration from her lip. "They have had a great many years of prison, both of them," she said, smiling at me. "My brother here," she said, and she motioned toward the boy, "has had nine months of it. I don't want him to have any more." There, within the first hour in the city, in the first exchange of words, were the walls erected word by word around those who spoke, and they stood high, cold, unscalable, so close that the air seemed difficult to breathe. Had we reached out our hands, we might have touched them, but instead we drew closer to one another, lowering our voices so that the echo might not ring out against their stone. "I am Manuel's wife," the young woman said quickly, softly to me. "We have been married only three years, so Manuel's sister would not have known."

The boy spun around on the piano stool, as if seeking a way of escape, but instead his fingers fell on the keys of the piano, and the lilacs trembled in their vase as he played the ballet motif out.

"Listen," he said, and he turned his lifted head in profile to us, the full dark lips parted as his fingers sought the notes and played. "Listen," he said, his head beating time, "can you understand it?"

"If Manuel walks by outside," the young woman said, "the music will tell him. It has been warning him for days now, ever since Alfonso was taken, that there has been trouble. When he hears this, he knows it is not safe to come home."

"Manuel plays the cello," I said, remembering.

"We met at music school," said the young woman, the eyes invisible behind the glasses, but the soft mouth giving the look of love away. "I dance professionally, so it is part of my work to practice. But Manuel and Alfonso had to make their living as language teachers, so they never had the time they needed to go on."

I opened the flat black bag that hung from my shoulder by its strap, and I took the envelope from one pocket of it. In it was the letter from Manuel's sister, and the square green pages of the French identity card, with the place still blank where the photograph should be. Inside the identity card, the yellowing paper of the Spanish birth certificate was folded, torn at the edges, and perishable as onion skin.

"She took this copy of his birth certificate with her when she left in 1939," I said, and I unfolded the papers one after another, spreading them out upon the bag that lay across my knees. "This, and the card, would establish an identity for him in France. In the letter, she gives him the name of the town, and the guide who will get him across. She worked for months to get him the card, and now everything is ready for him. She wants him to leave, to get out of here quickly," I said. The boy had stopped playing the ballet music, and he swung on the piano stool again to watch our faces and to listen to what we said. When the young woman leaned forward to touch the documents, she still did not take the dark mask of the glasses from her eyes. "All the directions are in the letter—the guide's name, and the place on the frontier," I said. "She's never stopped working for it—"

The boy sat on the piano stool, his long, big-jointed hands clasped between his knees as he leaned forward, watching us. Before he spoke, he ran his tongue along his lip.

"In France, Manuel would be free, he would be absolutely free, wouldn't he?" he said. He looked at his sister, and his eyes were dark and deep with transport, as if rapt and blinded by the sudden vision of franchise that he saw. "In France, he could work, make a living, not be arrested," he said slowly, holding the shape of each word a long time on his tongue. "In France, he would be a free man," he said.

The young woman put her fingertips to her temples, and with this gesture the embroidered scarf slipped from her shoulders and left them bare.

"But Manuel would not go. He would never go," she said, and the dark glasses masked her strength or her weakness or whatever her eyes might have betrayed.

"You say that because you don't want him to go, you don't want to lose him!" the boy cried out, and he twisted his interlocked fingers together as he leaned forward on the stool.

"No, it isn't that," she said, with her soft fingertips pressed to her temples. "For if he stays here, it is perhaps more certain that I lose him. But a man who has been strong a long time cannot be tempted by acts of weakness. He would not understand what you meant if you offered him the means to go."

"You women with your love, your demanding, absolute love!" cried the boy, and he twisted his hands together, and his voice seemed close to tears. "Can you think what it might be for him to step out a door a free man every morning, and to lie down in bed a free man every night? Can't you see that there comes a time when nothing but that matters—when country no longer matters, and women no longer matter? Can't you understand," he said, his full lips trembling, "that a man can come beyond his need for women or his love for women, can come so far beyond them in his desperation that he no longer knows they are there?"

"Hush," said his sister. "Neither you nor I can speak for him. This must be Manuel's decision." She put her hand on my arm again, and she went on saying: "You do not know Manuel, so it is not easy for you to see him. He is a very unhappy man, a good singer, very spirited, and the heart wide open. In the days of the liberation of France, we all of us became quite reckless with joy, but he became even more reckless. We said things openly that we would never have dared to say before. People shouted out things to one another as they read newspapers in the streets. Manuel said things openly during his lectures, talked to his students in the classroom as if now, after the French, our turn for liberty was coming next. We couldn't believe it wasn't just about to happen here. And then it didn't." She stopped talking for a moment, her hand still lying on my arm. "And when it didn't, Manuel began to become a little desperate. I think it is even possible that his heart closed a little to hope," she said, and her brother tossed restlessly on his seat, and twisted his fingers as if in pain.

For a little while we did not speak, with the choice that was Manuel's lying in silence between us, and I folded the papers over, the birth certificate, the identity card, and the letter, and put them into the envelope again. And then, as if to prevent the last door of escape from being closed to him, Manuel's wife said quickly:

"We—neither my brother nor I—we must not be seen walking in the streets with you. It would only make things difficult for you here. But there is a man—a friend of Manuel's—" She turned toward the boy, who sat with his dark, rapt gaze fixed on the vision still. "If she went to him, asked him for news of Manuel?" she said, and the boy nodded slowly, scarcely roused from the fabulous dream of proffered liberty. "If you leave by the other door there, and go directly the length of José Antonio to the square where the tables are set out for drinks, you'll find him. He'll be sitting at a table—"

She said he would be sitting, youngish and thin, brown-haired and certainly without a hat, reading a copy of the *ABC*, and probably drinking nothing. As he had only one suit, a grey one, that is the one he would be wearing. "If either my brother or I went there and talked to him, the police would pick him up for questioning," she said. "But you can go up to him quite freely, and say you know Manuel's sister, the one in Paris, and that you want news of Manuel." And I knew it was this that I would do. "And when he looks up at you," she went on saying, "you will see that his jaw is a little crooked, and he has a film of blindness over a part of his left eye. If anyone knows where Manuel is, he will know it, and perhaps he can take you to where Manuel is. Perhaps you will see Manuel," she said softly, and then she turned her head away. "For so many years there have been prisons separating us, separating Manuel and me, and separating other men from other women, and perhaps a frontier like this between us would not be the same kind of separation. Perhaps there would be a compensation in knowing he was free. But you must get the papers to him so that he can make his own decision. Once he wrote me from Carabanchel that a man without his woman is not much good to anyone, least of all to himself," she said, "and I know that a woman without her man is lost."

"So you would keep him here, doom him, condemn him!" her brother cried out. "You would have him behind bars here rather than let him go!"

She turned her head back to me again, and then she lifted one hand and took the dark glasses from her eyes. There was a red mark on the white skin of her nose where the glasses had rested, and now I could see the clear blue color of her eyes as they moved from feature to feature of my face.

"If you see Manuel, will you tell him that I shall believe in it, whatever his decision is?" she said, and we might have been alone in the sunlit room together, and her brother, with the down on his lip, not tossing in impatience beyond us on the stool. At the door, we paused for a moment, and touched each other's hands. "If there is news of him, will you come back?" she said, and in leaving her there was a sense of dual cleavage that could not be explained or named; perhaps that a portion of her torment moved with longing down the stairs and out into the hot, silent street with me, while a portion of my compassion remained there with her, soft as an arm around her waist.

Chapter Two

M ANUEL'S FRIEND was there, reading his paper at a table in the narrow alley of shade beneath the trees, and the dust lay white in the desert of the square behind him. He looked up at once from the words he was reading, his lids drooping like the weary eyelids of a camel, but, in spite of the lassitude, one knew that he made up his mind in the snap of a finger concerning woman or man or printed word. He folded the paper and stood up, neatly combed and rather dapper, the grey suit well made and clean, but the stuff of it gone as shiny as silk from the years of squaring his shoulders in it and buttoning it carefully over against imputation.

"I have come from Manuel's sister in Paris. I am looking for him," I said.

He pulled out the other iron chair for me, and, as we sat down, I saw there was nothing of drama or grief about him despite the blue film blemishing one eye, and the slightly twisted jaw.

"Paris," he said, and when he smiled you could see the teeth were gone from one side of his face. "I once lived six months in Paris, so if you like we can talk in French together." His sleek, narrow head with the swollen bulge of the forehead was inclined toward me, the eyelid drooping lower over his imperfect sight. "Since a year," he said, "a curious regulation has been in effect. Except at bullfights, a man may not appear in public without his jacket on. So if you should say to me now, 'Do take off your jacket and be cool,' and if I should do so, the officer you see at the end of the avenue would walk down and arrest me. I do not wish to be re-arrested. Now that you have come from Paris, I prefer to sit and talk to you." His thin arms in the sleeves of the grey jacket were balanced on the table edge, and his long dark, square-tipped fingers were laid together, tip matching tip, and his jaw hung sideways over them. "Manuel was given two weeks in solitary once for walking out in the prison yard at Alcalá without his jacket," he said, and the scars went deeper in his cheeks as his mouth twitched. "The prison authorities had overlooked the fact that Manuel had been arrested in his classroom without his jacket. Manuel," he said, still speaking French, "teaches languages in the same school in which I once taught chemistry. We have known each other fifteen years. He did not keep his last rendezvous with me. That was six days ago."

"I have brought a letter, papers for Manuel," I said. "His sister wants him to come at once."

"Yes," said Manuel's friend, as if it were these words he had been expecting to say. "Let me tell you what it is like," he said, going on with the story of the classrooms. "One morning you walk out into the hall, and there they are waiting just inside the door, and you experience at once that feeling of impatience with them—irritation because there they are again, come to interrupt your work, your life, to waste weeks, months, years of your time. Again, you think —so it is going to happen again. I won't be able to go on tomorrow morning with that problem on page 106, I won't be able to meet so-and-so tomorrow night and play that rubber of chess. Only when you are walking out between them do you begin to remember the details of what is going to come—the slivers of wood driven under your nails, your knuckles closed in the back of a door," he said in a pleasant, courteous voice, with the half smile hanging on his mouth. "I am telling you this," he said in apology for it, "so that the promise of release made to any one of us may be given its full measure of attraction. I have seen Manuel tortured for information which he could not give," he said, his eyelids drooping wearily, "as he has seen me tortured. It is possible that it is happening to him now."

The waiter had strolled down through the dust past the empty tables, and when he stopped beside us, Manuel's friend looked up at him.

"From Paris; the lady has just come from Paris," he said, speaking Spanish now, and then he motioned with one hand to the waiter. "We were in San Miguel de los Reyes nine months together, the period of time required to give birth to a friendship. He's on *libertad vigilada*," he said in a low, almost humorous voice. The waiter took a cigarette from the pack I held out to him. "Have you seen anything of Manuel Jerónimo?" said Manuel's friend, the smile not altering on his mouth, and the waiter shook his head.

"Liberty under surveillance, provisional liberty, and attenuated liberty are particularly nice today," said the waiter grimly as he leaned to light his cigarette from the match held in the other's hand. "Which one will you have?"

"Beer," said Manuel's friend, and the two men grinned at each other, and the laughter sounded softly in their throats. "Beer for the lady too?" said Manuel's friend, and I nodded my head. After the waiter had gone up the dust of the sidewalk again, he looked at me across the table, his head courteously inclined in the dappled light of sun and shade. "I am glad you came from Paris," he said, with his jaw slightly twisted in his face. "It gives one a whisper of hope. Even if this gallery of the mine has been sealed up with a handful of the living in it, your coming makes one believe that the others outside can still hear the rappings on the wall. If you have time to come with me, there are a few places I can take you to," he said and he might have been speaking of other cafés that we would move on to, and sit down in, and order drinks together, but this was not what he wished to say. "There are certain friends we have, Manuel and I and all the rest of us—old friends who live in the caves. They may have seen him."

The waiter brought the two glasses of beer and set them down before us, and Manuel's friend took out his ancient leather wallet and paid. His hands were dark and small, and the fingers long, and his nails on the brown peseta notes were clean as wax.

"I do not know Manuel," I said. "If we find him, what do you think he will do? Will he agree to take the papers and go?"

A tramline passed on the other side of the square, and now and again the single antique cars rocked slowly past, the passengers overflowing from the doors and standing two or three deep on the wooden steps of them, and the bells clanging in loud, wild clamor as they came. Manuel's friend moved one shoulder in the slick grey jacket of his suit, and he did not answer at once. He waited until the tramcar had rocked on down the avenue, and the noise of its passing had ceased.

"Once when we were in Alcalá together," he said then, and a little edge of foam lay white along his lip, "the order came through that political prisoners were to relinquish what was left to them of their identity, and put on the same prison garb the others wore. We had on the same suits we had been wearing when we walked out of our classroom three months before, Manuel, Alfonso, and I, and they were ours the way our private lives were ours. If they wanted us to give them up, they would have to strip them from us like our skins. We did not happen to be pickpockets, and we were not murderers, for such men had committed outrages against individual liberty, while it was our rather foolish reverence for individual liberty which had brought us where we were. We were close enough to being men of principle to be considered men of principle," he said, with the half smile hanging on his mouth. "So we told the authorities that if we had to wear the suits of ersatz cloth—which turned into paper after one washing or one fall of rain—then we would not eat. Not eating," said Manuel's friend, taking another swallow of beer, "is a punishment the flesh takes at the insistence of the will, but the strange thing is that under such duress, the will cries out for nourishment even more wildly than does the flesh. Nourishment of another kind, of course—approbation, recognition, or merely a little applause. As for me, I believe the whole gallery that went on hunger strike would have eaten before the six days were up if Manuel had not been like a mirror held up to reflect our own weakness or our tenacity. Manuel did not whimper, did not cry out, did not give in," he said, the humorous look of chagrin in his face.

"And in the end you won?" I said.

"No," he said smiling wryly. "The imprisoned never win. In the end we wore the clothes the others wore. You ask me what Manuel will do now," he said, and he shrugged one shoulder slightly again. "I have known him fifteen years, and he has never failed us." And then he stopped speaking, and he lifted his glass and drank down the rest of the beer.

We crossed the square together, walking casually as people do in Spain, as if nothing more than the next avenue of shade or a breath of cooler air were their destination, and we waited a moment at the curb on the avenue for the tramcar to come down underneath the trees.

"You have not checked in with the police yet?" said Manuel's friend.

"No. I got in at eight this morning," I said.

The tramcar was taking the corner now, tipping to one side as it came, with the seats of it full, and men hanging two or three deep to the sides of it, as bees cling to the hive. Manuel's friend put his hand beneath my arm, and we went toward it, and when it halted we slipped our feet in among the other feet on the step, and the bells clanged out in wild alarm, and we rode on with it as it rocked along the rails, clinging to it as the others clung.

Chapter Three

THE CAVES could not be said to have been dug in the earth, for the pale soil was as hard as stone under foot, and it seemed that the excavations must have been blasted out by a force more violent than the hand of man. But however they had been hollowed there, they honeycombed the golden soil that lay in a girdle around Madrid, with the mouths of their entrances black scoops of shadow cast on this desert of brilliant light. There were steps worn concave in the earth to mount to the dry, baked expanse of the plateau, and as Manuel's friend and I went up them we could perceive no movement of life. And then, abruptly, the gopher-like figures came erect, of a color with the soil in which they lived, and they waited at the entrances to the subterranean labyrinth, their eyes watching us approach, their bare, golden-skinned feet planted on the hard, dust-powdered soil. We might have been the first white people to have touched their continent, and because we were the first, they looked without fear or shame at us, in gentle curiosity.

"The Republican hotel is on the left," said Manuel's friend, the wry smile on his mouth, and he put his hand beneath my arm to lead me toward its door.

There was one man standing at the entrance of the cave to which we walked, a short, heavy-shouldered, bronzed man in a ragged shirt, with faded blue cotton trousers tied by a

cord around his waist. His bare feet were planted a little
apart, holding firmly and powerfully as if to the planks
of a ship's deck instead of to the hot, dry earth. His hair
sprang grey and bushy on his head, and under his wiry,
flourishing grey brows his eyes moved brightly and
shrewdly on us, and he put out his hand and shook first
mine and then the hand of Manuel's friend.

"Will you come downstairs?" he said, and, with the gesture of his arm, the rags of his sleeve fell like pennants from
his shoulder. Standing close to him, one could see the leather
of his brow, and cheek and neck, and the St. Christopher
medal hanging among the grey curls on his chest, its enamel
the same rich blue as were his eyes.

Manuel's friend went first, and once inside the arch of
shadow, he turned to take my hand in his, and the others,
standing in the sunlight at the doorways of their excavations,
watched us lower our heads and descend into the dark.
Below, there were the shapes of three men lying asleep and
we made our way in silence past their broken shoes, and
their legs, in trousers powdered white with dust, drawn up
in childlike weariness. A stool was set against the sloping,
earthen wall beyond, and in the half-dark Manuel's friend
motioned me to it.

"There is your seat," he said with courtesy, speaking
softly to me as if we had made our way into a theater box
after the hush of expectation had descended on the house.
"*Première loge de face*," he whispered, the voice humorous.
"The overture is finished. The curtain is about to rise."

"*C'est chic, eh?*" said the grey-haired man when he heard
the sound of it. He had come down the contrived steps behind us, and he stood in the semi-dark before the stool on

which I sat, jerking his thumb across his shoulder. "*Confort moderne*," he said, and he held his nose.

"So you're French, you're from the *Midi?*" I said, and I took the packet of cigarettes out.

"Marseille. And I'd give ten years of my life for a dish of *bouillabaisse* now," he said, with the laughter wheezing in his chest. He took a cigarette from among the others, standing short and stocky and faceless against the brimming well of light. "I'd lose my way in the Vieux Port if I went back. I crossed the border twenty years ago," he said.

Manuel's friend took the match quickly, courteously, from his pocket, and struck the head of it with his thumb nail.

"Who are they?" he said, holding the flame to the Frenchman's cigarette. With his sleek narrow head, he indicated the three sleeping men.

"They've been two weeks on the run," the Frenchman said, and he drew the smoke deeply into his lungs, and slowly let it go again. "When were you on the Cannebière last?" he said, speaking French still.

"In 1941. They hadn't bombed the port yet," I said, and Manuel's friend turned his blurred eye on the Frenchman.

"Any sign of Manuel Jerónimo?" he said.

"Manuel came past four days ago," said the Frenchman, as if it were nothing at all. "He slept the night here."

"And he went on?"

"Yes, he went on," the Frenchman said. Now that the eyes grew accustomed to the dark, I could see the leathery look of his neck and face again, and the high-bridged nose with the skin drawn taut across the bone. "I used to run one of those excursion boats out to the Ile d'If. Captain," he said, and under his bushy brows his eyes were on me, saying:

228

*See me in a leather-beaked cap and a brass-buttoned suit,
with the Mediterranean breaking behind me. See the boards
of a deck underneath my feet, and a sea wind slapping against
my face. Don't notice this cave, and the way it smells.* "I
know the whole coast, Cassis, La Ciotat, and all the rest," the
Frenchman said, the cigarette hanging on his lip. Beyond
him, on the beaten earth of the floor, the three men lay
motionless, sleeping the slumber of the nearly dead.

"Look," said Manuel's friend in his casual, half-humorous
voice, his head tipped towards the Frenchman; "this has
happened to Manuel before, and we didn't start combing
the caves for him. But this time things are different. This
lady," he said, his lids drooping wearily across his sight,
"she has come from Manuel's sister in France. She has
papers for him; she's brought him the means of getting
out."

"Getting out?" said the Frenchman, and in the half dark
his fingers sought for the medal hanging on his chest, and
found it among the iron curls of hair. "Getting out? Getting out of what?" he said.

"Out of the country, out of the situation here," said
Manuel's friend. His thin hands were in his jacket pocket,
and his narrow head was tilted courteously.

"Manuel get out of the country?" the Frenchman said,
and then he took the cigarette carefully from his lips,
and he began to laugh.

"Very well," said Manuel's friend. "But he has a right
to know."

"I fixed him up with a false identity the other night," the
Frenchman said. He put the cigarette back in his mouth
again, and he drew the sweet smoke in. "If they pick him

229

up, he's somebody else. I told him to keep away from home, and he has a chance. Maybe in two or three months things will be quieter, and then he can circulate again." The smoke drifted slowly from his mouth, drawn in a serpentine current up toward the opening, where the sun stood halted on the brink of hollow dark. "I told him to keep away from friends," the Frenchman said, and then the laughter began to wheeze again, as if hidden bellows fanned a tentative flame. "But he won't stay away. The police can always count on that. That's the trouble with Spaniards," he said, and he turned the cigarette carefully on his lip. "He'll be feeling good with the papers he's got in his pocket with another name and history on them, and so he'll stop in somewhere for a glass of wine. You'll find him tonight any time after ten, at Lamana's café where he knows the Flamenco entertainers. You'll find him sitting there, I tell you, watching the dancing and listening to them sing. You've seen Manuel dance?" the Frenchman said, and he thrust his elbow into the ribs of Manuel's friend. "Like a fool, eh?" he said, as if the memory of it alone could save Manuel from anything else that might be asked of him. "Just like a fool! You know what we say about him—that he's got music running in his veins instead of blood."

"I've seen his blood run, too," said Manuel's friend in a pleasant, courteous voice, and now one of the sleepers on the floor cried out in pain or terror as he stirred.

"Ah, don't talk like that, don't talk about blood!" said the Frenchman, and underneath his wild grey brows his blue eyes were turned to mine. "Have you ever seen Manuel dance? Have you ever heard him sing?" he said, as if these were Manuel's activities and nothing else besides. "Opera arias, street songs, warbles them like a bird. The night he slept here, he sang us any song we asked for, as quickly as you called the names out—French songs, Italian songs, anything that came into your head. I've known him ten years," he said, and he took the cigarette from his mouth and studied it shrewdly, as if estimating how many instants of smoking it might still contain. "Whenever he got tobacco, he'd bring it along, and coffee, if anyone sent him any. But I swear if you try to give Manuel papers to get him out of the country, he'll laugh in your face. He's Spanish, I tell you, he's crazy. He'd cut out his heart, if you asked him, but if you gave him a passport to get him away, he'd tear it in half—"

With solicitude, the Frenchman put the cigarette back between his lips again, and he drew a deep breath in. There might have been more he wanted to say, but now one of the three men stretched on the floor of the cave raised his head from his arms, and looked first at the golden mouth of sunlight which gave access to the ground above, and then turned his head to look with dazed eyes from the light to the darkness in which the figures stood.

"I must have had a dream," he said to the sight of the Frenchman and of Manuel's friend, and he passed his fingers through his hair.

He seemed a young man, but against the shining nimbus of the aperture, his features could not be clearly seen. He lay on his belly, both elbows propped under him, his head and shoulders dark against the golden light.

"Pando's gone out for food," said the Frenchman, turning toward him, and speaking in Spanish to him.

"Were you talking about papers—papers to get a man out

of the country, or was that part of a dream?" the young man said.

"That was true. We were talking about a man called Manuel, with a sister in Paris," said the Frenchman patiently, as if speaking to a child.

"Manuel Jerónimo?" said the young man, and the Frenchman did not answer for a moment. He took the cigarette from his mouth, and he studied the end of it again.

"Yes. Manuel Jerónimo," he said.

"He and my brother-in-law were together on Tuesday night," said the young man, speaking quickly across the semi-darkness of the cave. "Manuel and my brother-in-law, Eleuterio, were at dinner at my sister's when the police picked them up for questioning. I didn't dream that. It happened three nights ago."

For a moment after he said this, no one spoke in the cave. No one moved until the Frenchman dropped the minute end of his cigarette on the hard earth of the floor.

"How do you know the police picked them up?" the Frenchman said.

"I slept that night in the church," the young man said. Lying there propped on his elbows, he gave a jerk of laughter. "In the confessional box," he said. "My sister's two little girls brought me something to eat in the morning before I set off again, and they told me. They said the police had taken Eleuterio and Manuel Jerónimo away."

The Frenchman cleared his throat, and his fingers found the medal on his chest again.

"They can't keep Manuel, they can't do anything to him. His papers are too good," he said. "They might keep him twenty-four hours, but they wouldn't have anything on him, and after that they'd let him out." He said: "They can't pin anything on him with the papers he's got. His name is José Martín, a plumber, and the photograph and the thumb-prints are right. They'll see him through anything. I'll swear to that." He stood with his feet planted strongly apart, but however temperate was the sound of his voice, the gale was rising, the sea was running high. "They'd have to let him out," he said, and he lifted one arm and drew the tatters of his shirt sleeve across his leathery brow.

"Where did they take them?" asked Manuel's friend in his low, courteous voice, and beneath the drooping lids his blemished vision was turned towards the young man who lay, propped on his elbows, beside the two others still sleep-ing on the floor.

"My sister might know by now where they've taken Eleuterio," the young man said. "The girls said she didn't know then."

"Give me her name. Tell me where she lives," said Man-uel's friend. He stood with his sleek head bent, giving ear to the syllables as they were spoken, repeating the family name, and the name of the street, and the number, his jaw hang-ing slightly askew.

It was after two o'clock then, and we had not eaten, but we did not speak of this. It is possible that we did not think of it even as we crossed the parched plateau and went toward the avenue. And, as we walked, a hundred barefooted chil-dren seemed to spring out of the hard substance of the earth, rising, furtive as vermin, from the labyrinth of caves. Their voices rose and fell, murmuring the chorus of entreaty to us, and their feet ran quickly, soundlessly beside us, as if they were no more than the shadows of children fleeing, fleshless and dark, across a screen of brilliant light. Their avid fingers were at our clothes like the claws of birds, and the rags of their garments fluttered in streamers as they ran, murmuring to us: "Give something from your great wealth and your great kindness, Señor, Señora!" And even while their fingers touched our clothes, and the sharp bones of their shoulders pressed against us, their eyes were quick for the movement of the hand lifted either to strike in irritation at them or to toss the coins out on the ground. When Manuel's friend put his hand into his pocket, they fell back in wariness an instant, and then, in their eagerness, they knocked the money into the bleached dust and fell upon it like dogs on the quarry at the kill.

"They may have taken him to Carabanchel," said Manuel's friend, scarcely aloud.

Only three of the children came down the steps and onto the avenue with us, and when we stopped at the curb the separate beauty and torment of their faces was there in abeyance at our elbows as we paused. Their skins were dark as fawn hides, and their legs as brittle as those of fawns, and their eyes set prominent and wide as in a wild thing's skull. It was these brown, liquid eyes, craven with calculation, that watched the length and breadth of the street for the sign of a uniform, so as to skip from sight into the caves again if it seemed to come their way. "Give something out of the generosity of your noble hearts, Señor, Señor!" their voices murmured, and Manuel's friend felt with his other hand in the pocket of his grey dapper jacket, and took out the coins and the bits of paper money and gave these to them, his mouth half smiling. But he did not seem to see them there.

Chapter Four

THE YOUNG man's sister was named Señora García, and when she opened the door we saw the slight dark woman, in her early twenties still, girlish and slender and gypsy-like, wearing the purple cassock frock of those who fulfill a vow of gratitude to the Virgin Mary for her answer to specific prayer. The yellow silk cord of the tasseled belt was knotted above her narrow hips, and the two little girls who stood on either side of her were dressed alike in blue-and-wine-colored pinafores worn over short-sleeved, silky sweaters of the same clear yellow as her belt.

"Come in," she said, after Manuel's friend had spoken, and her voice was alive with a singular merriment. It was the sound of her voice and the extravagance of life in her delicate animated bones that endowed her suddenly with beauty. "Friends of Manuel Jerónimo's are very welcome here," she said.

We had come into the hallway of the apartment, and she closed the door behind us. And then the three of them—the daughters moving as the mother moved—turned as one person, their dark eyes on us, and waited quietly for us to speak.

"We have come for news of Manuel," said Manuel's friend.

"Ah, we were just leaving to catch the bus for Carabanchel!" said Señora García, and she stood smiling at us, her hands on the shoulders of the little girls. And on her

lips, the name Carabanchel might have been that of any
place but a prison, and the excursion a picnic on which the
three of them were setting out.

"So your husband is there?" said Manuel's friend.

"Yes, we got the notice last evening," she said. *And what
of Manuel?* said the silence in the hallway; *what of Manuel
Jerónimo?* But Señora García did not cease to smile.

"And the bus will leave—?" said Manuel's friend.

"In half an hour or so," said Señora García. As she moved,
the little girls moved with her, one on the right, the other
on the left, and they looked up at the clock hanging on the
wall. The ears of the mother and her daughters were pierced
by tiny gold rings, but around the mother's neck alone was
there a large oval locket, heavily embossed, hanging upon
a fine-linked chain. The heads of the three of them were
adorned alike with smooth black locks, and each head bi-
sected by a marble part; but the mother's hair was pinned
into a chignon at the nape of her curved slender neck,
while the hair of her daughters was drawn sharply up from
their thin-skinned temples, and held in place on either side
by small blue silky bows. "We are taking food out to our
Papa," said Señora García, and when she gestured towards
the baskets, the silver bangles moved musically upon her
thin dark arm. The baskets—the actual one, and its reflection in the mirror—stood on the table against the wall, with
the ends of the loaves of bread thrusting out from one end,
and the green horns of bananas from the other, and each
basket covered with a flowered cloth. "We're taking him
bread, as you can see," she said; "a little meat, some fresh
sardines that we grilled for him this morning, and a jar
of milk. What else?" she said, and she looked down at the

little girls who stood there in her skirts, their eyes grave and censorious, their mouths unsmiling, so that they seemed to bear a burden of age and responsibility that had not been given her to bear.

"A package of tobacco and his espadrilles!" the high voice of the younger child cried out, and when the mother and sister laughed at the sudden piercing sound of it, she hid her face in her mother's purple dress.

"We got the tobacco on the black market, and we used up our bread and meat ration for the week this morning," said Señora García, and she smiled in guilt.

"Then I'll go down and get some eggs, and some oranges for him," said Manuel's friend. He had turned and touched the latch of the door, but he did not open it. Instead he stood looking back at Señora García, holding her, bright, insouciant, gypsy-like, an instant in his filmed imperfect sight. "And Manuel?" he said.

"Ah, who knows? Perhaps he is there too. How can one know what they do with them once they take them off?" she said. Having heard the note of apprehension in his voice, she turned in sudden impatience from him, and her eyes looked through their veil of lashes into mine. *We, as women, have learned and forgotten more than they have ever set down in books*, her intolerance with him might have been confirming to me, and her dark thin hands moved on the children's shoulders restlessly. *We are sustained in our weakness by something they have never even heard a whisper of*, she might have been saying; *by a consecration to the very acts of hope, tenderness, love, whatever the name may be, but which no man has any share in*. She stood there on her black platform-soled sandals, in her purple cassock frock, ready to stamp her foot, having no patience with which to meet the troubled features of man's inquietude and man's incurable heresy. "Manuel has false papers, so they will let him out," she said as savagely as if she had said: *After four, six, eight years in prison what have any of them to fear?*

And now Manuel's friend went out the door, and closed it behind him, and the two women and the two little girls were left together in the hall. For a moment, the sound of the man's footsteps could be heard descending the stairs, and then they were silent, and the last sight and sound of man was wiped away.

"Do you know why they were after Manuel Jerónimo and our little Papa?" Señora García said. Her dark lively eyes glanced through their lashes at me, and I said I did not know. "They were in the balcony of a moving-picture theater, dropping leaflets down in the dark, our Papa, Alfonso, and Manuel. They must have been recognized on the way out. They must have been pointed out to the police. There's no other way they could have known."

"Señora," I said, speaking quickly to her. "I have come a long way to find Manuel. I must go to Carabanchel too. If I could speak to your husband for a moment, I could find out if Manuel is there."

"Then you will come with us!" she cried out softly, and her eyes were filled again with the look of strange dark secret joy. She glanced at my plain blue dress, and the white earrings in my ears, and the low-heeled sandals on my feet. "You will look like a Spanish lady when you put on another dress," she said; "and no silk stockings, of course, and very high-heeled shoes! It will be easy—my cousin's things are

238

here—" And then she started to laugh. *How straight and white your teeth are, Señora García, how long and beautiful your lashes are!* I did not say aloud to her. "I have my cousin's papers here, and they will get you past the gate. You don't look like her, but we'll comb your hair up, and it will do!" she said. She took my hand in her quick nervous fingers, and the children cast their dignity aside and ran with us as we fled down the narrow hall.

Señora García opened the door into the bedroom, and there, in the shuttered gloom, stood a great carved wooden bed, with a spread of coarse cream-colored lace laid over it. On either side of the bed stood a window, the ribs of their closed shutters striped brilliantly with outdoor light. But here in the room, the bed, the chairs, the patterned rug, the metal crucifix nailed to the wall were veiled with twilight. A massive wardrobe stood in the far corner in the crypt-like dusk, and as Señora García crossed to it with running steps, her own muted reflection in the purple dress hastened to meet her in the mirror as she came.

"Come!" she called softly. "Come with me!"

When Manuel's friend returned, here was this other woman to open the door for him, and he stopped still for a moment with the two tall paper bags of oranges held in his arms, and the smaller one of eggs borne in his hand. The cousin's shoes were high-heeled, and the dress was of silk, striped in three colors, pink, grey, and green, and finely pleated from the hips. When one walked, it closed and opened like a fan.

"I am Señora García's cousin going to Carabanchel with her and her children," I said.

"Yes, you look like a Spanish woman now," said Manuel's

friend, and Señora García laughed in delight, and put her thin bangled arm through mine. "Now you are Spanish, and you belong to us," said Manuel's friend.

The children did not take their grave condemnatory eyes from us, for we were as possessed with ourselves and as foolish as two girls setting out together for a costume ball. And as I looked at Señora García's thin laughing face, my own guilt said suddenly: *Is it possible for levity to dilute the quality of drama? Must drama remain forever overcast to be rendered its full and terrible due?* But Manuel's friend had set down the bags of oranges, and lifted the flowered napkin from the basket, and fitted the paper of eggs in with care; and now there was no time to seek an answer. Señora García and I went arm in arm out the door, and started down the stairs, and behind us came the sober children. And Manuel's friend followed, bearing the covered basket in his hand.

He did not come any farther than the corner with us, for there, where the high grey bus stood empty, a group of people had set down their hampers and packages to wait, and we too put down the things we carried and waited with the others under the green boughs of the shady avenue. The faces of the men who had come this far were marked, as was the face of Manuel's friend now, with a similar dereliction, like those of men who have come to a gate that is closed, and who linger a while before it, knowing they cannot go beyond. For the cards in their pockets bore, with their names and their likenesses, the dates of their incarcerations, and the varying stages of liberty—"provisional," "under surveillance," or "attenuated liberty." It was only the women and children who continued past the barrier, who entered the kiosk and laid their papers on the counter, bearing their baskets and bundles between them, and waited before the official faces for their names to be written down.

"I shall leave you here, then," said Manuel's friend, and, for the first time, the drooping lids, the twisted jaw, lent a sheepish, a nearly craven look to his face. The uniforms—the black shoulder-straps, the boiled cardboard hats with the brims turned up in back, painted black as pitch—were just beyond, and his blemished sight moved carefully toward them, and away. "Tonight—about ten o'clock," he said, looking at me, "will you come to Lamana's? I shall be at a table, near the dancers. I'll wait for you there."

Behind him stood the other lingering men—the brothers, the cousins, the grandfathers on their canes, the friends who could go no farther. They watched from a little distance as the women and children went hand in hand past the barrier, past the kiosk, past the uniformed men, and hoisted their baskets of bread and fruit up the steps of the high grey bus. And then they turned, like outcasts, and went off slowly down the avenue.

Señora García had shown her papers to the officials seated there, and she and the two children moved on, carrying the basket between them. I stood the bags of oranges on the desk, and I took the cousin's papers from the pocket of the pleated skirt, and laid them down upon the wood.

"Object of the visit?" said the officer, his hand copying the name out still, his eyes not looking up.

"To see my cousin, Eleuterio García," I said.

Chapter Five

THE WARM LIGHT breeze came through the open windows from the blazing world without and lifted the tendrils of Señora García's hair at her temples and her brow. She leaned forward from her seat to touch the children's pinafores and smooth their hair ribbons in her fingers, saying their names—"Manolita, Juanita"—like the notes of a stringed instrument plucked softly on the rushing air.

"Manolita, my Juanita," she said, her eyes admiring their dark locks, their delicate brows, and their pale creamy skins. "My little Juanita, my Manolita, my loves."

The bus was full, for as women of another country will press into a motion-picture theater of an afternoon, taking their children with them, so these women had crowded into the seats, some dressed as city women are, and some in bright colored skirts with artificial flowers in their hair. Infants vowed to pink or blue rode in their arms, and children slept on the seats beside them in the heat, but the women's faces were lifted, not in submission to a silver screen on which passed the shadows of a Bergman or a Cary Grant, but afternoon after hot afternoon, and month after month, their eyes were turned in patience to the current stage on which the drama of the prisoners might be played.

"Manolita had rheumatism all one year, so I took the vow then," Señora García said, and the bus went swiftly across the flat parched land. "I promised the Virgin that if she were cured, I would wear the Habit of Jesus until it fell to pieces and could no longer be worn. And that night, when I lit the candles, Manolita sat up in bed with no more pain, and she was cured." She leaned quickly forward in the swaying bus, and her gypsy-nimble fingers touched Manolita's ear. "Dirt in it," she said. "You can only see it in the sun." Sleep had begun to drift across the children's faces, weighting their lids so that the dark lashes hung heavily on them and drew them closed. "Our little Papa will be happy to see Juanita and Manolita," Señora García said, and now her hand moved to the locket that hung around her neck, and her sharp narrow thumb-nail pried the two laminae apart. "Here is Eleuterio," she said, and she tipped the locket on her breast so that I might see the tense small face, tight-lipped, tenacious as a fist, with the broad dome of the forehead overhanging it. Because of the height of brow, the eyes seemed placed in the exact middle of the skull, black, bead-like, intent, and yet they met one's own with a deep unbroken look of love. "Our Papa has only one arm, gone beneath the shoulder," Señora García said, and her nail showed the place in the locket where his right arm should be. "He lost it at Toledo. He was in the Republican army then," she said, and the silver bangles on her arm made their light temporal music as she snapped the locket closed again.

Our bus was not the first to reach the gate of Carabanchel that afternoon. There were others drawn up, empty now, on the white road before the long, low, adobe portico where the women waited with their children and their baskets in the shade. Over the tiled roof of the portico, the still unfinished portions of the prison could be seen—red brick walls, strong in color, standing in jagged malediction against the sky's deep violent blue. Señora García and I crossed the road, bearing the basket between us, and Manolita and Juanita came behind, the bags of oranges in their arms. We took our place in line behind the other women, and Manolita and Juanita moved forward step by patient step with us, asking no favor as children of another country might, voicing no word of protest against the mandates of this world of adult incarceration and adult penalty.

"After we give our names," Señora García said, speaking as if in secret to me among the others, "it will be twenty minutes before the men come up from their cells and into the public reception place. They wait for the visitors there, the ones who have been called, behind a double ring of bars—like a bull ring," she said, telling this softly to me as if none of the others there must know. "The visitors are in the arena, and the men wait in the stalls. And although your man seems near to you beyond the bars, nearly close enough to touch, you have to shout your questions very loud to him above the sound of the other people's voices, or else he cannot hear." Her eyes were filling with pleasure again as the line advanced more quickly, and she turned and put her hand out to the little girls. "And I will ask him about Manuel at once," she whispered to me, "and if he says Manuel was brought here with him, then we will ask them to let us see him. And if Eleuterio says he is not here, then Eleuterio will tell us where to go." *However it turns out, we will have played the trick on them,* she may have stopped herself from saying, and she put her dark thin beautiful face against my shoulder, laughing as wantonly as a gypsy who has just picked their pockets clean. "And whatever

there is to do next, I will help you, I will go with you wherever it is," she said.

We were close to the wicket now, and her eyes were alive
again with the strange dark look of delight. *In twenty minutes I shall see Eleuterio's face*, she kept herself from saying;
I shall hear his voice above the other voices. She had come
to the wicket, and she opened her identity paper out flat
on the wood, and she ran her tongue along her lip as if her
mouth were dry. And then we both turned and drew Manolita and Juanita close to the ledge, the bags of oranges in
their arms, so that their faces might be seen as well.

"To see my husband, Eleuterio García," she said, and her
voice and her hand did not tremble, but the blood had
bleached from her nails as she held to the counter watching
the guard behind the wicket scan the records for his name.
And then, as the pen moved over the square of paper, writing the pass out, the blood ebbed darkly back under the
small flakes of her nails again.

It was my turn now, and I stood before the wicket in a
dress that was not mine, and I passed the papers that did
not bear my name across the wood and under the wire to
him, and the guard looked up into my face. Beyond, Señora
García and the children waited with the others where the
examination of the baskets took place. The mother had a
comb in her fingers, and she did not turn her eyes to look
at me, but she leaned over her two daughters, combing out
their hair.

"I have brought some food to my cousin, Eleuterio
García," I said to the man behind the wicket.

His face was a sad face, lonely-eyed, bony, long, and it
hung between the heavy braid epaulettes like a horse's head

in weariness between the shafts. It might have been he who was committed to solitary confinement in this cage, condemned by his own impotence, his own indecision, to the abjectness of being guard instead of prisoner, with the names he sought on the records those of his jailers, and freer, more ruthless in their judgment of franchise than he. His blunt nail was on the name of Eleuterio García still, and now he took the pen up, and wrote the second paper out.

At the end of the portico was the door, with another guard standing by it, and the visitors moved slowly toward it, one behind the other, and through it, their passes in their hands. Once I had followed them through, I faced with the others the wide dusty expanse, part vacant lot, part roadway, which lay the length of the prison wall. The parched earth that stretched away was rutted by cart wheels that had passed there in a wetter season, the deep troughs of them baked hard as sculpture now, wiped clean as asphalt of vegetation. Across this ground the narrow railway tracks ran from the strip of shade cast by the portico to the corner of the prison wall, and there passed through the open gateway and out of sight to a terminus that lay beyond. The coupled cars which had begun to roll slowly down the tracks were packed high with the baskets of bread and fruit, the hampers, the bundles which the visitors had loaded onto their double tiers.

"Manolita, Juanita, quick, quick, the oranges!" Señora García cried out, and we ran after the slowly moving miniature train. We lifted the basket up onto the last of the double-decked cars, and, still running, the children set the bags of oranges upright beside the basket, and then we paused a moment, watching the train go.

Before us, the women and children moved in scattered procession across the wasteland of heat and light, some walking singly, some hand in hand, following the way which the train took towards the gateway standing open in the prison wall. We began to walk now, and the children followed us, over the dust, in the direction in which the others walked. And beside us, over the prison wall, were the new buildings taking shape, the new façades reaching upwards toward completion under the blue candescent sky. Brick by brick, and with trowelful after trowelful of slapped wet cement, were the prisoners building their prison stronger, higher, more invulnerable, erecting their own sepulchers, as if sealing themselves alive within them as they worked.

"It is going to be seven times larger than its present size," Señora García said. "Eleuterio worked two years on it, he and Manuel and Alfonso together. That is the work political prisoners do."

We passed through the open gateway, as the others did, moved with the stream of people to the door of the building on the right, showed our passes to the third guard stationed there, and entered the bare low-ceilinged crowded room. And here Señora García turned quickly to the children.

"Let me see your hair, let me fix your ribbons, Manolita," she said. "We'll see Papa in a minute." She took a handkerchief from the pocket of her purple cassock dress, and wet the corner of it with her tongue. "Come to me, Juanita; dirt all around your mouth," she said. And she took the comb out in her narrow nimble fingers again, and drew it through their hair.

The heat lay like a blanket on the people crowded in the

room; you could not get from under it, you could not cast it away. *In fifteen minutes,* the voices said, and the soiled colored handkerchiefs were lifted to wipe the sweat from necks and brows, and the mouths were smiling; *in fifteen minutes the door will open.* The low wide room was drained by a corridor at one end, and the double doors at the end of that corridor would be flung open when the time had come, and the women carrying their infants in their arms, and with their children at their skirts, moved down the bottleneck in hope. *In fifteen minutes,* the promise was made; and they would ride in then on the tide of eagerness to the reception arena where the prisoners waited, as audience, in the arena stalls. *In fifteen minutes, only fifteen minutes,* said Señora García's bright lively eyes.

It could not be said when the other whisper began to run from mouth to mouth, from ear to ear in the crowded room, but from instant to instant the sound of it ran faster, louder, and the heads turned uneasily on the shoulders, and the look in the faces altered as the whispered words came clear. *Hunger,* the telegraphic message went; *the political prisoners are on strike. On hunger strike.* And the women lifted their infants higher on their shoulders, and looked into one another's eyes.

"Our men are on strike," said a woman close to me in the press of the room. "Our men are on strike," said the other voices.

The political prisoners are on hunger strike, the words rang louder, clearer. *They are to be punished. There will be no visitors allowed today.*

"But perhaps some of them will be allowed to come up!"

said Señora García, rejecting the unconditional terms of it. "Perhaps not all of them will be punished!" But a small white bloodless ring of pain or fear was cast around her mouth.

And now the women with their children pressed forward down the corridor, as those who are left above will press to the entrance of a mine, hearing the far deep muffled detonations of disaster. Whatever time was, or had been once, or whatever its customary demands might be, there was no recognition of it left as they moved forward to the brink, asking mutely that word be given of the men trapped below. It might have been an hour that passed, or two or three, in which only one infant roused from sleep and cried in hunger for a little while. *Ah, hunger, hunger,* said the disembodied voices, sounding the note of mourning now. *Our men are on hunger strike! We have brought food to them, food scraped out of a week's or two weeks' ration, bartered for on the black market, a trainload of food, and they cannot open their mouths and eat!*

They could not have seen the guard step from the blazing sunlight of the courtyard into the room, for their backs were turned to him, but a ripple of cognizance ran through the waiting women when he came. They turned their faces, dry-eyed and drawn and weary in the heat, to where he stood dwarfed and puny on the threshold, reaching up on his toes to see across their heads.

"The visitors!" he called out to the packed sweltering room. "The visitors will leave the hall and go out through the gate by which they entered! They will surrender their passes to the guard outside! All visits have been cancelled for today!"

"All visits, all?" said Señora García, refusing it still. She had made her way near to him, drawing the children behind her.

"All. There are no exceptions being made," he said, and he took off his official hat and mopped his streaming brow.

And patiently the women turned, and in patience took this other direction, moving submissively out into the brilliant day again. They stood there, their eyes dazzled for a moment as are the eyes of women who have stepped in stupor from a motion-picture theater, and they looked about for the train of food.

"Where are we going?" Juanita cried out in sudden distress.

"We must get the basket and the oranges," Señora García said.

"We must take the food back with us. We cannot leave it here." *The prisoners are on hunger strike*, went the whisper along the walls and through the dust, but the women's mouths were silent. "When Manuel was at Alcalá, his wife hardly ate, all those years she hardly ate," said Señora García scarcely aloud, and now something which could not be precisely named had begun shaking like the cold in her flesh. "She brought everything to him," she said, "three times a week, in the afternoons like this—" And *hunger, hunger, hunger*, repeated the hot dry wind as it blew through the women's hair.

We were standing on the outskirts of the crowd, a little apart from the others, when the butterfly came towards us down the current of the air. It was not a large butterfly, but one with pure white wings, and it fluttered forward and alighted on Manolita's hand. It trembled there for a moment before beginning its promenade from Manolita's wrist up to her elbow, its wings upright and quivering variably, like the sails of a sloop tacking to the breeze. And then its clinging feet advanced up Manolita's small bare arm, the face quite visible, twisted and venomous as an old man's face, the legs arching like a circus pony's as it climbed. When the minutely feathered feet entered the hollow of Manolita's arm, she began to laugh with pleasure, laughing out loud, her lips turned up with laughter in her smooth pale cheeks. And Juanita too burst into laughter, and Señora García touched the locket which hung around her neck, and her fingers clung to it as she stood there laughing as if nothing as ludicrous as this had ever, in her lifetime, taken place.

Chapter Six

I T WAS AFTER TEN, and the little woman in the
black and yellow silk dress writhed slowly, voluptuously
under the artificial lights, dancing the Flamenco dance
to the music of the piano and the violin. She was scarcely
larger than a child, but her face was hard and evil and no
longer young, and the short little muzzle of it was painted
in imitation of a young girl's face. But it was the face alone
that was scarred by the acid of age, for the dress was cut
low between her breasts, and there was her firm satiny flesh
revealed in soft denial of the mask above it, even the throat
smooth and unblemished, and the bare shoulders glossy as
if covered by a young girl's skin. In her ink-black hair
bloomed scarlet loose-petaled flowers, their stems entwined
in the trellis of the upright tortoise-shell comb that did not
tremble as she danced. There seemed to be no bones in the
velvet of her writhing limbs, and yet the wooden platform
shook under the deliberate fury of her heels stamping out
their arrogance and petulance.

The music played in Lamana's café, and the woman
danced, and her partner in his snuff-brown, short-jacketed
Basque suit, topped with the clerical collar and the brown
ten-gallon hat, sang as he sauntered back and forth across
the boards. He was a strong high-chested man, and the comb
in the woman's hair did not reach to his shoulder. The cloth
of his trousers was drawn tight across his heavy thighs, and

his feet in their polished ankle-high boots were manipulated as subtly as kid-gloved hands. He strolled back and forth on the platform, his head raised, looking beyond her as she writhed in controlled convulsive precision before him, and his wild unbroken voice sang aloud the humorous legend of man's pride and potency. Even when the woman twisted, as if in pain, against his flanks, he did not glance at her. His eyes were fixed on the people seated at the café tables, and as he sang to them of the sovereignty and invincibility of man, the men called out in acclamation to him. His head was that of a strong man, with the brows heavy and black, the nose large, and when his voice clung powerfully to the high marvelously protracted notes, the blood stood dark and static in his face, and his great curved nostrils flared.

This was Lamana's café, and Manuel's friend was seated alone at a table on the raised gallery that overlooked the platform where the performers and the musicians played. The elbow of his slick grey jacket leaned on the railing, but he was not watching the woman dance, or listening to the words sung out. Under his weary drooping lids, his eyes were on the doorway, and when he saw me he stood up and made a gesture with his hand.

"Good evening," he said when I had made my way through the crowded tables to him. "It is half past ten. One begins to wonder when people are late," he said, and the side of his mouth was empty of teeth as he smiled.

The chairs had been set on one side of the table only, so that those who sat there might face the players, and Manuel's friend and I sat down beside each other, and he lifted the little half-bottle and filled my glass with wine.

"I am hungry," I said, and the word was wrong. It was

as if a skeleton had taken a chair and sat abruptly down with us, for there was wine on the table, and music playing, and there was no place for him there.

"I can order fried fish, smoked ham and bread for you," said Manuel's friend, leaning forward. But his eye on the bottle might have been counting the drops that remained to see how much food they would wash down.

"Let us have another half-bottle, and fish for both of us," I said. I took out the hundred-peseta note, and his face was startled.

"Don't do that," he said, his eyes not on it. "I am not in the habit of eating much. It is better not to stretch the stomach. Please put anything like money away."

It seemed to me that we had been a long time apart, and that there were many things to say, but the music had begun again, and we did not say them to each other. I took a swallow of wine, and I looked around at the other tables on the gallery, and at those in the café rooms below us, and Manuel's friend leaned one elbow on the table.

"Manuel is not here. I have been watching. But there is time yet for him to come," he said.

Each number they played out on the platform began temperately, quietly enough, as if beginning in slumber. The woman would stir a little to the first bars of music, her monkey-like face masked with somnolence, her arms beginning their weaving, as sleek and boneless as snakes. And then, step by sinuous step, she would move towards the seated man, her knees bent, her body sloping backward, her arms never ceasing their weaving, her high heels rapping soft as a finger on the floor. In a moment, the man in the snuff-brown suit would stretch his legs and get up from his chair beside the piano, and stroll indolently back and forth, adjusting the shirt cuffs at his wrists, straightening the brim of his hat as he looked out across the tables, nodding to those he knew in the room, and then he would begin to hum behind his teeth. There were no castanets in the palms of the woman's hands, but her pliant red-nailed fingers snapped sharply as the crack of a whip, and she stamped louder now, seeking to rouse the sleeper from his dream. But he did not look at her as he began to sing the quick confidential words, this time of the young bride and her bridegroom who had never consummated love before. And, as he sang, the woman was nothing more to him than a streetwalker slinking and writhing past him, leaving the same effluvium of fard and musk upon the air. And, singing, he lifted a chair in one hand, and spun it on two legs until its back stood to the audience, and then he seated himself astride it, and the notes sprang from his throat as rapidly and violently as argument. His dark eyes moved boldly on the people at the tables, and his tongue and hands dealt equally, first to the right, then to the left, the histrionics of the humorous tale of virgin love.

"*Olé!*" the men seated at the tables called out as his voice rose in high strange beauty. "*Olé! Olé!*" they cried, and they struck the tables with their open hands.

He sat with his legs astride the chair, and his hat tipped casually across his brows, his voice singing intimately to them now; and the woman stamped faster on the boards, circling slowly, painfully around him, her hips writhing, her back curved perilously, her body arching with lust. Her red underlip pouted in her small evil face, and her arms wove sinuously the length of her torso and loins, and as the music of the violin and piano accelerated, she danced in precise and vicious fury before his continence.

"*Olé!*" the seated men called out, and in the farthest corners of the café rooms they got up from their chairs, and stood, clapping their hands, and stamping their feet upon the floor.

The dancer was misshapen, almost crippled now in the agony of her desire, twisting her soft boneless body before him in the tight-bodiced, full-skirted, swinging dress. But he had taken the high muffled note in his teeth, he was holding it hard within his throat, his lungs, his belly, holding it until it seemed the veins must fill to bursting in his throat and temples. He had got to his feet, stepping carefully in his soft low leather boots, and he twirled the chair with a motion of his wrist and set it behind him; and still he had not taken breath, and the note had not faltered or broken yet, but had instead increased in power as it mounted within his skull. The nostrils were dilated wide, and the blood rose darker, reaching the point of ebullition in his face, but still the note held longer, sweeter, sharper, the thread drawn tauter until it seemed for another prolonged moment that it must already have reached and gone beyond the violent moment of its release. And now the woman writhed faster, more wildly before him, but still he did not relinquish the note, but stood with his lips closed tight upon it, and then, as if the lungs themselves had burst, his mouth opened and the tremendous volume of sound poured out across the café rooms. And instantaneously, and as if for the first time perceiving her there, his eyes fell on the woman dancing the distorted crippled dance of love before him, and he reached slowly, deliberately out and drew the small soft writhing body against him, and there her movement ceased, and her voice cried out in anguish as his mouth closed on her mouth.

It was after the second number that the singer came to the railing and shook hands with Manuel's friend across it, leaning close on his heavy folded arms so that one saw the separate hairs of his thick black brows, and the hairs that sprang in his ears and nostrils, and smelled the odor of dampness from his flesh. He jerked his dark clefted chin towards the bottle and glasses and the crescents of fried fish left on the plate.

"I'll come around and have a drink with you," he said.

We watched him go the length of the platform in his soft svelte boots, and at the steps he flung himself around the railing, and made his way quickly through the tables to us. He picked up a chair standing empty at a table as he passed, and bore it with him, and he pulled it into place under him and sat down beside Manuel's friend. Then he looked up and snapped his fingers for the waiter.

"Bring me a beer," he said.

They did not begin talking at once about it; they spoke of other things first, such as the price of white wine and smoked ham now; and the singer said, shrewdly, matter-of-factly, that entertaining was a business as variable as any other. He spoke of voices, of entertainers, of the songs in season, as if they were produce you fingered in the market, discarding some because of the price, and others because they had been bruised or soiled by use. There were furrows slashed across his brow, and down each side of his well-cut, embittered mouth, and as he talked one felt the marrow and blood of action rich as a gold mine in his flesh. He sat there clothed in his smart Basque suit and his subtle boots, with the vehemence held in abeyance in him. The waiter came back and set down the glass of beer, and in the same fearless voice, the singer said:

"There's been trouble out at Carabanchel."

"I heard there was something," said Manuel's friend, and he turned the glass stem in his fingers. Beside the pure male brooding power of the singer, he seemed a frail little man.

"Rioting in three of the galleries," the singer said, and he took a drink of beer. "Protest against the food. The old story: the prison cooks selling the prisoners' rations on the free market." The fantastically long pointed nails of his yellowish fingers drummed on the table. "Yesterday we got word that the guards had them under control," he said. "They thought they had it settled. They went through the galleries and picked out every third man, no matter what he was in for. There's been no word of them since. To-day, the rest of them went on hunger strike, and they say they'll hold out until the others are given counsel or are freed."

He took another drink of beer, his bold eyes moving absently from table to table across the rooms, not seeking for women, not seeking, perhaps, for any familiar face.

"What of Manuel Jerónimo? Has he been in here this week?" I said.

"Jerónimo and I are in the same category. Another one on *libertad vigilada*," he said. He reached back to his hip pocket, and he took out the wallet, and opened it on the table, and he selected the identity card from among the other papers in it. "Liberty to breathe," he said, not lowering his voice, "provided you don't breathe deeply; liberty to sleep, if your conscience permits it; liberty to work, if

258

not too many questions are asked." He pushed the card across the table to me, and there were the dates of the terms he had served stamped on it, and there was the photographic likeness, but the face was not that of a man who might stroll across the boards singing aloud the words of man's invincibility, or who might take a woman in his arms, while the music played, and slowly kiss her mouth. It was, instead of a likeness, the mask of outraged and humiliated man, with the full, sharply cut lips set, and the male eyes bulging in the heavy handsome skull at the immensity and the flagrancy of his betrayal. The lips were closed, but this time not closed upon the high vibrant prolonged note, but closed almost in terror, almost—except for the last full measure of man-hood and resolution in them—closed upon weak and woman-ish outcry against pain. "If Jerónimo were a free man tonight," he said, "he would be here." The violinist was tuning up now, a white handkerchief folded under his chin, and the singer watched him from the corner of his eye and took another deep swallow of the beer. "That's what I was six months ago," he said. When he jerked the flexible thumb of his right hand toward the photograph, I saw that the nail was gone from it, and in its place was calloused, corrugated flesh. "That's what I was once, and that's what I'll be again when they pick me up again and put me through it for what I know or do not know."

"If you see him," said Manuel's friend, "tell him this." I saw now that in the time I had not glanced at him, he had eaten the ends of fried fish and the bread, eaten them quickly while we talked, and the plates stood empty before him. "Tell him there is a friend of his sister's here from Paris," he said, and he turned his blemished sight away in guilt from the empty plates. "She has papers for him—papers to get him across the frontier."

"And what will he do with them?" the singer said.

"He will make the choice," I said after a moment in which no one spoke. "He will make his own decision." But the words had lost their taste on my tongue, and their sound was hollow in my ears.

"No," said the singer. "You are mistaken. It is much simpler than that." On the platform below us, the violinist softly plucked his strings to the piano's steadily repeated *A*. "You are either every third man who is taken out and shot, or else you are not," he said, "but one is not permitted a decision. There is no choice that he can make, except the profounder choice which lies between good and evil, and that choice Jerónimo has made." The singer got to his feet now, and he leaned above the table a moment, one strong sallow hand bearing his weight on the cloth. "A brave man likes good things—drink, women, music, in their proper proportion," he said, "and Jerónimo's as brave as any of us. If he were out, he'd be here tonight at a front table, asking for the music he wanted. And I'd sing it for him. If you're a man, you get up on a stage and bellow your heart out, you don't skulk in the wings," he said, and now the music began to play.

We sat watching the singer go off, tall, heavy-shouldered, powerful, making his way through the tables. He swung down the steps and around the railing to the platform, and he crossed the boards and picked up the ten-gallon hat from the piano and put it on the side of his head. *So this is the answer to the uneasiness and guilt,* I did not say aloud, and I remembered Señora García's and the children's laughter.

This is in itself the answer, the final outwitting of them, the thing which they have sought to touch and have not touched. It is levity that gives drama a noble face, and yet saves it from its own depravity. The dancer had put on a white dress for the final number, and pinned white lilacs in her blue-black hair, and her heels rapped softly across the platform.

When we walked out into the darkened street, the strip of night above our heads was filled with summer stars.

The meeting with Manuel's friend was fixed for eleven in the morning, but I was early, and as I walked down José Antonio to the dusty square, I saw he had not come yet to the tables in the avenue of shade. I sat down in the place where we had met the day before, and the waiter strolled down through the dust of the sidewalk to me, the napkin folded over his arm.

"The Señora is alone today?" he said. I said I was meeting my friend at eleven, and he brought the newspaper to me and laid it down on the white of the table top. It had been opened, and the inside page was folded outside now, and the soiled rim of his fingernail lingered a moment at the lower corner of the page.

"They got them," he said, and he stood looking across the square at the tramcar rocking down the rails, with the people clinging to the steps of it.

The little square of print said there had been rioting among the prisoners at Carabanchel, and it added that several executions had been carried out. I sat reading down the list of names of these men who were strangers to me, reading the small print down through the Josés, the Vicentes, the

Ricardos, until I came to the eighth name, and at that instanc
I believed in each individual death, and the look of the sky
as it must have been to them then, and the last trembling
moment of defiance. The eighth name was that of Eleuterio
García, and the tenth was Manuel Jerónimo's. I did not
know the others who had died.